# SHE-CRAB
# SOUP

## Dawn Langley Simmons:

### Autobiography:
All For Love

### Biographies:
A Rose For Mrs Lincoln
Rosalyn Carter
Margaret Rutherford

### Juvenile:
The Great White Owl of Sissinghurst

## Gordon Langley Hall:

### Biographies:
Princess Margaret
Jaqueline Kennedy (with Ann Pinchot)
Golden Boats From Burma
The Two Lives of Baby Doe
The Sawdust Trail:
    History of American Evangelism
The Gypsy Condesa
Lady Bird and Her Daughters
Mr Jefferson's Ladies
Vinnie Ream — The Girl Who Sculptured Lincoln
Osceola
William, Father of the Netherlands
Dear Vagabonds
The Enchanted Bungalow

### Play:
Saraband For A Saint

### Humor:
Me Papoose Sitter
The Day Mrs Weller Flew To The Moon

### Juvenile:
Peter Jumping Horse
Peter Jumping Horse At The Rodeo

# SHE-CRAB

# SOUP

by

Dawn Langley Simmons

**ACME PRESS**
Westminster, Maryland

ISBN 0-9629880-2-2

Library of Congress Catalog Number 93-72370

First printing November 1993




ACME PRESS
1116 E Deep Run Road, P. O. Box 1702
Westminster, Maryland 21158




1 2 3 4 5 6 7 8 9 10
Printed in the United States of America

For

Judith Marotta

and

Pamela Pike Standhaft Jackson

# She-Crab Soup

### (the recipe)

1 tbsp butter
1 quart milk
1/2 cup whipping cream, whipped
1/3 tsp mace
1/8 tsp pepper
1/2 tsp Worchestershire sauce
1 tsp flour
2 cups crab meat and crab eggs
1/2 tsp salt
4 tbsp dry sherry

Melt butter in top of double boiler and blend with flour until smooth. Add in the milk gradually, stirring constantly. Add crab meat and crab eggs, and all seasonings except sherry. Cook slowly over hot water for 20 minutes.

To serve, place one tablespoon of warmed sherry in individual soup bowls, add soup and top with whipped cream. Sprinkle with paprika or finely chopped parsley.

Serves 4 - 6.

Maree Schwerin
Charleston, SC

[Editor's note: Last we heard it was illegal to catch female crabs, and what a shame that is.]

# 1

Mr Pee was preserving his virginity for marriage. This was a bit hard on me, as we had been engaged for the past ten years, ever since 1959 when my Godmother, Miss Annabel Pincklea, had died and left me her mansion on Tradd Street, and I had arrived from my native Britain to live in the Holy City of Charleston.

Mr Pee's mama, Miss Henrietta, and his ancient black nurse, Maum Sarah (she had suckled him in the days when wet nurses were in vogue), were both equally determined that when The Time finally came, Mr Pee should go to the altar the most spotless of bridegrooms. You really couldn't blame Miss Henrietta, for she had been crossed in love by her own husband — cuckolded not by another woman but by a man, one of those fancy decorator types who had descended on Charleston determined to make their fortunes.

It didn't last, mostly because the decorator failed to make his expected fortune. Within a year, he left Mr Pee's

Daddy for a flamboyant gourmet chef, with whom he opened a reasonably successful bed-and-breakfast inn.

Before anyone could breathe a sigh of relief, however, Mr Pee's Daddy went off the deep end again and married a wealthy divorcee, Miss Jessie-Belle, who owned a chain of intimate garment stores.

Thereafter, Mr Pee's Daddy kept his attachment in high style in a green shuttered house on East Bay Street where it was rumored by those in the know that Wife Number Two had a finer set of monogrammed silverware than Wife Number One, to say nothing of the upper drawing room ice-blue crystal chandelier that had come from the late Russian Czar's summer palace in St Petersburg.

This relationship, sad to say, also folded when Miss Jessie-Belle ran off with a circus lion-tamer, leaving Mr Pee's Daddy all alone, except for a mistress or two whom he maintained on the side to see him through these stressful transitions.

When Mr Pee's Daddy took desperately sick with galloping consumption, it was Miss Henrietta, Wife Number One, who had to nurse him, for Maum Sarah — who had also been *his* nurse and referred to him as "my baby" (and to Mr Pee as "my baby's baby") — had decreed that in spite of his extramarital adventures he should expire graciously in his own bed. And in the big white-columned mansion next door to mine, her word was law. Even Mr Pee went so far as to say that Maum Sarah was the conscience of his family, and that next to his Mama, his faithful horse Estella, and finally me, he loved her best of all.

When Mr Pee's Daddy died very properly in his Charleston-made carved rice Honduras mahogany four-poster bed, Miss Henrietta made a vow on his casket that their son should walk in the paths of chastity. As a confirmation gift when he was twelve years old, she sent him on a trip to Rome with his tutor. When they returned with an enormous nude statue of Samson in chains, a pose which left nothing to the imagination, Miss Henrietta nearly fainted. While Maum Sarah temporarily covered the crucial spot with her big black Sunday church-going umbrella, Miss Henrietta phoned Mr Aloysius Haskell, the monument mason, to come at once to the mansion as there was a dire emergency. When he arrived in his special funereal top hat, she ordered him to please ignore the chains and carve Samson a pair of white marble under-drawers...and while he was at it, to carve marble fig leaves for all the little cherub figures in the garden. When Maum Sarah complained that her old arms were aching from holding the enormous umbrella in place, Miss Henrietta sent the cook up to Woolworths on King Street to buy the biggest pair of boxer shorts she could find for Samson to wear until his marble ones were finished.

Having been brought up in a succession of historic houses in England, I felt pretty much at home in the Pincklea mansion. It was much more spacious than anything I had been used to, and an ideal place to pursue my career as a writer of gardening books and articles. I was a hopeless romantic, and just knew that, any day now, a dashing gentleman like Jane Eyre's Mr Rochester would appear to sweep me off my feet.

My godmother was a maiden lady who had attended boarding school with my own mama in England, and always treated me like one of her own family. When I took over her home, I also inherited her two trusty servants — Mr James, the butler, and Miss Frances, the cook. And just as Maum Sarah always had the last word in Miss Henrietta's home, so did Mr James have in mine. Of uncertain years, Mr James always wore a black patent leather chauffeur's cap indoors and out, even when he was serving at the table. An outsize pocket watch swung from a gold chain like a pendulum as he nimbly served the meals. Once it hit Miss Topsey Piddleton smack in the forehead during the fried okra so that she

3

needed five stitches, and he wouldn't even say he was sorry. Miss Topsey, being a good Episcopalian and, to hear her tell it, a personal friend of the Archbishop of Canterbury, had graciously forgiven him. Mr James had been unimpressed. "That woman got a head bigger than her body and it's got no business taking up the small amount of air space God has allotted to my watch!" I had to remind him that Miss Topsey was a guest in my house, and that out of respect for me if nothing else, he should in the future try and avoid her head, even if it did offend him.

Mr James had watched Mr Pee grow up, for there was a great kinship among the old family retainers. Shortly after my arrival, Mr Pee fell over my wall while pinching my late Godmother's prize figs, only to be invited into the kitchen for liquid refreshments. I recall being rather put out, because Miss Frances and Mr James never allowed me into their kitchen, even to make myself a cup of tea.

It turned out that there was an ulterior motive in Mr James' gesture. In due course, having been fortified with two mint juleps, Mr Pee was ushered into the lower drawing room (all the best houses in Charleston had two) where Mr James formally introduced us. How was I to know that the ultra-conservative Mr Pee was the prize catch in Charleston, when all he could talk about was Estella, his beloved white horse. He reminded me of the legendary Ashley Wilkes in *Gone With The Wind*, minus his Confederate uniform. Mr Pee had a slim, lithe physique, a sulky bottom lip, a delicious little smile and, as I soon was to learn, he was the epitome of a perfect Southern gentleman. Maybe a little *too* epitomous.

His mother seemed to like me also, to say nothing of his old nursemaid Maum Sarah, who asked me right out to recite the Ten Commandments. When I did so without hesitation, she up and announced that I was the girl she had decided her baby's baby should marry. As Miss Henrietta always seemed to agree with everything Maum Sarah decided, we were forthwith declared engaged to be married. The engagement was formally announced on the Court (Queen Elizabeth's) page in the Times of London but not in the Charleston News and Courier, for no true Charleston lady allowed her name to appear in print except when she was either married or buried.

It was to be a long engagement, for every time a date was set for the wedding, Miss Henrietta came down with the vapors, or Mr Pee suddenly discovered that the date conflicted with an important polo match, until Maum Sarah threatened to go and live with her niece, the Reverend Mrs Carmen Suck, who was a lady minister up in New York State where they put up with such things. It didn't take long to realize that Miss Henrietta had developed a rather jaundiced view of marriage, and that Mr Pee himself was less than enthusiastic about relinquishing his independence.

Once a year Miss Henrietta went north to have her face scraped, so that while all the Charleston matriarchs of her generation turned yellow over the years, Miss Henrietta retained her own pretty pink and white cherubic complexion. At such times, Maum Sarah borrowed Mr Pee's Boy Scout tent and had Mr James drive her and her old tabby she-cat, Miss Landine, to the country to fish in the Edisto River. When everyone was away, Mr Pee would turn up on my doorstep, his under-butler carrying his best white cotton pajamas as carefully as if they were the Confederate flag. Before we got into bed, Mr Pee would carefully arrange two pillows down the middle, to make sure, he explained, that neither of us was tempted by carnal lust. He had decreed that we should behave like brother and sister until our wedding...which was taking longer and longer to materialize.

When I mentioned this to his cousin Alexis from Ridgeland, a would-be actress still awaiting discovery, she

5

nearly had a hysterectomy. "If any man tried to pull something like that on me, I'd boot him out the door in a flash!" And to be honest, Cousin Alexis knew whereof she spoke, having been through four husbands before her fortieth birthday, with another on the way (husbands, that is, not birthdays — time had essentially come to a halt for her on her thirtieth, when she stopped every clock in her house and never wound them again; she would have done the same to the clock in the tower of St Philip's if the rector had let her). In addition to her husbands, a steady parade of men had tried unsuccessfully to meet her insatiable demands. Whether those demands had any bearing on the premature demise of the four husbands is anybody's guess.

Determined to resolve my dilemma, Alexis went to see Devious Julius, Maum Sarah's cousin and a conjure man who lived on one of the sea islands, to see if he could do something to hasten the marriage, or at least effect its consummation so that her procrastinating cousin would have to marry me or run the risk of eternal damnation.

Devious Julius charged her ten dollars and she returned to the Pincklea Mansion with a black voodoo doll that looked as if it had been made out of an old black stocking. It had extra long pins stuck through all the unmentionable places so that Cousin Alexis had to be careful not to prick herself as she carefully placed it between the two pillows on our bed. She then personally arranged a bouquet of spider lilies which she had picked in Miss Henrietta's garden for romantic effect. Then, having set the scene for what she hoped would be a night of belated fulfillment, she retired to the guest room, where at two in the morning she — and everyone else in the house — was awakened by such hog-sticking screams that she thought someone was being murdered.

It seemed Mr Pee had a habit of sleeping with his favorite childhood teddy bear between his legs, and somehow, reaching out in the darkness, he had grabbed the voodoo doll instead. Cousin Alexis, acting as chaperone, drove us to the hospital emergency room in her bright red Thunderbird while Mr Pee in turn cried, hollered and groaned. Cousin Alexis kept telling him to be brave and remember how their Great-Great-Uncle Obadiah Middleton had to have his right leg cut off with no anesthetic after the Battle of Shiloh, but it didn't seem to help.

At the hospital, a doctor extricated the pins which had transferred themselves from the doll to Mr Pee's lower extremity, and patched up the lacerated portions of his anatomy. At this point we were free to take him home...but not before Cousin Alexis had seduced one of the male attendants and was turning her attention to the doctor.

News travels fast in society circles, especially when socially prominent people show up at the emergency ward in night attire. Everybody who was anybody in Charleston thought that now Mr Pee would *have* to marry me, as I had been publicly compromised. But still he made excuses.

In due course, Miss Henrietta returned with her new face, while Maum Sarah and her cat, Miss Landine, came home with enough fish to last the household for a month. Outside in the garden surrounded by blushing camellias, Samson stood resplendent, masked discreetly by his remarkable white marble drawers. Maum Sarah charged tourists fifty cents each to observe him (two-fifty without the drawers).

The gorgeous spring of 1968 passed, followed by a string of June weddings at those two Episcopalian bastions of propriety, St Michael's and St Philip's. Mr Pee dutifully gave his favorite cousin Alexis once more in marriage, but with a bit of a difference. This time her mother, known familiarly in the family as Poor Aunt Greta, announced that enough was enough — she had now paid for five wedding receptions, including the liquor, and her days as Mother of

The Bride were over. She had decided to enter a respectable Episcopalian Convent in Atlanta where she would take the veil and forthwith be known as Sister Doubting-Thomas Greta.

As a departing gesture, which I thought was mighty generous of her considering the nuptial record of her only child, she gave Mr Pee and me what she described as a "premature wedding gift", a portrait of herself portraying a live oak tree in the Pageant. Even now I have it hanging among the family portraits in my dining room.

Meanwhile, I watched helplessly as one by one my friends marched resolutely to the altar, while I remained engaged but husbandless. Below Broad Street, where most of the best families sequestered themselves, I was referred to over cocktails as the Last Foolish Virgin.

Everybody in the Holy City seemed to know of my lovelorn predicament, even the flower women selling their bouquets of purple, red, yellow, and pink posies as I passed them down by the post office. The sweet suggestive smell of yellow jasmine and ginger lilies only added to my frustration.

Not that Mr Pee was ever unfaithful...and God only knows some of those high-bred debutante hussies pursued him relentlessly. But they quickly lost interest when he offered to show them his collection of birds' eggs instead of his bed.

Maum Sarah and Mr James, those arbiters of our joint virtues, took every opportunity to remind me that it wasn't every lady, properly engaged or living in sin, whose fiance rode over on his white horse to present her with a blossom of white magnolia. Why, in his wide-brimmed straw plantation hat he could have stepped clear out of the nineteenth century...

...And into my house, as he did each day punctually at noon, tossing his hat to the waiting Mr James who was always there to catch it. He would stay for three-o'clock dinner, still a local ritual, and then take a two-hour siesta on the cooling couch, where my late Godmother's family laid out their glorious dead. Outside, his horse Estella would break forth with the loudest of whinnies, a signal for me to take her a sugar lump. Thus satisfied, she would trot riderless back to her air-conditioned stable next-door.

# 2

My home was known as a Charleston single house, the stucco-over-brick painted an appropriate shade of pink in honor of my late Godmother's illustrious family. There were two large columned porches called piazzas, each running the full length of the house. From the lower piazza the front door, complete with Mr James' pride and joy — the highly polished brass lyre-shaped doorknocker — opened directly onto the street. At the opposite end, steps led down into the garden that had been set out like a series of three rooms, each opening into the other. There were small brick-edged flowerbeds with an inner lining of box-wood, each filled with bright splashes of azalea and camel-lia in springtime. A triple fountain, from which water splashed merrily into large cuplike receptacles, stood near the center.

Beyond that was an area shaded by hollies and bushes of baby's breath. There was a stone seat over which tiny green salamanders slithered and then disappeared on warm days, and a large feathery agave or century plant, which Mr James told wide-eyed tourists would up and die when it reached its hundredth birthday. Behind everything else, by the wall which bordered on Miss Henrietta's property, grew a large hackberry tree which, with its thick branches, had taken over that end of the garden like a giant octopus, devouring the light and causing the ground cover to wither and die. When I told Mr Pee that perhaps the offending monster should be cut down, or at least trimmed, he simply wouldn't hear of it.

"That's where I had my tree house when I was a boy!" he exclaimed in a horrified voice. "Some of my happiest times were spent there."

He smiled in recollection. "Cousins Alexis and Hepzibah would come over to play. Alexis was my favorite cousin. She always let me play with her dogs as long as they were not the boy ones. Cousin Hepzibah wouldn't let me play with anything. She was as nasty then as she is today. No wonder that Baptist minister she married ran off and left her. I felt right sorry for Reverend Jones — especially since he had the misfortune to be a Yankee."

On the matter of the tree, Mr James agreed with him, as he always did. Sometimes this got a little frustrating. "Why is it you always side with Mr Pee?" I demanded. "Is it because he gives you double what I do every Christmas?"

"Now you got no call to say that, Miss Gwendolyn," he replied. "After all, weren't it me introduced you to your own true love in the first place?"

"Well, let's not make it sound so one-sided," I countered. "Didn't *I* pay for the caskets of your two wives, when they both died of influenza the same week? As I recall, you were similarly afflicted and survived. Then you picked out the most expensive copper casket for Miss Lillybelle, she being as you said your 'legal wife of the flesh', and the purple plush-covered chinaberry one for your fancy

11

woman, Miss Olabelle. Why, you ordered me not to spend more than three hundred dollars on the poor woman because you said she wasn't worth any more! Besides, Maum Sarah told me you got a handsome commission from the undertaker for bringing him so much business at one time — enough, I believe, to put four brand new tires on your ancient fire-truck-red Cadillac."

"Now don't you go callin' my Miss Olabelle a fancy woman!" he said, jumping up in his stockinged feet, since he had been polishing Mr Pee's church-going riding boots on my period Chippendale dining table. "I fancied her and she fancied me. Besides, I got sick and tired of hearin' that Miss Lillybelle singing hymns in bed. Nuthin' worse than somebody screaming 'Onward Christian Soldiers' in my good ear."

With that, Mr James spat for the final time on Mr Pee's best church-going riding boots, missed, and hit the Venetian compote instead. Then, holding the boots at arm's length, he marched out of the dining room, presumably to the sanctuary of his butler's pantry.

In spite of his occasional surliness, Mr James and I got along quite well. And, fortunately, he got along very well with Miss Frances Washington, the cook. Miss Frances was a large, statuesque black woman who wore a spotless white uniform and a pointed cap — she could easily have passed for the matron of a hospital.

She had been raised to respect her elders, however difficult they might be, but I knew the cook-housekeeper's true worth. Miss Frances was an organizer; while Mr James ranted and raved over a trivial detail, it was she who kept things running smoothly at the Pincklea Mansion. Although Charleston-born, she had been sent to New York to be raised by an aunt, returning as a woman of thirty to claim her rights, as she said, which meant taking up the role her mother, Miss Shiloh Alice Lee, had just vacated by her death. Miss Frances was well and truly installed in the house by the time Godmama died and I arrived to take over.

Mr James and Miss Frances were united by a happy conspiracy in which they ran the house like it was their own. "Don't you worry about anything, Miss Gwendolyn," Miss Frances once told me. "You just stay up in your sitting room and work on your books, and one day you might be famous like my favorite author, Miss Barbara Cartland." — she always read her romances at breakfast — "Then you can dress up all in pink like she does, and you might even get on TV...or be invited to Buckingham Palace."

Miss Frances was tall, Amazonic, and bossy. She might well have been a Nubian prince in a former life, but even she had her weakness: a young man, several years her junior, by the name of Big Shot Calhoun.

All I knew about Big Shot then was what Mr James and Maum Sarah had told me...and that was plenty. He was the son of a self-ordained Baptist minister at the church where Miss Frances was choir director. In addition to his ministerial duties, Big Shot's Daddy also fixed rich people's roofs at cut-rate prices and sold pickled pigs feet as a sideline.

Big Shot himself had no visible means of support, though he drove around town in a big silver Cadillac. Maum Sarah informed me she happened to know that lovesick Miss Frances had put up the down payment for the car. She was always showering him with gifts, having just recently bought him a subscription to *Playboy* magazine, since he did so like to read about sports and cars. Mr James noted that, standing beside Miss Frances, Big Shot looked like a dwarf, for he barely made it up to her shoulders. And he went even further by calling Big Shot "Miss Potty's Pimp".

Miss Potty was a Charleston institution. She ran what she called her "Health Club" over on Radcliffe Street, where even the palmetto trees move in suggestive rhythms. Mr James used another term for Miss Potty's enterprise, which as a Charleston lady of the old school (if only by adoption) I am not at liberty to repeat. Suffice it to say that for a fee which varied according to color and age — for it seemed that whatever they were doing, the old men always took longer — Miss Potty and her girls dispensed the pleasures of the evening... which included her famous stuffed shrimp plate preceded by the most extraordinary she-crab soup. I know this from personal experience because Mr James brought me some of his leftovers to taste, as he had been raised not to waste anything.

Although black herself, Miss Potty's clientele was not limited to gentlemen of her own race. Her clientele of white gentlemen-callers boasted some of the best names in the Holy City. She practiced occupational integration before it became fashionable and Charleston hired its first black police chief. The hostesses were described in Miss Potty's Health Club flier as "all good Christian girls. Our Miss Wilhemina also teaches Sunday School, dutifully preparing her lessons between her loving duties here. Enjoy her and save your soul at the same time."

For some strange reason, Miss Frances Washington did not seem to object to her true love Big Shot Calhoun's close proximity to Miss Potty, for, as she once remarked to me, "Their work brings them together." Actually, it brought them a little too close together, for a few years ago Miss Potty bore Big Shot a son, Rhett Cartland. (Miss Frances was allowed, in return for a small donation of $25.30 to the Health Club Girl's Retirement Fund, to choose his middle name.)

"Never mind," Miss Frances rationalized. "It is only natural for a gentleman to stray, and Big Shot is no exception. Besides, Big Shot and I are engaged, although I did have to buy the ring." As Big Shot's Daddy said, "I'll marry you to my boy myself, Miss Frances, as soon as you come up with the five hundred bucks for the second-hand stained glass window for my church." Miss Frances promised that she would do her best to fulfil her pre-nuptial agreement.

Although up until that time I had not met Big Shot, I did have the pleasure of meeting his daddy, who showed up one day — wearing blue overalls and a clerical collar, his gray hair standing on end — to negotiate the repair of my so-called carriage house roof, rather a genteel name for what had been the former slave quarters.

After giving me what I thought was a very fair price for a new red tin roof, he presented me with a jar of his famous pickled pigs feet. They were ghastly looking little things — I would have preferred a live pig, which are such intelligent creatures and make better house guards than any watch dog.

Big Shot's daddy then sat himself down under the fountain where he proceeded to tell me about the trials and tribulations of raising his only son.

Big Shot's childhood had hardly been a conventional one, I was told. "Why, he walked out of school when he was twelve and was found three days later at Miss Potty's Health Club, where he duly informed me he was learning the trade. Well, that was a bit awkward, as you might imagine...especially as I spend a good deal of time at that establishment myself — strictly in a soul-saving capacity, you understand.

"And if that weren't enough," he went on, "about that time, Big Shot's plump little mama, my own sweet wife Miss Archangel, began to act strangely. She used most of the housekeeping money to buy art supplies, and began to draw the most amazing portraits of men and women, all buck naked and with several eyes, each a different color. All this was done with the most vivid poster paints she could find. She said she heard voices telling her just how many eyes to give each of her subjects, and what colors they were supposed to be.

15

"Then one day, the voices apparently told her to go and sit in the Old City Market among the fruit, vegetables, and sweet grass baskets offered for sale, where a tall thin white man with stringy hair and blue eyes...which he could pop out of his head...would come and find her. She was to obey his instructions to the letter."

Big Shot's Daddy didn't much go for the idea when she told him, but he knew from experience that to oppose her was to ask for trouble. "She would stomp, scream, and give my grits to the stray cat. And out of clear nastiness she gave my big red silk underdrawers, the Goodwill pair I always wore to preach in on All Saints Day, to a visiting seaman."

The way Big Shot's Daddy described it, the Old City Market was a much more lusty place than it is in its sanforized state today, with all of those prissy little gift shops crammed in among the brick arches to please the tourists. Then there were round-faced black women selling the fat tomatoes and cabbages that they had grown on John's Island, all chattering away happily in their Gullah dialect which their ancestors had brought with them from Africa. The walls smelled of saltwater and in spots oozed green slime, while at night the men relieved themselves on the walls. On a damp morning when the tide was out, the air was sickly sweet with the smell of pluf mud, which the natives took for granted but the visitors found to be somewhat disturbing.

"And there," Big Shot's Daddy went on, "by one of the entrances, my dear Miss Archangel set up her easel and drawing board that Big Shot had bought her with Miss Potty's generous Christmas bonus, and started to draw. And sure enough, just like the voices had told her, a tall lanky white man with long straggly yellow hair appeared carrying a camera and leading an enormous brown poodle dog named Miss Ruby. He took one look at Miss Archangel's work and said, "I must have it!" He gave her a twenty dollar bill which she carefully folded, and then turned and hid it in the top of her baby blue drawers while he was inspecting her portfolio.

"Then, to her amazement, the man reached up to one of his eyes and pressed...and something popped out into his hand. To Miss Archangel, who had never seen a contact lens before, this was irrefutable proof that the voices had been right.

"The yellow-haired stranger announced that he was Mr Charles Baxter, a New York art gallery owner, and would she like to accompany him and Miss Ruby back to New York City where he would represent her work, and between them they would make a fortune. So after Mr Charles Baxter bought her a long blonde wig and a red tutu petticoat, she packed two cases and three hat boxes, put her fixed tomcat Mr Jeremiah in a special little carrier, and set off for New York City with Mr Charles Baxter and Miss Ruby. There she was billed as 'Sister Archangel Who Hears Voices'."

Big Shot's Daddy sighed. "She never came home to Charleston again. And at last report, she now owns her own high class condominium in Greenwich Village, while Mr Jeremiah sports a real diamond-studded collar. Of course there was nothing for me to do but divorce her for desertion and adultery, although there was really no proof that her relationship with Mr Charles Baxter was anything but businesslike.

"It was a darned shame, Miss Gwendolyn," he said sadly. "Why, if we had been living in Biblical times, we could have taken her down to the Battery and stoned her."

Big Shot's Daddy finally returned to the subject of his son, of whom he was very proud. "Just look at that nice big car he drives. You'd never know that as a little boy he was painfully shy. I recall one Halloween, I let him go with the bigger boys for their annual visit to Magnolia Cemetery — that's where the rich folks are buried. All the best white

17

ghosts live there, I told the boy. Poor little fellow — somehow he got lost among all those graves and headstones, and when he disturbed an irate owl from her perch on top of an old rugged cross, he ran screaming for dear life.

"Then he tripped and fell. And when he looked up, he saw a big white marble angel, wings outstretched. And Miss Gwendolyn, my boy swears on my dead grandma's grave on Edisto Island that marble angel *smiled* at him.

"He stopped crying, picked himself up and said 'Thank you Ma'am' to the white marble angel, then climbed bravely over the cemetery gates and went on with his trick-or-treating. I always have said that was a *special* angel — why, she made a little man out of my boy!"

I was soon to learn just how special that angel really was.

# 3

With early summer, the soft rains came and the crepe myrtles burst into bloom — pink, purple and white. The black women walked down King Street with their big umbrellas. Later, when the rains ceased and the sun came out, the umbrellas would protect them from the sun's searing heat. It was a time of reflection for me as I sat writing in my study, the rain splattering on windows and shutters alike.

Mr James came in without knocking to bring me my mail. On top was a letter from the head of our family, Cousin Matilda-Madge — the Honorable Matilda-Madge, I should more properly say — from her castle in England. The implications of this were rather disturbing, to say the least; although my cousin means well, she just happens to behave like a bull in a china shop. As Mummy used to say, "Poor girl — that expensive finishing school in Switzerland didn't do her a bit of good. She looks like a man, talks like a man, and behaves like a man. And most men are afraid of her."

Cousin Matilda-Madge's letter (or directive) read as follows:

Dearest First Cousin Gwendolyn

Has that shrinking violet Mr Pee set the date for your holy nuptials yet? Or is he still waiting for that reconstructed mother of his to pass away, to say nothing of that nasty old witch of a nurse. No wonder he turned out like he did, a model of annoying indecision. However, that does not help your position any or your poor family's either. Why, even his Grace, the Archbishop of Canterbury, asked me at lunch — confidentially of course — if you were any nearer to God's blessed altar. As you well know, there are some Jeremiahs who maintain his Church of England is cracking at the seams, and some day there might even be women priests. So just in case it does explode, you cannot wait forever.

We need babies, Cousin Gwendolyn — little babies for heirs, to inherit this noble, crumbling old castle (dear old thing —I do love it so). You are our only hope, skinny as you are, to save our family tree, which as you are fully aware can be traced right back to William the Conqueror. I have given up on Cousin Judith, who was lost to procreation the day she used her legacy from Great-Aunt Gertrude Hall to make that fatal trip to those racing stables in Virginia. How were we to know that she would fall in love with a horse and never come back? Now she's so busy breeding horses in upstate New York that she hasn't got time to do the same for her own species — I can hope for no progeny from her.

As for me, you well know — because I have repeated it to you on many occasions — I just do not fancy the male animal. Ever since our cousin Ronnie Ticehurst pushed me into the mineral springs at Royal Tunbridge Wells when we were both seven, I've hated them. Poor Daddy, he did try, lining up everyone with a title in the county, but in spite of all his efforts, nobody could be inveigled into marrying me. After he had exhausted the list of minor nobility, he tried out the gentry. Then came the doctors and even a dentist...but all to no avail. So he turned in desperation to the lawyers, and finally the clergy, where he managed to corner a little curate in Cranbrook. But it was a dead end. The young man told Daddy in no uncertain terms that he would rather go as a missionary to the headhunters in New Guinea. And as a matter of fact, he did. And that's the last anyone ever heard of him.

So when Daddy finally admitted defeat in all attempts to hitch me, he sank into a decline and expired on my thirty-seventh birthday. His dying words were for me to produce an heir somehow, even if I had to do it by artificial insemination. When I told this to the Archbishop, he nearly went into sanctified labor.

So, unless that damned horse of Cousin Judith's falls and breaks its bloody neck, it is all up to you. Give Mr Pee a lady-like ultimatum. Ten years is too long for any engagement, especially when it has been announced in the Times of London. If he still refuses to set a date for the wedding, then dump him in the oleander bushes and accept the proposal of any man with all his faculties who asks you.

Your affectionate cousin,
Matilda-Madge

What an unfortunate day to have received such a mandate from Cousin Matilda-Madge. A group of visiting Baptist ministers and their wives had written Mr Pee's domineering Cousin Hepzibah, the bane or his life (to say nothing of mine), as head of the Save-The-Poor-Horses League, for a private house tour in return for a generous donation. A Charleston tradition, house tours were normally held in the

Spring, when floral-wise the city looks its best. By now most of the old families had already closed their historic homes and fled to Flat Rock, North Carolina, to escape the summer heat. So Cousin Hepzibah was hard put to find volunteers who would open up their homes at such short notice.

She approached Mr Pee's mama, Miss Henrietta, first, but old Maum Sarah flew into a tizzy, since Miss Landine, her old she-cat, had unexpectedly given birth to twins, which she blamed on that ginger tomcat with the extra toes they had encountered on their fishing trip to Edisto — a logical conclusion, as the twins arrived with all his physical characteristics except those associated with girls. Maum Sarah declared that having tourists trample through the house would probably induce Miss Landine to hide her kittens, and that would be most undesirable as she had chosen conveniently to have them in a Hepplewhite Martha Washington armchair in the lower drawing room.

Maum Sarah didn't like Cousin Hepzibah anyway, which harkened back to the days when she was a baby and Maum Sarah was employed as her wet nurse. Cousin Hepzibah was over a year old before they could wean her, by which time she had grown a full set of teeth. Obviously disgruntled when Maum Sarah ran dry, Cousin Hepzibah, for sheer nastiness, up and bit her, costing Miss Henrietta a heap of money for Maum Sarah's plastic surgery at the Mayo Clinic in faroff Minnesota.

With Maum Sarah's rebuff, Cousin Hepzibah turned up on my piazza to announce that the tour would have to take place here at the Pincklea Mansion at two o'clock that very afternoon. "I know you won't refuse, since I am your very best friend...and besides it is your duty to Estella, Mr Pee's faithful horse, to oblige the Save-The-Poor-Horses League."

Let me say right off that Cousin Hepzibah was *not* my best friend, and the obligations I felt to Mr Pee's horse were questionable. But one simply didn't argue with Cousin

Hepzibah. For one thing, her imposing size and brusque, assertive manner made her an intimidating figure. And she had always had her own way, even as a child. "She used to kick me in the cradle that Maum Sarah rocked us in," Mr Pee once told me. "She had very sharp toenails even then."

She then ordered me to lock up Miss Margie, my German Shepherd, as she had never gotten over the embarrassment when the dog had grabbed the bottom of that Bishop's wife from Grand Rapids, Michigan, who was touring my house, relieving her of a sizeable chunk of apple-green polyester.

When Mr Pee's cousin had departed, I informed Mr James, who had the dining room table covered with all the silverware he was cleaning, of the impending tour. Then I told Miss Frances, the cook, who was pasting clippings of Barbara Cartland into an already bulging scrapbook. They both vigorously protested, until I reminded Mr James of the tips that the tourists invariably gave him when he told them about the ghost of Robert E. Lee, who was supposed to rush through the house on the anniversary of the Battle of Gettysburg looking for his bedsteps. We kept these in a place of honor in the Victorian bedroom, in case he took a notion to get into bed, which he is said to have done only on one occasion...and then only when it was warmly occupied by Cousin Alexis. As she said primly afterwards, even the ghost of Robert E. Lee could not resist a true daughter of the South.

With all the commotion, we quite forgot that Mr Pee was still asleep in the Federal bedroom, having had an altercation with Maum Sarah when she refused to allow him to hold the new kittens. He had arrived, still sulking, to spend the night...so there he was in my Charleston ricebed, chastely clothed in his virginal white pajamas and clutching his teddy bear which, since the unfortunate episode with the voodoo doll, he had relegated to a safer anatomical position.

When the tour reached the bedroom, Cousin Hepzibah, though somewhat surprised, took it all in stride. "This is the Federal Bedroom," she explained coolly, "and that is my first cousin in bed. He is so romantically involved that after a long and adventuresome night he quite forgot you were coming."

The Baptist ministers and their wives seemed quite delighted with her torrid explanation, although one woman with dyed blue hair emitted such a loud giggle that her husband gave her a nasty look.

It was with some relief that I saw Mr James finally close the street door on the last visitor, then retire to the butler's pantry to count his tips. Afterwards he announced he was going to Edisto to visit his late Wife Number One, Miss Lillybelle, in the Presbyterian graveyard where he had planted her. Miss Frances was back in the exciting make-believe world of Miss Cartland, while Mr Pee slept soundly on with Miss Margie, the German Shepherd who had been highly insulted at having been shut up in a bathroom, lying blissfully beside him.

With everyone in the household so occupied, I had a few quiet moments to think more about Cousin Matilda-Madge's letter. She was right, of course — Mr Pee, a Southerner and a gentlemen, just had to do the honorable thing and marry me, for Cousin Matilda-Madge needed an heir and it was up to him to help me produce one. Otherwise, God forbid, she might turn up in Charleston where, short of a shotgun wedding, she would pick me a husband herself!

That night Miss Frances gave me frozen fishfingers for supper, although she knew very well how much I hated them. She was in a terrible mood, for she had just found out that Big Shot Calhoun had gone to Miss Potty's annual summer picnic to Folly Beach with all the girls and hadn't even asked her. He had, however, invited his Daddy to go along, and had even purchased a matching pair of father-and-son red bikini swimming trunks in which to perform on the beach. Big Shot later apologized to Miss Frances, and promised to call for her at seven tonight to escort her to a revival meeting at his Daddy's church, where the Reverend Mrs Carmen Suck, Maum Sarah's niece from New York City, was the featured speaker.

By eight o'clock I had, with some effort, liquidated my frozen fishfingers, followed by a sloppy egg custard dessert, and still no sign of Big Shot. Miss Frances was furious. She took off her crown-like cook's cap, pulled a straw hat over her ears, and without even saying Good Evening, stormed out of the house.

Five minutes later, the doorbell rang and I went down to the street door to answer it. There, wearing a crumpled white teeshirt and the most suggestive red bikini, was a short, stocky, barefooted black man with broad shoulders and a great big smile.

We stood there for several moments, me in my white crepe de chine and he in his flaming bikini. Slowly, he put out his hand, as if unsure whether I would reciprocate. But I did, so that our fingers eventually touched.

"*My angel,*" he murmured. "My angel in the cemetery, come to life..."

Then, saying no more, Big Shot Calhoun disappeared like a dripping tomcat into the warm, blue street.

It stormed and rained all night, and the next morning the garden looked like a battleground. Branches and leaves littered the red brick walks while the banana fronds were slashed as if with a giant knife. Little yellow loquat fruits had been stripped from their branches to lie orderly on the ground. Mr James declared that God must have been mighty disturbed about something to have made such a mess.

25

I hadn't slept well, but not just because of the storm. The strange tingling sensation I felt when Big Shot's hand touched mine had persisted for hours, and all night long I tossed and turned, dreaming fitfully of angels and tomcats. After breakfast, I tried to do some writing, but I couldn't concentrate.

To make matters worse, Miss Frances turned up for work in a most disheveled state, her large eyes swollen from weeping, her usually immaculate white uniform looking like it had been slept in. The oatmeal was cold, the coffee a disaster and, to complicate matters, Cousin Alexis arrived with her favorite cousin and confidante, Cousin Lewis. A Civil War buff, he was dressed in a sky blue jump suit with a hole in the seat and a Confederate colonel's gold braided uniform jacket. He kept complaining that he had left Ridgeland in such a hurry that he had forgotten his sword.

Cousin Alexis always maintained that Cousin Lewis was her first and only true love. He had flaming red hair, a throwback to their common Irish ancestors. Years ago, they had announced to Cousin Alexis' mother, Poor Aunt Greta, that they wanted to get married. She was so shocked that she nearly fainted, and absolutely forbade the marriage, fearing that as first cousins they might have silly children.

After that, neither was quite the same. Cousin Lewis took to drink and had to be given three cups of black coffee before he was fit to go to St Philip's on Sunday mornings, while Alexis made a career of multiple marriages and extramarital affairs. She said it was only done in retaliation for her mother's cruel refusal to let her wed her one true love, Cousin Lewis.

Even Poor Aunt Greta said that each husband was worse than the last. But it was Cousin Alexis' confession, after drinking some spiked eggnog at Thanksgiving, that she and Cousin Lewis had sinfully consummated their unrequited love in General Wade Hampton's bed, that Poor Aunt Gretta had a nervous breakdown, which the family discreetly referred to as religious mania and which prompted her retirement to the convent in Atlanta.

Not that things were any better for Cousin Alexis, who hadn't produced a single child out of all her many husbands. Her current one wasn't any better, which was the reason for her sudden unannounced visit with Cousin Lewis that morning on their way to see the family lawyer. It seemed that Husband Number Five had just been found in bed with a church secretary from Aiken, South Carolina. The discovery had been made by a private detective financed by Cousin Lewis, who had then even offered to pay for what Cousin Alexis was sure would be another divorce.

"No man has ever *dared* to be unfaithful to me before," she declared " — and to think we were married in St Philip's. At least two of my former husbands had the good taste to commit suicide, making me on each sad occasion a respectable widow."

Cousin Lewis agreed. "I always told Alexis that her latest was no gentleman. Why, even after his recent deplorable behavior in Aiken, he even refused me the pleasure of a duel."

Mr James, who was listening in the background, nodded vigorously. "Mr Lewis, sir," he roared, "you should have skewered him!"

Finally, after Cousin Lewis had helped himself liberally to the sherry on my sideboard and Cousin Alexis had spent forty-five minutes in the downstairs powder room apparently improving her makeup, they left for Mr Stoney Buger, the family lawyer down on Broad Street, leaving me to piece together the shocking events leading up to Miss Frances Washington's ghastly appearance.

Having waited so long for Big Shot to collect her in his long silver Cadillac the previous evening, she had no time

27

to go home and change clothes before going to the revival. When she arrived at the redemption tent, it was so crowded that she had to push herself through to the front. She made her way past numerous familiar faces, including most of Miss Potty's Health Club girls, for whom a spiritual purging was one of the better forms of weeknight activities.

There on the stage were Big Shot's Daddy and the Reverend Mrs Carmen Suck, wearing identical purple robes and white clerical collars. They were flanked on either side by Maum Sarah nursing Miss Landine, her old she-cat, and the two girl kittens, along with Miss Henrietta, Mr Pee's mother, who had invited herself because it reminded her of all the revival meetings she had attended as a little girl with Maum Sarah back on her daddy's plantation.

When, by sheer brute force, Miss Frances (or, as she was known in that august establishment, Sister Frances) had grappled her way to the front, she felt herself rudely brushed aside by none other than the missing Big Shot himself, still most inappropriately clad in his skin-tight red bikini drawers and tee shirt. But before she could open her mouth, Big Shot hollered out in a voice loud as a Cooper River foghorn, "Reverend Missus, I want to confess!"

A cry of "HALLELUJAH!" went up from the crowd, including Miss Henrietta. Miss Landine, who was used to these outbursts, only hissed at the Reverend Mrs Carmen Suck, because ever since Maum Sarah had told her niece she could take one of the girl kittens back to New York to become the Church Cat, the old she-cat had taken a violent dislike to the lady preacher.

As Miss Frances stood speechless, Big Shot mounted the raised wooden stage. An expectant hush fell over the audience, as everyone knew of his association with Miss Potty's establishment, and eagerly anticipated that his confession would include some salacious details.

28

Tears rolled down his cheeks as he began: "I have sinned, Reverend Missus!" he said between sobs. "My flesh was so weak it took an *angel* to show me the error of my ways!"

Then he turned and looked squarely at Miss Frances and declared, "Sister Frances, I hereby disengage myself from you. And, as a gesture of brotherly love, you may keep the ring." — apparently forgetting in the heat of the sanctified moment that it was she who had paid for it.

He grabbed her right hand and gave it a chaste brotherly kiss, then marched manfully out of the tent, while his daddy shouted from the pulpit, "Son, you can't do that! She ain't finished paying for my stained glass window!"

For the rest of the day, the sound of Miss Frances' sobbing and the ceaseless ringing of the telephone shattered the usual peace of the Pincklea Mansion. It was raining again, and a sense of gloom hung over the darkened rooms. Mr James' nerves were frayed, and he jumped each time the telephone rang. He never allowed me to answer my own phone, in case it was somebody calling to tell him he had just won the numbers. Obviously he hadn't, for I could hear him mumbling something about Miss Potty's Health Club having some nerve calling his missus.

Between tears, Miss Frances did manage to get a dinner of sorts together before Cousin Alexis and Cousin Lewis returned for the afternoon meal, looking like a pair of drowned rats. Their spirits, however, were upbeat. In spite of Mr Stoney Buger's entreaties that perhaps it was just a little marital misunderstanding, Cousin Alexis had filed for divorce on the grounds of adultery.

To celebrate the occasion, Cousin Lewis had taken his true love shopping on King Street to buy a friendship ring in which the little diamonds and rubies were intricately shaped to portray the Confederate flag. It must have cost him an entire month's allocation of his Trust Fund. He also was thoughtful enough to buy me three new typewriter ribbons and a bottle of wine to have with our dinner.

Hours later, after the meal and coffee, they departed for Ridgeland, where they planned, Alexis said with a lacivious wink, to make an early night of it. I returned to the dining room for another cup of coffee and found the candles were spluttering. Suddenly there was a loud crash of thunder and the electricity went off, so that, with the exception of the dining room, the house was in total darkness. Outside, the sky had turned a frightening greenish black.

As Mr James puttered around with more candles, we heard a door slam. Somebody had arrived by the kitchen entrance, so he hurried out to see who the intruder was. Over more claps of thunder, I heard the sound of raised voices, followed by smashing china, as if a table had been overturned. Mr James was shouting — "You'll pay for this, you carpetbagger! Just you wait 'til I find my gun!"

"Use this!" I heard Miss Frances scream.

Then the door of the dining room flew open to reveal Big Shot Calhoun, clutching a pail full of sensuous orange calla lilies and pink crepe myrtle, all dripping wet. He was followed in quick succession by Mr James, brandishing a rolling pin, and Miss Frances Washington with a huge carving knife. Round and round the table they ran until Mr James tripped, grabbing the tablecloth and taking everything on it with him. The cook stumbled over him, the knife flying out of her hand and impaling the portrait of the late General Pincklea right through the heart.

As I collapsed into my upright Chippendale dining chair, Big Shot Calhoun poured his flowers all over me. I felt like Ophelia in the drowning scene in *Hamlet*. Then he fell to his knees and announced with true sincerity, "My angel, I am yours! I will never leave you again."

The same, however, was not true of Miss Frances. She demanded her paycheck and Christmas bonus right then and there, then quickly packed her collection of Barbara Cartland paperbacks and deliberately hung her cap on the newel post in the foyer. Suitcases in hand, she marched to the front door.

"VENGEANCE IS MINE, SAITH THE LORD!" she shouted. "I WILL RETURN!"

Then she grabbed an umbrella and stalked out of the house, slamming the door behind her, causing the vases and chandelier to rattle.

A split second later the sky lit up outside, and we heard a shriek. Rushing to the door and flinging it open, we saw Miss Frances standing in the torrential rain, wisps of smoke curling up from her tattered clothes, her hair standing up in frizzles on her head, a twisted skeleton of an umbrella in her hand.

She glared at us with bloodshot eyes, then sloshed off into the stormy darkness.

"Never mind, Angel," Big Shot said, putting his brawny arm around me. "You have lost a cook, but gained yourself a husband."

# 4

Big Shot was determined to marry his angel as soon as possible because, as he said in no uncertain terms, I was his and he was mine — it was simple as that. At least to him.

It wasn't that simple where I was concerned. I was being asked to marry a black pimp, the father of an illegitimate child whose mother ran a bordello? I reasoned, I argued, I cajoled — with myself as well as with Big Shot — but to no avail. I couldn't convince him that this was the most insane idea anyone could *possibly* come up with. More significant, perhaps, was the fact that I couldn't convince myself either. In the ten years I had been engaged to Mr Pee, nothing he ever said or did had generated anything like the response I felt from Big Shot's brief, gentle touch. It was a new, wonderful sensation, and I didn't want to loose it.

Neither did he intend to quit his job at Miss Potty's because nobody, but *nobody* — black, white or indifferent —

was going to say that he was only marrying me for my money.

When news of the momentous event that was about to happen spread through the Holy City, all hell broke loose, for until that time there had been no legal marriage between a black man and a white woman in the state of South Carolina. Of course, from plantation days, there had been countless instances of mating between members of the two races, by choice or otherwise. There was even an Episcopal church in Charleston that was built for the children of such unblessed unions.

And then there was the old dowager about whom polite society still talked about only in whispers. She had contracted a marriage of convenience with a respectable member of her own white society while keeping her handsome black lover on as her butler...which worked well for both of them since her husband was gay. For years they all lived together in a pleasant *menage a trois*.

In fact, a shaken Big Shot's Daddy asked if we couldn't do the same. What if the irate opposition blew up his church? — then all his life's work would be for nothing. Better yet, why didn't we just move to New York?

I telephoned Sissinghurst for Cousin Matilda-Madge's valued advice. She didn't hesitate with her reply: "Marry the stud. We can always say he's an African diplomat."

With this word of encouragement, I asked Mr James to take back Mr Pee's ring, which had been on my engagement finger so long I needed soap to remove it. Mr James utterly refused to be the bearer of such ominous tidings. "Missus, we shall all be shot!" he kept insisting. "Or *worse!*"

Finally, fortified by three sherries and the promise that I would pay for his burial insurance for the next six months, he was persuaded to deliver the ring with a letter which read:

33

Dear Mr Pee

It is my sad duty to inform you that because of your ten years of procrastination, I have decided to break off our engagement, which I should have done five years ago when I wrote *Dear Abby* for advice and she said that in her opinion you were in love with your mother. My Cousin Matilda-Madge in England, the matriarch of my family, needs an heir which, owing to a frivolous state of nature resulting in her hatred of men, she is unable or unwilling to provide for herself. I am tired of waiting for Miss Henrietta to expire so that you can assume your intended role and fulfill my cousin's desire. I will always respect you.

Yours, like the Confederacy, In chaste remembrance,
Miss Gwendolyn

Well, don't let anyone try to tell you that hell knows no fury like a woman scorned. Just wait until it's a man. Mr Pee was *furious*, especially after giving Mr James two dollars and thirty-five cents, all the money he had in his riding breeches at the time, to inform him who the serpent was who had bitten into his personal apple.

"*Big Shot Calhoun*?!" he is reported to have hollered. "Why...that man's a *pimp*! And besides, he's...he's..."

Mr Pee then ran outside and pulled up the ivy geranium I had given him for Christmas and ordered Mr James to return it to me immediately.

Family reaction was swift and predictable. A distraught Miss Henrietta said I should be sent to live with Poor Aunt Greta in the Episcopalian convent, while Maum Sarah wanted me burned at the stake — no vain wish, as I have it on good authority that she phoned her cousin Comfort Jenkins on Edisto to cut her a truck-load of firewood. Mr Pee's nasty Cousin Hepzibah nearly had a stroke — "Hells bells! Is that woman out of her *mind*?!" — and demanded that Devious Julius conjure up a spell to turn me into a spotted toad.

I was immediately made the scapegoat for everybody's misfortunes. Big Shot's Daddy got a curt letter saying his new church had termites, which he unhesitatingly blamed on me; and Miss Potty complained that business had suddenly fallen off by ten percent. Worst of all, one of those glossy magazines in New York declared that I had shaken the very cradle of the Confederacy, for wasn't it in Charleston that the Civil War began?

Fortunately, not everyone reacted so negatively. Mr James didn't agree with my decision, but loyalty came first and he declared his intention to see the thing through. Mr Pee's Cousin Alexis, who had bounded into one marriage after another, said reassuringly, "Well, you've got to start somewhere." And even Miss Potty, mother of Big Shot's child, didn't seem too upset: "Long as it don't keep him from his work...and that's not likely."

Through all this worrying period, the only one to remain unshaken was Big Shot himself, so that when I developed a case of nerves he announced without wavering, "Get the license, Miss Gwendolyn. I'm making an honest woman of you *tomorrow*." And so, God bless his sweet unpredictable self, he most certainly did.

When I got to the Surrogate Judge, he grumbled that he would have to start a new filing cabinet because of me. Prior to my disrupting appearance in his office, there had been two — one marked BLACK and the other WHITE. Then, being the nice Jewish judge he was, he bubbled, "Well, my dear, welcome to the minority."

"One way or another, I've always been in the minority," I assured him.

Thus fortified, I returned to the Pincklea Mansion where the telephone had been ringing incessantly. Mr James was furious. He called Miss Potty's Health Club for Big Shot, who was being given a bachelor party that evening, and told the recipient in no uncertain terms to send two of the girls over to answer the phone, and two more to sort the mail — an entire truckload having just arrived. The correspondence fell into two categories; those that approved the marriage and those that didn't. A telegram arrived from London that the Queen, God bless her, was sympathetic.

A hasty call was made to the castle at Sissinghurst for Cousin Matilda-Madge to fly over at once to give me away, but regretfully she couldn't on such short notice, as she was guest of honor at the gamekeepers' annual feast and nobody could carve the venison as well as she. She did promise, however, to drink a toast to me on consummation night.

Big Shot's Daddy finally agreed to perform the ceremony, but only after he learned that the New York *Daily News* was sending a photographer. It was agreed that the ceremony should take place in my lower drawing room, but we were not really safe even there. The night before the ceremony, the fire alarm — which had only been recently installed — went off. The fire was quickly traced to the crawl space under the house. Mr James extinguished it with his garden hose, but not before he singed the bottom of the new blue jeans that the Reverend Mrs Carmen Suck had brought him all the way from New York — "for old times sake", whatever that might mean.

Two small boys standing outside the iron gates said they saw an old witch with long yellow hair scurrying away from the scene of the crime. After Mr James inspected the brushwood with which the fire obviously had been set, he declared it to be from Edisto Island, where I was to be burned at the stake. It didn't take much imagination to conclude that Maum Sarah must have borrowed one of Miss Henrietta's blonde wigs and set the fire.

Everything had to be done in such a hurry. Miss Potty made the cake, stuffing it with lucky dimes and two fifty-cent pieces, one of which Mr James got in his slice, breaking a wisdom tooth in three places. My original white lace bridal gown had been languishing in storage for the past ten years, so that was the least of my problems. I also had Godmama Annabel Pincklea's wedding veil, resurrected from a hat box in the Victorian bedroom packed between layers of white tissue paper and faded rose petals. Poor dear, she never did wear it, as her betrothed thoughtlessly died of the measles a week before the wedding — all the more tragic since she was denied the solace of an open casket because his handsome face was covered with ugly red blotches.

Miss Potty's girls sent me a real lace handkerchief and a lucky rabbit's foot which, from the looks of it, hadn't long left the rabbit.

Cousin Alexis telephoned to assure me that, in spite of strong family opposition from all quarters, she had decided to follow her conscience and be matron-of-honor. She had already chosen her formal gown of cherry red lace with matching headdress and bouquet of white gardenias and baby's breath from Joe Tucker, the society florist on Queen Street, and was bringing Cousin Lewis along in his full Confederate colonel's uniform, complete with sword with which Big Shot and I could cut Miss Potty's cake. Since he was half Yankee on his daddy's side, Cousin Alexis said he had a perfect right to attend the nuptials without having to ask his Deep Southern relatives for permission.

Big Shot asked if I would mind if his little son Rhett Cartland could serve as page boy, in spite of his mother's reservations — Miss Potty insisted that he wasn't properly toilet trained and might have an accident in the middle of the service. Big Shot's Daddy offered to pay for the child's outfit out of his church's discretionary fund.

Although Mr James persistently grumbled over having to help me get ready for what he called my "bloody singsong," I managed to solicit his cooperation...but only after promising to pay for the solid gold thirty-year commemorative pin his lodge was selling at cut rate. He helped arrange Aunt Gertrude Hall's French marquetry and ormolu table for an altar, while Big Shot's Daddy contributed the brass Maltese cross borrowed from a tombstone near his church.

Flowers had begun to arrive from everywhere, so many in fact that we filled the lower piazza until it looked and smelled like a funeral parlor. Then Mr James began hanging the larger floral tributes on the big iron gates outside. While the Flag of the Confederacy flew at half mast in front of Miss Henrietta's house next door, Mr James ran up the Stars and Stripes and the British Union Jack at ours.

There were a few unfortunate incidents. Somebody phoned in a bomb threat and we had to call the local police, who sent down a detective to search under the house. Fortunately, after two hours, three coffees and a plate of hush puppies, he found nothing.

Then a telegram arrived from Detroit: "May all your children be silly and all your chickens die." It was unsigned, but we were all quite convinced — especially Mr James, whose six chickens over on Edisto had up and croaked for no apparent reason — that Miss Frances Washington, the unforgiving cook, had gotten wind of the news.

Promptly at five, Cousin Alexis arrived with her old Nanny, Miss Queen Esther-Lee, a tall ramrod-straight woman with steel gray hair. A no-nonsense individual who took great delight in Alexis' numerous marriages, she heartily approved of my unconventional engagement. She had us both stand barefoot in our real silk shimmies while she inspected first our teeth and then our ears to see if we had cleaned them properly. Satisfied that we passed muster, she helped first me and then Cousin Alexis into our gowns. At that moment, Miss Potty arrived, dressed in tight red satin, a mink coat, and a large brimmed red hat that sported three large peacock feathers which she claimed would ward away the Evil Eye.

"It's a really nice evening," she greeted me. "The tide's out and the pluf mud's ripe." Then, leaving Miss Queen Esther-Lee to dress her screaming little son Rhett Cartland in his white satin suit, Miss Potty went downstairs to the makeshift wedding chapel to solicit business. When the boy bit Miss Queen Esther-Lee, she up and regally bit him back. Then, when she finally had him looking like an angel, he announced that he had to go to the bathroom.

Cousin Alexis had engaged the services of Monsieur Horace West, who came all the way from Savannah to fix our hair and put a chaplet of white lilies on her head, and Godmama's wedding veil complete with pearl orange blossoms on mine. The poor man's face was ashen white from his fear of being crushed to death by the hordes of people outside. He had nearly fainted when Mr James, in top hat and tails, greeted him at the front door with a shotgun. And when he had to explain to Miss Potty that he was a Jehovah's Witness and therefore could not possibly accept her invitation to visit her establishment, we thought we'd lost him.

Together with Cousin Alexis and Miss Queen Esther-Lee, we took turns at peering through the shutters at the crowd outside. Cousin Alexis spotted Miss Topsey Piddleton, camouflaged with a brunette wig and a Scarlet O'Hara bonnet, in the front row. Miss Topsey, a squat athletic spinster whose inclusion into local society circles had resulted from her late father's prominent position as ambassador or something to Great Britain, was an accomplished church organist, but had been pressured by Cousin Hepzibah, among others, to boycott the occasion. Her appearance today was probably due in part to curiosity, and in part to the imminent arrival of Cousin Lewis, on whom she doted shamelessly.

Maum Sarah was also spotted in the crowd, puffing a smelly black cigar and wielding a large sign, upon which was crudely scrawled: "THROW JEZEBEL TO THE DOGS!!"

"How unladylike," sniffed Cousin Alexis.

Then Cousin Lewis arrived, shouting "Make way! Make way!" He was dressed to the teeth in full Confederate uniform and riding Cousin Alexis' horse, Miss Penelope, which he had borrowed for the occasion, since his own horse, Mr Sylvester, got into a hornets nest and was still indisposed. He dismounted and tethered Miss Penelope to our gate, where the horse immediately began making a meal on the waiting floral tributes. Miss Topsey Piddleton's eyes lit up, and she elbowed her way through the crowd, just as Cousin Lewis spotted Maum Sarah and gave her a hearty pinch on her skinny little bottom. Maum Sarah screeched and swung at him with her sign, but missed and clobbered Miss Topsey instead.

In the melee that followed, Big Shot's Daddy arrived, looking like a bishop, complete with red cassock, white surplice, clerical collar, and two husky bodyguards. Big Shot followed five minutes later amidst a hearty shout from the crowd, many of whom were clients of Miss Potty. She had bought him a brand new black tuxedo, complete with white turtle-neck shirt, for he absolutely refused to wear a tie, saying that it would only cramp his style.

Miss Topsey Piddleton was carried onto the piazza to regain her senses, which required an inordinate number of tumblers of brandy. Then she wobbled into the mansion, planted herself at Godmama Annabel Pincklea's old organ and began to play a medley of sprirituals, a throwback to her plantation days.

Now it was time to begin, after a minor delay in extricating little Rhett Cartland from the Hepplewhite bathroom, where he had locked himself in. Promises of ice cream and cake finally did the trick, and Miss Topsey obligingly switched to "Here Comes the Bride."

The procession began with Cousin Alexis sashaying downstairs, bowing to everyone and throwing random kisses as if she were the feature attraction. Little Rhett Cartland then managed to drop the wedding ring that his father had bought me at Sears Roebuck (We should have listened to Miss Queen Esther-Lee and pinned it to that ridiculous little white satin cushion).

Finally it was my turn. But the person Big Shot's Daddy had chosen to give me away — Deacon Aloysius Jaspars, a political hopeful with his eye on the state legislature — suddenly got cold feet and left me standing bereft at the top of the stairs. When Big Shot's Daddy found out, he sent the two bodyguards up to get me, which they did, guns in hand. Miss Topsey Piddleton immediately rose to the spirit of the occasion and struck up "The Battle Hymn of the Republic". Thus fortified, I was led downstairs, as Miss Potty said later, like a bewildered guinea pig, to where Big Shot Calhoun, the bridegroom, was patiently waiting.

There was one panicked moment when all my doubts about this whole enterprise came rushing back, and I hesitated halfway down the stairs. But the serene sight of Big Shot's confident smiling face — along with Cousin Matilda-Madge's voice somewhere in my head urging me to get *on* with it for heaven sake — put my fears quickly to rest.

The two bodyguards hustled me into place beside Big Shot and Cousin Lewis, who had graciously agreed to stand in as best man... since the bridegroom, in his unswerving eagerness to get married, had forgotten to get one. As his ceremonial sword kept slipping, requiring that he hold it in place with both hands, he was forced to grip the wedding ring between his teeth, so that there were times when I feared he would swallow it.

41

I must say that Big Shot's Daddy gave us a very nice service, including a forty-minute sermon on Sarah and Abraham and Isaac and Rebecca, but purposely leaving out Adam and Eve for, as he noted at the beginning, they were both practicing nudists and he didn't want those New York tabloids accusing him of advocating pornography. He ended his discourse at last by inviting everyone to buy a church raffle ticket, the first prize being a live pig.

After finally pronouncing us man and wife, Big Shot's Daddy had us sign the marriage certificate, and Big Shot proudly led me back upstairs and out onto the upper piazza so that the crowds below could get a look at us. Mr James was terribly nervous, and he was quite right when he said some screwball might shoot us. He stood well back from the balcony as we acknowledged the well-wishers.

Then Big Shot told me to throw down my bouquet of pink roses and violets, which I would have preferred to place on my Godmother's grave up in Magnolia. But since they probably would have to fumigate the flowers first, I did what Big Shot suggested. Miss Topsey Piddleton, having rejoined the crowd, leapt up like a mountain goat to successfully catch it. She squealed in delight, then looked around for Cousin Lewis, but he had already begun sampling the potent punch in the reception area.

Mr James then threw open the door to invite everyone in, friends and enemies alike, for Champagne and cake. In spite of all the problems, the reception was extremely well attended, for in Charleston, personal animosity is quickly forgotten when somebody is giving a party. Even Maum Sarah, the old hypocrite, parked her Jezebel sign behind a banana bush and took her turn in line for refreshments. She even asked Mr James for an extra piece of cake to take home for her old she-cat, Miss Landine.

At last it was over, and Mr James locked up for the night. Cousins Alexis and Lewis commandeered the Art Deco bedroom — they felt it was too late to go home to Ridgeland, and they didn't dare turn up on Miss Henrietta's doorstep.

Mr James had laid out Big Shot's special matrimonial pajamas which Miss Potty's girls had thoughtfully given him, with a picture of Tarzan imprinted on the back. While he was undressing, I retired to my boudoir to put on my blue silk nightgown festooned with sequins.

I can only say that my new husband appeared more at ease than I did when we met formally on the landing, where he professed a sudden desire for a nice glass of milk, which he associated with virility. So, since Mr James had gone home, we went down to the kitchen, which had always been off limits to me. Then with his big glass of milk, Big Shot led me into the lower drawing room, still adorned as a wedding chapel with appropriate lilies. And there on Miss Annabel's cooling couch, our marriage was consummated at 2:25 in the morning. We were still blissfully sleeping there when Mr James found us the next morning.

# 5

Promptly at ten in the morning, Big Shot's Daddy arrived, minus his church collar, to spend our first honeymoon day with us. He was soon joined by Cousin Lewis, nursing a hangover and very upset because Miss Queen Esther-Lee had insisted in chaperoning Cousin Alexis throughout the whole affair. Cousin Alexis wasn't too happy about this either, as she managed to seduce only three of the male guests during the reception, including the TV cameraman.

Mr James gallantly cooked breakfast for everyone as we all watched the news of the wedding on TV. He nearly burned the toast watching for glimpses of himself on the screen. Cousin Alexis managed to get into nearly every scene, posing extravagantly, and Miss Topsey Piddleton, clutching the bridal bouquet, could be seen stuffing her face at the banquet table.

There was even some international coverage, including some scenes at Cousin Matilda-Madge's castle in Sissinghurst. She was dressed in her Girl Scout Guide uniform, with boots and upturned hat like a soldier in the Boer War. She had graciously thrown open the castle grounds to the surrounding neighborhoods to share her joy at my wedding to Big Shot and the prospect of getting herself an heir without the nuisance of making one herself.

Interviewed in a windswept scene on top of one of the castle battlements, she said: "I am scrumptiously delighted with my new cousin-in-law, and it doesn't bother me in the slightest that he is not the color of a chaste arum lily. In any case, there are several precedents for mixed marriages in our noble family, all highly successful...one even producing a bishop of the cloth.

"Many generations ago, while on one of the Crusades, an ancestor named Rudolph — known in our immediate family as Rudolph the Reckless — wed a raven-haired Saracen maiden he had rescued from a sultan's harem. Reckless Rudolph was so impressed with her beauty and her skill with a broadsword that he married her straightaway, and together they survived the rigors of fighting the war and still found time to produce fourteen children. They are buried together in the family vault along with their faithful dog Iago.

"Then there was Reverend Elias Elijah, who captured the heart of an American Indian maiden known as Gathering-Sparkling-Raindrops until the family changed it to Ethel-Fay. She was responsible for designing both waterfalls down by the lake."

The last glimpse we had of Cousin Matilda-Madge was as she was about to cut a giant iced wedding cake when she was suddenly called away to the telephone for a call from Buckingham Palace.

At this point Big Shot excused himself to run down to Miss Potty's. Although strictly speaking he was on honeymoon leave, he felt it his duty to stay on top of things in his place of business.

45

While he was gone, his Daddy continued his eloquent transversal of all the famous Biblical couples, while Cousin Alexis bemoaned the frustrations of dealing with her five husbands. While I was vascillating between historical romance and modern frustration, the phone rang. Mr James answered it. "It's Miss Henrietta," he whispered to us.

"Mr James," she said, "as the noble Christian that you are, please leave that den of iniquity for a few minutes and come over here and minister to my poor cuckolded baby, Mr Pee. He tried to drown his sorrows in Maum Sarah's homemade chinaberry wine, and we simply cannot revive him."

Mr James agreed, reluctantly, to come over and do what he could. He left, armed with a jar of our strongest coffee, just as Big Shot returned from Miss Potty's. I asked him if everything was okay.

"Never better, my angel," he replied, hanging up his sailor cap on the coatrack. "Although her number-one girl, Big-Ass Mabel, seems to be coming down with the measles."

Cousin Alexis shuddered. "That woman could use some plastic surgery on her you-know-what. I cannot think what the gentleman callers see in her."

Big Shot shrugged, grinning. "Why settle for a sardine when you can have a whale?"

Big Shot and I were just sitting down to dinner when Mr James returned with the news that Mr Pee was coming around, but that his temper was still none too good. I expressed concern for Mr Pee, since I had never known him to be this aroused by anything.

"Don't worry, my angel," Big Shot said reassuringly. "He'll blow off his anger for a day or so, and then things will be back to — "

He was interrupted by a deafening blast, as one of the dining room windows shattered and the little radio which was playing Elvis Presley's "Love Me Tender" was blown across the room. Big Shot and I dove for the floor.

A moment later, Mr James dashed into the room carrying his ancient shotgun, tossed it to Big Shot, and grabbed Godmama's Daddy's own weapon which hung over the dining room mantle. "We got problems," he said, unnecessarily.

As the two of them crept toward the front door, I edged over to the window and looked out over the piazza, just as a second blast rent the night air. This one, however, blew away the whole top of a streetlight near the road. It was followed immediately by yet another, which shattered the chapel window of the convent which stood sedately across the street. Instantly, the lawn outside was filled with a flock of screaming nuns.

I could barely make out a figure standing in the street, weaving around in circles and pointing a large shotgun. The weapon discharged once more and flattened the tires of a car parked nearby. Nuns and bystanders dropped to the ground, hands over their heads.

I knew immediately who the figure was, and ran to the front door, where Big Shot had already gone out to confront the invader.

"Now just calm down, Mr Pee," he said quietly. "There's lots of innocent people around here, and we don't want nobody hurt."

Mr Pee stiffened and muttered something about "family honor".

"Yes, well, why don't you just let me have that gun," Big Shot said soothingly, "and we'll go inside and have some coffee and talk about all this."

Mr Pee shook his head vigorously. "...Not going into that den of inquitity...intiquity...in..." He reached down and fumbled with the bolt on the gun.

47

"Now, Now, Mr Pee..." Big Shot began, reaching for the weapon. "No more of that. Besides, you already used up all the ammunition...the gun is empty."

Mr Pee looked down at the gun in his hands, a puzzled look in his eyes. A moment later, Big Shot's hands closed around the barrel. Startled, Mr Pee jerked back on the gun.

Big Shot was wrong. The gun was not empty. There was a flash, an explosion of sound...and Big Shot crumpled to the ground.

Mr Pee stared in horror, then fainted dead away.

And so did I.

"People are starting to arrive to offer condolences," Big Shot's Daddy said quietly, his hand on my arm, as Mr James handed me a cup of coffee. "Think you're up to it?"

I nodded. I was too numb at this point to feel any more distress. The police, ambulance and coroner had left, and only a few news reporters were outside taking pictures of the scene of devastation. Maum Sarah had taken the shaken Mr Pee back to his house. Mr James had called Cousins Alexis and Hepzibah. Big Shot's Daddy was doing his best to comfort me while dealing with his own anguish.

The visitors were all very supportive. Several of Miss Potty's girls, who had known Big Shot since his earliest days there, reported that Miss Potty herself had collapsed at hearing the news. I wondered if and when Miss Frances Washington, my former cook and fiancee of Big Shot, would learn of the tragedy, and how she would react.

Cousin Alexis arrived and extended sincere sympathy. Having buried two of her five husbands — although none under such violent circumstances — she could readily identify with the problems.

"I have to warn you," she said. "Cousin Hepzibah will be less than sympathetic with your bereavement. She was on Maum Sarah and Miss Henrietta's side from the start in thinking that you did our Cousin Pee wrong. And they're going to be even less happy about all the new controversy."

She was right. Promptly at midnight, like three witches, Cousin Hepzibah, Maum Sarah and Miss Topsey Piddleton (having been recruited to fill in for Miss Henrietta, who was nursing the distraught Mr Pee) arrived at my door. Maum Sarah carried her silver-headed cane, which she poked into every corner as she slithered into my living room like a small crocodile. Cousin Hepzibah and Miss Topsey wore white summer mourning, while Maum Sarah wore black, which was her standard color anyway.

Mr James served them all coffee. In addition, Miss Topsey requested several essence-of-ginger cookies to help the indigestion brought on by the tragic events.

Cousin Hepzibah cleared her throat. "It's a terrible tragedy, my dear, and you know you have our deepest sympathies. If there's anything we can do to see you through this difficult time..."

Miss Topsey Piddleton fidgited uncomfortably. Maum Sarah tapped her cane impatiently on the floor.

"As your best friend," Cousin Hepzibah went on, "and with only your best interests at heart, I would suggest an extended trip somewhere...just until things settle down a bit, you understand. Feelings are still running high at this point, and your continued presence might only serve to acerbate them. After all, there is the family honor to consider..."

I stiffened. "If Mr Pee's behavior is any indication of how one considers his family honor..."

"In Charleston, the old families always look out for their own. We do not solicit scandal, but when it comes — as it did when you decided to put aside my Cousin Pee for another...person — we took it in stride, dealing with it once and for all in our own way."

49

It was obviously pointless to argue with her. I drew a breath. "As a matter of fact, I have given serious consideration to returning to my home in England..."

She slapped her wide knees. "An *excellent* idea..."

"...until, as you say, things have calmed down a bit."

"Hmmph...yes... *Well*," reaching for her white beaded purse, "all of this is going to cost you a pretty penny...to say nothing of funeral expenses, legal fees, living costs back in England... We want you to be comfortable, not feel rushed..." She withdrew a check and handed it to me as casually as she would offer me a cigaret.

The check was for fifty thousand dollars, and was signed by Mr Pee's mother, Miss Henrietta. I sat looking at it as Cousin Hepzibah closed her purse and settled back in her chair, a smug look on her face. Then I asked Big Shot's Daddy to kindly lend me his pen.

While they all stared, I endorsed the check and handed it to my wide-eyed father-in-law. "Go buy yourself a new church," I told him.

Miss Potty tacked a notice on the front door of her health club:

## CLOSED

## OWING TO A DEATH IN THE FAMILY

and then put all the girls to baking shrimp rolls for the wake. The funeral home did a real nice job fixing up Big Shot, whose face was unmarred in the fatal blast. He lay peacefully in his copper casket in that same lower drawing room where we were so recently married. Big Shot's Daddy arranged for three large ladies, dressed all in white, to be in attendance in case anybody collapsed; they were hard at work all the evening. Miss Potty managed to faint in Mr

James' arms three or four times. At one point, while all three white ladies had their arms full, Miss Wilhelmina, the Sunday School teacher, knocked over our potted palm in a swoon.

We fed everybody in the dining room as my late husband would have wished, while Cousin Alexis fed Miss Margie and her own little poodle, Miss Gloria (after her movie idol, Gloria Swanson) in the Butler's pantry. She and Cousin Lewis were the only white persons in evidence besides myself, for Miss Henrietta had issued an edict that everyone who valued his or her reputation in the Holy City had better stay away.

Next morning, Cousin Alexis accompanied me to the airport. Mr James promised to look after things until my return — which at that point I wasn't even sure would ever take place. We stood like two large black beetles in our mourning clothes, watching Big Shot's casket being loaded onto the plane. I had decided to take his body with me, to be buried in my family plot at Sissinghurst, rather than leave him in the proximity of those who had effectively done him in. Big Shot's Daddy had no objection to this, and Miss Henrietta and her crew sighed in relief.

Just as I was getting ready to board the plane myself, Cousin Lewis came dashing up, in such a hurry that he had forgotten his Confederate jacket. "Cousin Pee just had a heart attack," he announced breathlessly. "Everyone's at the hospital."

"Oh, dear!" Cousin Alexis exclaimed. "Is he...?

"He's resting comfortably," her cousin assured her. "Apparently it was only a minor attack. But I think you'd better come along to the hospital."

Cousin Alexis hugged me, then hurried over to the waiting car. Cousin Lewis hesitated, then said, "I'm very sorry for all that's happened, Miss Gwendolyn. Cousin Pee is, of course, very dear to us all. But in the long run, I think perhaps he was amiss in his treatment of you. And I respect you for following your heart. I just wish I could do as much with Cousin Alexis, the only true love of my life."

He looked at his watch. "I must run. And you have a plane to catch." He took my hand. "Cousin Alexis and I will do all we can to see that all this unpleasantness is put behind us. And you must do the same. And you must return to us as soon as you feel able."

I hugged him, and told him to give Mr Pee my sincere wish for a speedy recovery. At least I think it was sincere.

# 6

We buried Big Shot beside my mother in the small green cemetery behind the village church at Sissinghurst. It is a special place where the wild robins steal the red berries from the holly wreaths at Christmas time, for as Cousin Matilda-Madge often reminded me, "Succour the living as well as the dead."

Cousin Matilda-Madge was an imposing figure of a woman — stocky, burly, like the portraits of Henry VIII. She was a tower of strength to me before and after the funeral, insisting that I stay with her until I decided what I wanted to do.

Her home was a huge medieval castle with all the trappings — parapets, turrets, battlements and courtyards. A long yew-lined road led to the entrance, and standing regally beside the front steps was an enormous white marble statue of a horse.

Once she took me with her to the top or the tower to oil the clock which, as she carefully explained, she had to do herself, for clocks were very fussy as to who fiddled with their innards. Three hundred and sixty five steps, one for every day of the year, led up to the battlements with the royal bedroom underneath. "The last Queen who stayed there had to be carried down on a stretcher. Nobody thought to tell us she had a weak heart — well, you know how secretive royalty can be. It's a wonder all those stairs didn't kill her."

"Can we look inside?" I begged, and Cousin Matilda-Madge was only too happy to oblige, taking an enormous iron key from the chastity belt at her waist. The heavy oaken door slowly opened with much creaking to reveal a chamber of great beauty boasting tall mullioned windows with panoramic views of hopfields and apple orchards stretching for miles over the flat Kentish Weald. All the furniture was draped in dust sheets like courtiers around the massive cherub-carved Elizabethan four-poster bed.

"Daddy and Mummy spent their wedding night in it," my cousin giggled. "And I was the result...for better or whatever." Her double chin quivered.

"What a perfect place for a honeymoon..." I remarked.

The medieval part of Hastings clings like a giant limpet to the foot of a white chalk cliff surmounted by the ruins of a Norman castle. There it dreams of days when it was a bustling seaport with its two grand churches, St Clement's and All Saints, that attested to the inhabitants' prosperity. Somewhere in Regency and Victorian times had come the rows of gray stone and neat red brick villas, the large hotels for summer visitors, the pier stretching out like a long alligator into the English Channel itself, and the paved seafront stretching as far as neighboring St Leonards.

The old town where I found my small Tudor house on Church Street seemed alien and aloof from the new. There I spent my days writing and coming to grips with my grief, finding at last a measure of peace. On stormy nights the wind blew in from the rough sea rattling the diamond window panes while I sat in the warm security of the chimney corner savoring my own log fire. Little Margie, glad to be done with her six months quarantine — the British law to prevent rabies — was glad to be home, enjoying our long solitary walks on the sands when the tide was out. There, far from the intrigues of Charleston society, I awaited the birth of Big Shot's child, so in a way he seemed very close.

Manigault Calhoun was born on the sixteenth of October, 1973, in the sprawling hospital at Hastings. She was a lovely child with brown curly hair and brown eyes speckled with green. Cousin Matilda-Marge was as elated as if she had given birth herself, flying both the British and American flags from her tower top. She drove down from Sissinghurst for the candlelight christening held in St Clements, built in the twelfth century, followed by tea and iced cake in my little old house built with the timbers of a long salvaged wreck. I was determined to enjoy this child, for when she smiled it was Big Shot's smile. Thus comforted, I felt that at least part of him had come back to watch over me.

With Miss Margie on a leash and the baby in her pram, we were a familiar threesome on the narrow streets of Hastings' old town. On Friday afternoons, Cousin Matilda-Madge herself arrived, as she explained, "for a whiff of fresh air", taking over the pushing, charging along the seafront, her pearls flying out in the breeze.

When Manigault was two and in a push chair, she fell madly in love with Ocky the Octopus who lived in a tank in the pier's aquarium. There was no peace, even on wet mornings, until we had visited Ocky. We were such frequent visitors that the attendant often let us in for nothing.

It was a pleasant life, but I knew in my heart that good things did not last forever, that one day the Holy City of

Charleston would reassert itself into my life...as in due course it most certainly did. A cable arrived from Cousin Alexis, now on her sixth husband, Number Five having been respectfully drowned she-crabbing at Folly Beach. The cable read:

SADLY INFORM YOU MISS HENRIETTA SUCCUMBED
TO ONE FACE SCRAPING TOO MANY. FUNERAL
FRIDAY MAGNOLIA CEMETERY. MR PEE SAYS ALL
IS FORGIVEN. PLEASE COME HOME.

It wasn't clear exactly who was doing the urging to return, or for that matter who was supposed to be forgiving whom. I had anticipated this dilemma for some time, and was never really sure how I would respond when a decision had to be made. I was comfortable here, but there was much about Charleston which I sorely missed.

Cousin Matilda-Madge thought I was quite mad, but granted that I must have my reasons. "Make them eat crow," she insisted. "Especially Mr Pee." I could understand her point of view, but I wasn't one to hold grudges, and I could only hope the same was true for the residents of the Holy City.

So I left my little Tudor house in Hastings, employing a good neighbor as caretaker, and bade farewell to cousin Matilda-Madge, with the promise that I would bring Manigault, her heir, back for a visit every summer. Then I flew off with Miss Margie to America.

Awaiting us at Charleston Airport was Cousin Alexis, dressed as I last remembered her, in funereal black with a waist-length veil, and attended by her nanny, Miss Queen Esther-Lee. Mr James was sporting a bowler hat, and accompanying him was a gangley young black man who looked to be about seventeen years old.

"This," announced Mr James with an air of importance, "is Miss Glory-Be, your new under-butler, who fortunately can also cook. His mama used to work for your grandmama, but has just gone to live in heaven with Big Shot, so it would be Charleston etiquette to give him a job."

Miss Glory-Be was loose-limbed, and his joints seemed to be suspended by strings like a marionette. He shook my hand daintily and said he'd heard *so* much about me, and it was just so *thrilling* to be working for me.

I stammered my thanks. Then, as the funeral was imminent and there was no time to even go home and change clothes, I left Manigault, now a boisterous four year-old, and Miss Margie, agreeably relieved that there was no wretched quarantine to contend with this side of the Atlantic, in the care of Miss Queen Esther-Lee, and was whisked by Cousin Alexis in her new white Rolls Royce (a wedding gift from Husband number Six, a financier from Wall Street) to the realm of the glorious dead, Magnolia Cemetery.

There, among the hundreds of tombstones and expensive monuments commemorating the cream of Charleston society, we were met with a most extraordinary sight. Mr Pee and Maum Sarah were sitting in identical chrome-plated wheelchairs, Mr Pee sobbing loudly and Maum Sarah screaming, "My baby, Miss Henrietta, don't leave us!" Mr Pee looked a good bit older, and was sporting a small Adolph Hitler mustache and wearing a large black band on his sleeve. Maum Sarah looked more like a witch than ever. I noted that although Miss Henrietta was not yet in the grave, Maum Sarah was already wearing her most expensive wig.

They were supported by a great crowd of Charlestonians, both white and black, led by a grim-faced Cousin Hepzibah and Miss Topsey Piddleton, who was seated at a portable organ playing "Swing Low Sweet Chariot".

Cousin Hepzibah greeted me cordially — there's no other word for it — as if I had been out of town for only a few days. No mention was made of the events leading up to my departure, and I could only hope that things stayed that way.

Mr Pee looked up at me from his wheelchair, tears in his sunken eyes, then reached out hesitantly to take my hand. My heart went out to him, and I leaned down and kissed his cheek.

The casket, Cousin Hepzibah duly informed us, had already been opened six times, and now the lid was being raised for the seventh. Inside lay Miss Henrietta, a little shrunken it seemed, her face swathed in bandages like an Egyptian Mummy. Her favorite volume of *Beauty Tips for the Ever Young*, conveniently opened at "The Fine Art of Face Lifting", was gripped in her small hands, which were appropriately encased in white gloves, without which no respectable Charleston dowager would be seen before 4:00 in the afternoon, even in her coffin. Her size four white satin wedding gown with Brussels antique lace veil still fit perfectly.

Miss Topsey then struck up "Onward Christian Soldiers", presumably to hasten us out of the cemetery in time for lunch. The casket was closed for the last time and gently lowered into its final resting place beside Mr Pee's Daddy, her adulterous husband. Then I took my place behind Mr Pee's wheelchair while he was still bawling his head off and wheeled him to the waiting limousine, while overhead a flock of herons rather inappropriately sounded their mating calls.

Suddenly, something made me look up, and I found myself staring into the eyes of Big Shot's white marble angel.

He had been quite right — she really *was* smiling.

☆ ☆ ☆ ☆ ☆ ☆

It seemed like a time capsule, as if the years had just taken a brief holiday at the Pincklea Mansion. The garden paths were neatly swept, the lyre-shaped door knocker polished to perfection, and my ill-fated fountain was still spouting water. Only the century shrub had changed — it was in full bloom. Now I wondered what would Mr James tell the tourists, for it gave no sign of dying.

The house, the rooms, the cooling couch all seemed to be waiting — for what I didn't know, for in Charleston the past was married to the present, the future a mystery.

Mr Pee lived on in what was now his house, attended by the indomitable Maum Sarah, who treated him like a chronic invalid, although he seemed to have recovered well from his heart attack of nearly five years before. She no longer allowed him to play polo, or even to ride his faithful horse Estella for that matter. The only freedom he had was when she took off for Edisto, at which time he quickly appeared on my doorstep.

He never mentioned Big Shot. And, prudently, neither did I.

It came as no surprise when he confided to Cousin Alexis that he was prepared to let bygones be bygones and marry me properly, this time at St Philip's. He would even look after my child. My feelings were decidedly mixed, but at least this time I had the advantage over him; I could wait patiently for his six months of mourning for Miss Henrietta to be over before making any decisions.

Maum Sarah, who had not even been asked, absolutely refused to have anything to do with my daughter Manigault, which was fine with me. Our new under-butler, Miss Glory-Be, had an aunt, Miss Viola-Ball, who was more than pleased to become Manigault's nurse.

Big Shot's Daddy was more prosperous than ever with his brand new church, complete with air-conditioning and a slide projector with which he illustrated his sermons on

Sunday morning. He had not given up his roofing and pickled pigs feet enterprises, although he had relegated others to run them. His ambition was to have his own television show and sing gospel songs just like his favorite, Sister Beulah Rose.

Likewise, Miss Potty had prospered, having added a recreation room and pink marble restrooms to her Health Club in memory of Big Shot. Several of her girls were new, since some of the regulars had followed current fashion and learned to type and become secretaries and thus upgraded their personal careers. Even Miss Wilhelmina had married a visiting evangelist and gone to live in some cold place called Utica, New York.

Miss Potty asked if I would kindly donate two bright orange polyester recliners for the new recreation room which had fake paneled walls. This I was only too happy to do.

Miss Glory-Be now did my cooking, coming up with some most unusual dishes he had learned from a French chef with whom he had once enjoyed a pleasant affinity. When Miss Topsey Piddleton gave a party to commemorate the day she was presented at the Court of St James, he made a large sherry trifle with whole peeled bananas, like a miniature Stonehenge, encircling the top.

Of his jilted culinary predecessor, Miss Frances Washington, we heard nothing.

# 7

Nothing had rocked Charleston society as much since my unorthodox wedding to Big Shot. Cousin Hepzibah and Miss Topsey Piddleton arrived together at my house, breathless with the news. They rudely interrupted Mr Pee right in the middle of his breakfast, Maum Sarah having conveniently taken off to Edisto with Miss Landine, her old she-cat, and Miss Fiddle-Dee-Dee, Miss Landine's surviving daughter (the other one, Miss Praise-the-Lord, had been shipped to New York City to take her place as the Reverend Mrs Carmen Suck's church cat. Trouble was, Miss Praise-the-Lord turned out to be a tom and had to be fixed and renamed Mr).

"A *French Princess* is reported to be looking for an old mansion in Charleston that she can restore to its original pristine condition," announced Cousin Hepzibah. "What's more, she intends to move to Charleston and live in the house."

Mr Pee sniffed, carefully removing a spot of egg from his starched white pajamas. "As an environmentalist, I don't like the French — they eat frogs legs."

"You always were a spoil-sport," grumbled Cousin Hepzibah. "Besides, I have already extended her an invitation to serve as Vice-president of my own glorious Ban-Aluminum-Siding-in-Charleston Society."

Mr Pee frowned. "I thought Miss *Gwendolyn* was made Vice-president, seeing that she was the only one brave enough to vote for your motion to send a piece of siding to the Mayor in lieu of a Christmas card. Even Miss Topsey voted against it."

"It seemed so unladylike," whimpered Miss Topsey, snitching a hot biscuit when she thought Mr Pee wasn't looking.

Cousin Hepzibah ignored her. "I'm sure Miss Gwendolyn is prepared to make this sacrifice as a gesture toward arriving royalty."

Mr Pee slammed down his fork. "You have no right to treat Miss Gwendolyn so callously!" I was aghast — it was the first time in his life that Mr Pee had ever stuck up for me. "Besides, you have no way of knowing whether this...this princess will even accept the position."

At that moment, Mr James charged in with two bowls of grits, pushing one in front of Mr Pee and planting the other in front of Miss Topsey. Her face lit up. "For me?"

"Better'n havin' you sit there with your tongue hangin' out," he replied. She huffed, and proceeded to blow on her grits.

"Does this French Princess have a husband?" I ventured to ask. Mr Pee gave me an odd look.

"Passed on," Cousin Hepzibah replied, crossing herself. "Princess Frances is a widow."

"That's nice," noted Mr Pee. "Maybe she could marry Cousin Lewis. He needs a wife."

I frowned at him. "I don't think your cousin Alexis would appreciate that."

Mr Pee only grinned and called for more coffee. This time Miss Glory-Be rushed in to accommodate him. My new little under-butler had formed a very sweet attachment for my former fiance.

"I've never heard of a princess named Frances." I mused. It always gave me pleasure to annoy Cousin Hepzibah. "Now, if Princess *Margaret* were coming to live on the East Battery, that would really be something. We might even get to see her sister Elizabeth."

"I was presented to their grandparents, King George V and Queen Mary," Miss Topsey reminded us for the thousandth time. "I was a chaste sight to behold in my three feathers, dutifully sacrificed by Mr Wilfred, Mummy's pet ostrich."

"My, my — just like Sally Rand!" Miss Glory-Be giggled, receiving such a murderous look in return that he danced off to the kitchen.

"In the old days," snapped Miss Topsey, "insolent servants were sent to the old city jail to be whipped."

"Times change," sighed Mr Pee, buttering another piece of toast. "And not always for the better."

"Never mind the servants," grumbled Cousin Hepzibah. "I shall expect you both at the ceremony I've arranged at the airport two weeks from Wednesday. "We have to show Her Royal Highness what a real Charleston welcome is."

"How very exciting," yawned Mr Pee, and was promptly told by his cousin to shut up.

"Miss Topsey, kindly loan me your Holy Bible.... I hope it is the King James version."

"Of *course* it is," replied Miss Topsey, somewhat peevishly. "I am a royalist." She rummaged around in her large handbag to retrieve it.

63

"Hold up your right hand," commanded Cousin Hepzibah, and rather than offend a guest — even a less-than-welcome one — I did as I was told.

"Repeat after me: I, Gwendolyn Annabel Whittington (she pointedly omitted the Calhoun) do hereby agree to act as chaplain to the Ban-Aluminum-Siding-in-Charleston Society as a consolation prize for having graciously moved over so that Her Royal Highness, the Princess Frances, might legally occupy her seat as Vice-president."

I repeated her words exactly. I didn't care that much about the position anyway, and I had no wish to provoke Cousin Hepzibah.

But Mr Pee's demanding cousin was not finished with me yet. "Your first duty in your new holy capacity will be to deliver a cake to Maum Sarah for her eightieth birthday when she returns from Edisto tomorrow. Had to bake the damn thing myself, since my cook quit yesterday. Third one this month. Cook, that is, not cake"

I looked at Mr Pee for his reaction, but he simply shook his head and sighed.

Cousin Hepzibah's butler, Mr Solomon Jake, brought us Maum Sarah's birthday cake, carefully wrapped in a brown paper bag together with eighty little red candles that looked better suited to a Christmas tree. It took Miss Glory-Be all of twenty minutes to arrange them in a fussy pattern on the iced top. Then we set off for Maum Sarah's, leaving Mr Pee safely upstairs in the Victorian bedroom because, as he said, Maum Sarah would be too busy opening her presents to miss him.

Miss Glory-Be wore a white linen jacket, black pants, and a red baseball cap that some player had once given him — "in appreciation" (of what we were never sure). I followed with my open parasol and best white gloves. I was very uneasy, for I knew how much Maum Sarah hated me. But I was determined not to show it.

Maum Sarah's house stood on the grounds of the late Miss Henrietta's mansion, whose property bordered my own. In years gone by, before modern kitchens were installed in the house itself, all the cooking was done in kitchen quarters some distance away. Above were the servants sleeping quarters. As Miss Henrietta's family had quite a number of servants (known as slaves before the War of Northern Aggression), the building was much larger than usual in order to house them. This was now Maum Sarah's home.

Cousin Alexis had told me that Maum Sarah's domain was better equipped than some of the big houses around it. She even had a whirlpool jacuzzi in which to soak her corns.

Miss Glory-Be balanced the cake in one hand while he rattled the door knocker, which was shaped like a little black angel upon which Maum Sarah had made Mr Pee paint a pair of respectable orange breeches. After several loud knocks, a raspy voice shouted, "Come in! You dun interrupt my exercises."

The sight that greeted us was bizarre. In a large room, which was really three small ones knocked into one, was housed an unbelievable collection of antiques, a kitchen set consisting of a table and four red plastic chairs, Mr Pee's old wooden rocking horse, and a chest of drawers made by Thomas Elfe, Charleston's most famous cabinetmaker of the 18th century (which by rights should have been in a museum). The walls were covered with all the colored pictures that Mr Pee had ever made from kindergarten through the 8th Grade. In the middle hung a valuable oil painting by Jeremiah Theus, Charleston's most revered artist, of a very flat-chested lady who seemed badly in need of a substantial meal.

65

In the center of the room sat Maum Sarah's pink-tiled jacuzzi in which was lazily swimming a live duck who had already laid its egg for the day in a wall-papered cardboard box close by. The tub was surrounded by fake water lilies, a pink plastic flamingo, and a potted rubber palmetto tree to give the illusion of a tropical shoreline.

And in the midst of all this, Maum Sarah, attired in one of the late lamented Miss Henrietta's banana yellow jumpsuits and sporting a red poodle-curl wig, was peddling away for dear life on the exercise machine that Miss Henrietta had willed her.

At first she pretended not to notice us. But when Miss Glory-Be put down the cake on the scarlet formica tabletop, then proceeded to light all eighty candles with the silver Coca-Cola cigarette lighter that had been Big Shot's when he pimped for Miss Potty, she suddenly stopped dead and stared at the cake. "Who's that from?" she demanded.

When we told her that Cousin Hepzibah had sent it, she jumped off her bike and began blowing out the candles as fast as Miss Glory-Be could light them.

"Miz Gwendolyn," she hollered, "I got nuthin' personal 'gainst you, spite of you marryin' that womanizin' Big Shot Calhoun and runnin' off to Yankee-land like some white trash camp follower. But I fear bodily to partake of this cake, knowin' who sent it. Here...." and she picked up a small pearl handled knife, a relic from Mr Pee's childhood. "I aim to try it out on Miz Landine and see does she survive it."

Miss Landine, who had an extremely sweet tooth for an old she-cat, dutifully obliged, taking one bite of the patriotic Confederate gray icing. Abruptly, she gagged and threw up.

Maum Sarah nodded her head. "Like I suspected. Last time that big-boned hussy sent me somethin' she made I was laid up for three days. Dunno whether she just never learned to cook or she's actual tryin' to do me in."

She picked up the wounded cake and handed it to Miss Glory-Be. "Take it back and throw it down the commode," she ordered. Then she went over to her ancient TV set and clicked it on. "I got to watch my soap operas now. Must keep up with them New York hussies, always getting raped by their dentists."

As we were leaving, she picked up the duck's egg and handed it to me. "A present from Miz Stacey. For Mr Pee's breakfast." Then she slammed the door behind us and pulled the bolts.

Rather than face Cousin Hepzibah's wrath at such unwarranted rejection, I sent Miss Glory-Be with the cake over to Miss Potty's Health Club by taxi. When he returned, he was shaking his head.

"That's one strange lady, Miss Gwendolyn. First she's thrilled to death by the cake, saying how kind and thoughtful and all you are to send it. Then she gets all riled up and starts talking about Big Shot, and how you stole him from her. But then she turns right around and says how much she respects you, and didn't she send Big Shot straight from her own warm bed to be on time for his wedding. *Then* she says how sorry she feels for you, being a widow woman and all, but she just *knows* Big Shot's last thoughts were of her. *Then* — "

"Miss Glory-Be," I interrupted, "I think I've heard all I really care to hear. You're right, she's a strange woman, and as unpredictable as they come."

"Anyway," Miss Glory-Be said, unwrapping a package, "she sent you this..." He held up a colored embroidery in a frame constructed from beer can tops. In crimson letters woven by Miss Potty's own experienced hands was one word: REPENT. "She said it was given to her by her preacher man, who created a stir by dying right in her bed."

Miss Potty's present was as puzzling as her motive in giving it to me. But I resolved not to waste good time worrying about it.

# 8

In spite of his advanced years, Mr James still drove like a maniac. After an afternoon of running errands, I was a nervous wreck when we turned in our driveway, nearly taking one of the bronze lions with us.

Miss Glory-Be was there to greet us at the front door, wearing a pink frilly apron and wielding a feather duster. Miss Margie was at his heels, accompanied by her new friend, an orphaned basset hound named Miss Judith-Josephine (soon to be shortened to Miss J-J), which some white trash varmints had thrown out of a truck one Sunday morning while I was en route to get my New York Times. She had followed me home, and was subsequently adopted as Miss Margie's feminine companion.

"You sure did miss a treat, Miss Gwendolyn!" Miss Glory-Be exclaimed, excitement in his shrill voice. "Mr Pee came by with a *present* for you. He came the back way, over the wall — so Maum Sarah wouldn't see him, I expect. Then he carried it all the way up to the piazza himself." He snickered. "I never saw him carry anything bigger than his toothbrush."

"He brought me a present? Why would Mr Pee suddenly do something like that? Unless...it must be an anniversary present."

"What anniversary?" grumbled Mr James. "I don't know nuthin' 'bout no anniversary."

I nodded my head and smiled. "The anniversary of our first meeting, I suspect. When he was caught stealing my figs."

"I surely wish somebody would give *me* a present," complained Miss Glory-Be. "I have anniversaries all the time, and nobody bothers to send me anything."

"Well, let's go see what he brought," I said, proceeding out to the piazza. "We do need another reading lamp to put on his side of the bed..."

"Well, he'll have all the light he needs now to read his Nancy Drew mysteries," Miss Glory-Be giggled. "He has given you a *real Waterford chandelier* that belonged to his daddy's Wife Number Two."

I recognized it immediately — it had been in Mr Pee's possession since his infamous daddy died. "Mr Pee means well but, with all due respect to Miss Henrietta's memory, she couldn't stand that chandelier. Even Maum Sarah refused to hang it over her whirlpool jacuzzi. Miss Henrietta said that anything even slightly relating to Wife Number Two was sheer anathema to her more delicate senses."

"Nasty scarlet varmint, that Miss Jessie-Belle," Mr James growled, "cavorting with her lion tamer boyfriend right there in the garden while Mr Pee's Daddy was away at the Kentucky Races."

"What's past is past," I reminded him, hastening to change the subject. "The problem now is where to put it."

Mr James frowned. "The only place that *doesn't* already have somethin' hangin' in it is the foyer."

70

"The perfect place!" Miss Glory-Be tittered. "Mr Pee will see how much we all appreciate it every time he uses the bathroom."

"I hope no one expects me to hang it from the ceilin'," snapped Mr James. "You know very well I can't endure heights."

"It's going to need some work first anyway," Miss Glory-Be said. "Mr Pee left a trail of crystal teardrops all down the path, getting it over here. And he dropped three more in the visitor's commode. I'm afraid to flush it."

"Well," Mr James sighed, snatching up an 18th century solid silver serving spoon from the sideboard, "I guess this old man had better go fishing..."

"Mr Pee said he would return for tea at four," Miss Glory-Be informed me. "And we're also to expect his cousins Hepzibah, Alexis and Lewis. And that uncouth Miss Topsey Piddleton."

"Why so many people?" I asked. "Mr Pee and I usually just have a nice quiet tea by ourselves."

"Who knows?" Miss Glory-Be chimed, grinning cryptically. "Maybe it's a *special occasion* or something." Then he flitted out of the room, holding his left hand up in front of him, fingers spread, as if he were examining something beautiful.

There's something strange going on here, I thought to myself. First, Mr James has been acting peculiar, then Mr Pee abruptly gives me a present, and now Miss Glory-Be acts like he's hiding something from me. It's time to get to the bottom of this...

When Mr James returned from his salvaging operation in the downstairs bathroom, I collared him. "I get the distinct impression that something is going on behind my back," I informed him. "Would you mind telling me what it is?"

He sighed and nodded his head, a solemn look clouding his countenance. "I guess it's time to discuss a vital issue..."

I folded my arms, sensing an impending revelation. "And that issue is...?"

"Next month, God willing, I'll reach eighty-three." The old hypocrite wiped away a fake tear. "Missus, I'm 'bout ready to take off for celestial parts."

He sank into a Chippendale armchair opposite mine, carefully unfolded a large white handkerchief and pretended to weep, sobbing so loudly that he sounded like a bullfrog in heat. "You know and I know, when Gabriel blows his golden trumpet I got to get up in his chariot and leave you to make your own grits in the morning. Then when Saint Peter signs me in as a repented sinner and gives me my halo, there's no coming back. I got to stay on and take lessons on the harp."

"Mr James, you're *not* about to die," I assured him. "Your doctor told me you were as healthy as a suckling piglet. Why, you haven't even got a prostrate condition or a weakened bladder like most men your age."

"Never you mind my prostrate condition or my bladder!" shot back Mr James. "Didn't I promise Big Shot on your wedding day never to leave you, long as you needed lookin' after? Well, now I don't need to wait no longer. Mr Pee dun gone and proposed."

I blinked. "Proposed? To whom?"

"To *me*, of course! I'm your butler! I run this family. Only right and proper he should ask me for your hand."

So that was it. I can't say the proposal was unexpected, but the manner of its delivery was a little unsettling. I would have to give careful thought to an appropriate response...

"'Bout time he made you an honest woman," Mr James went on, "'steada slinking over here under cover of darkness like some mangy old he-dog. 'Bout time he showed *me* some consideration and saved me fixin' separate trays. I'm an old man, Missus — Gabriel's a-tootin' on his horn and I'm all ready to go...but not before I marry you off once and for all to our own Mr Pee."

Mr James folded his wrinkled hands and smiled bliss-fully. "Then I can sprout my wing feathers and fly off in peace."

"Amen!" said Miss Glory-Be, returning all a-tingle. "I can hear the bells of St Philip's ringing out already, Miss Gwendolyn. Besides, you can't jilt Mr Pee a second time — not even a Charleston lady would be that cruel."

"Jilt!" snorted Mr James, placing his white handkerchief in the top pocket of his jacket, having folded it carefully as if were the Confederate flag. "This time it would be breach of promise, 'cause I have already accepted."

At this point, a proper Charleston lady of the old school would doubtless have fainted...or at least reached for her smelling salts. I settled for collapsing into a cushioned chair. Miss Glory-Be snatched a copy of *Southern Living* and be-gan fanning me.

When I had sufficiently recovered, I turned upon the old butler. "Mr James, with all due respect to the Angel Gabriel, not to mention his calling trumpet, that was very *presump-tuous* of you!"

Mr James hung his head. "Maybe I was a little hasty, Missus...but I was only thinkin' of your own good. I can't be comin' back from the Great Beyond every time the sil-ver needs polishin'. 'Sides," he grinned, "I 'spects you al-ready made up your mind to let the poor man do right by you."

"Well, I — "

"Thought so. Now look, Missus. What's past is past — you just told me so yourself. Life must go on...and all that sort of thing."

"I won't say no," I admitted. "But it must be understood that any further negotiations will have to be between Mr Pee and myself."

By the time 4:00 rolled around, I had pretty much decided to accept Mr Pee's proposal, unorthodox as it was. I was briefly tempted to reply in kind by sending Mr James over with my decision, but finally decided that it would serve no useful purpose — Mr Pee was Mr Pee, and not likely to change in either of our lifetimes.

For the most part, Mr Pee was extraordinarily predictible. At the stroke of four, he arrived at the front door, leading his faithful horse Estella. Clenched in the horse's teeth was a white satin ribbon that Maum Sarah had pinched from somebody's funeral wreath, and dangling from the other end of the ribbon was a large diamond ring.

Mr Pee was accompanied by Cousin Alexis, who announced that there was nothing she enjoyed more than a romantic entanglement, and Cousin Lewis, who was so inebriated that twice he fell into the camellia bushes.

"Where is Cousin Hepzibah?" I asked.

"She will be late," Cousin Alexis explained. "She had several important matters to attend to, and said she would have some exciting news for us when she arrives."

At that moment, a large Harley-Davidson motorcycle, spewing black exhaust, roared up to the curb. The short, stocky, leather-jacketed, booted rider revved the engine a few times, and dismounted.

"Good heavens!" Mr Pee exclaimed. "We're being invaded by Hell's Angels!"

"I don't believe so," I reassured him. "It's only — "

The figure stalked up to the door and unbuckled the straps on an oversized helmet.

"I might have known," Mr Pee sighed. "Miss Topsey Piddleton."

"Mr Pee," she said, brushing the soot from her jacket, "you should trade in that nag of yours for one of these — lots more *horse*power!" She snickered.

As Mr Pee turned to retrieve the ring from Estella, Miss Topsey winked hugely at Cousin Lewis, almost causing him to fall into the Camellia bushes again.

There was a momentary problem when Estella, perhaps in reaction to Miss Topsey's remarks, stubbornly refused to relinquish the ring. When it was finally extricated from the horse's jaws, we repaired to the living room where tea was set up and waiting.

As the guests stood by, Mr Pee nervously slipped the ring onto my waiting finger...but not before accidently dropping it in the teapot. The ring turned out to be much too small, having been his mother's and grandmother's first, both of whom were unusually tiny. So it ended up, rather unconventionally, on my little finger instead. The size of the diamond, in contrast, was quite large, eliciting admiration from everyone. Mr Pee was urged to kiss me, but he said that he had only once kissed his mother in public and that was the last time that they had opened her casket. And so out of a genuine respect for the dear departed, he was not about to create a precedent.

Miss Topsey, who had been eyeing the buttered scones since her arrival, then cried out, "Now can't we *please* have our tea!" She insisted that she was hungrier than usual, having spent all morning at the organ practicing the hymns for our coming nuptials.

Mr James, resplendent in his white serving jacket, did the honors, his large gold watch swinging recklessly from its chain whenever he bent over to pour the tea. Miss Topsey cringed each time he approached her, holding her cup out at arm's length.

The talk was mostly about engagements, weddings, receptions and the like. Miss Topsey kept making eyes at

Cousin Lewis, and suggested that the two of them perform a duet at the wedding — she on the organ and he on his handbells, which he had learned to play at his finishing school in England. He winced and poured another dollop of gin into his tea cup.

At that moment, Miss Glory-Be waltzed into the room and announced with great flourish: "Mistress Hepzibah Pincklea Ravenal Jones."

The words were scarcely out of his mouth when Cousin Hepzibah rushed in and tossed him her mink coat. He barely managed to catch it, and dashed over to General George Washington's Chippendale mirror to model it.

"Your engagement is already the subject of responsible gossip in all the better social circles," she informed me. "As your best friend, I felt it my duty to disseminate the news in the most favorable manner possible...given its unfortunate precedent."

She removed her white gloves. "I stopped off briefly in Magnolia Cemetery to tell Miss Henrietta the news, and I am now in the process of compiling the guest list. Furthermore, I have booked the rector for the Fourth of July, and you have a dress fitting next Wednesday in my bedroom."

"She can't wear white," reminded Miss Topsey.

"And why not?" demanded Cousin Hepzibah. "Even a practicing member of the Church of England can make mistakes. I did — I married a Baptist, but I'll be more careful next time. A good Episcopalian."

Mr James offered Cousin Hepzibah some tea, but she shook her head. "I prefer vodka. Miss Glory-Be has a bottle hidden under the rose chintz cushions of the wicker armchair in the maid's private sitting room." She glanced slyly at Miss Glory-Be. "A little bird told me."

"Little birds tell you *everything*," pouted Miss Glory-Be.

Cousin Hepzibah carefully settled her tall sturdy figure into the delicate lines of a Martha Washington armchair.

"Now for my other news...having already dealt with yours." She paused for effect, looking over at Cousins Alexis and Pee...Cousin Lewis had already passed out on the cooling couch. "I have just sold our Aunt Minnihaha's white elephant for a million dollars cash."

We were all stunned. The late Miss Minnihaha Wragg's old mansion was in a terrible state of disrepair. Miss Minnihaha was as cheap as they come — it was said that she would have denied a coughdrop to Camille — and steadfastly refused to put a nickel into its upkeep or modernization. It had twenty-seven rooms and only one-and-a half baths...plus an array of outside privies used by the occupying Yankee soldiers in the Civil War.

"She must be turning somersaults in Magnolia Cemetery," Mr Pee remarked as Miss Glory-Be returned with a small glass of vodka for Cousin Hepzibah, instead of the whole bottle she was doubtless expecting. "All that *money*...Who in his right mind would pay a million dollars for that battered old house?"

"Could be Royalty," Miss Glory-Be sang, pouring my sherry.

"*Miss Glory-Be!*" snarled Cousin Hepzibah with such malice that the under-butler took cover behind my chair. "Which of my traitor friends told you?"

"A little birdie," he giggled. "Same one that told you about the bottle of vodka."

"You mean the *French Princess*?" I asked. "The one who was looking for a house to buy in Charleston?"

"The very same. She is even sending to Greece for white marble with which to repair the Corinthian columns. Now — " she polished off the vodka and gestured for Miss Glory-Be to get her another " — Her Royal Highness will be arriving here tomorrow to inspect her Union privies. Cousin Pee, you will escort Miss Gwendolyn to the airport, with Maum Sarah and Mr James in attendance, for we have to

77

keep up appearances, don't we? I, of course, will accompany His Honor the Mayor. And together we will welcome the Princess Frances."

At this point the tea party terminated and the guests departed — Miss Topsey Piddleton to her motorcycle, Mr Pee to take his afternoon nap, Cousin Alexis for a "hot date" with a Coast Guard officer who promised to show her his lighthouse (Cousin Lewis raised no objection, as he was still fast asleep in the couch).

Cousin Hepzibah, having arrived late, remained to nibble at the leftover pastries while finishing her vodka.

"I am pleased that you were able to sell the Wragg mansion," I said. "I just hope the Princess won't find it in unacceptable shape."

"If she had cared, she wouldn't have bought it sight unseen," Cousin Hepzibah shrugged. "Besides, being royalty, she's got the money to fix it up. The *important* thing is, that by purchasing the home from me, she automatically becomes part of our own social circle. Instant prestige. For us, that is."

She poured herself another vodka. "I'm so looking forward to tomorrow. I just *know* it will be an occasion we will never forget..."

# 9

The Hosea Pincklea Mansion
Dearest Cousin Matilda-Madge

I am completely exhausted from meeting Her Royal Highness, the Princess Frances, who has bought Cousin Hepzibah's late Aunt Minnihaha's crumbling old house for the enormous sum of one million dollars, The heat was suffocating at the airport as we waited for the royal plane to fly regally in. Mr Pee, bless his heart, went personally to buy me a frosted strawberry ice cream cone, completely covered with multi-colored sprinkles. He is a real Southern gentleman, even if he did go over the edge that awful night a few years ago. Mr James complains he can still smell the gunpowder.

Cousin Hepzibah was in her element, having stayed up most of the night before making last minute arrangements, then planning all the local committees on which she wants the Princess to serve. "Can't you see Her Royal Highness arriving in my carriage for the St Cecilia Ball?" she asked rhetorically.

Of course, this was before we actually *met* Princess Frances in the flesh, but I will explain all that in due course. When Miss Glory-Be arrived at the airport in a bright blue pickup truck with a huge rusted cannon in the back, Mr Pee recognized the ancient weapon immediately. "Cousin Hepzibah," he addressed her somewhat reproachfully, "Your cannon looks mighty familiar."

"*Our* cannon," she corrected him. "I borrowed it temporarily from the family plot. Nothing is too good for the Princess, including mementos of our glorious dead."

Mr Pee had to agree, for money talks in the Holy City. Under the explicit terms of their Aunt Minnihaha's will, he and Cousin Hepzibah had inherited her home equally, with the proviso that they give two of the Civil War privies to the Smithsonian. Cousin Alexis had been effectively disinherited, not so much for her matrimonial record as for committing indiscretions with Cousin Lewis. Since he was her godchild, Aunt Minnihaha had weakened somewhat and left him her pet bull dog, Mr Winston, and Mr Roberto, her pet albino rabbit.

I had to admit that Mr Pee looked really sharp in the white planter's linen suit his daddy had bequeathed him. He wore a wide brimmed straw hat with distinction, in a rather futile effort to hide his receding hairline.

"Sugar honey," he whispered to me, "kindly hold that sprinkled ice cream cone in your other hand. I want you to display dear Mama's engagement ring."

The dignitaries were beginning to assemble — the Mayor of Charleston, sweating profusely in a boyish navy blue suit; all the members of the city council, mostly in seersucker suits; Miss Topsey Piddleton, swathed in that same historic white lace gown left over from the Court of St James, but minus three feathers; two Catholic bishops, three Methodist ministers, two Baptists, six Episcopalians, two Lutherans, three Presbyterians and a Reform Unitarian; six shrimpers from Mosquito Creek and a large contingent of reporters, photographers, local bands and curiosity seekers.

Big Shot's Daddy, looking dapper as ever in his white clerical collar and a crimson bib borrowed from a Bishop, made a bee-line for me. "Daughter, you really must do something about your Mr James," he complained. "He refused to come with me to the airport and be my deacon. Said he had silver to clean, and had no time to meet some white-ass Princess."

Mr Pee agreed, insisting that Mr James' attitude was most irresponsible. "Our social obligations must come first — the family silver can wait."

I reminded Mr Pee that he had complained of being so tired himself that morning that he would gladly have slept through the whole occasion. At this, an anxious look came over his face. "In my haste, I believe I left my bunny slippers under your bed. Do you think that your dog, Miss Margie, will destroy them, as she did my best hunting cap?"

The arrival of Cousin Alexis at this point caused almost as much excitement as would that of Her Royal Highness. Wearing white crepe de chine to match her Rolls Royce, she was attended by six young men, four blonds and two redheads, who in turn were chaperoned by Cousin Lewis in full Confederate uniform. He had warned them, wielding his jewel-encrusted sword threateningly, to mind their manners with his beloved or suffer his wrath.

I had allowed Miss Glory-Be to assist Cousin Hepzibah for the morning, because he had threatened to join the Marines if I didn't. Dressed in powder blue tights and tickle-pink jacket, he was to be in charge of the cannon, and also to supervise the little flower girl and boy — lily white and jet black respectively ("So ecumenical," beamed Big Shot's Daddy). Miss Glory-Be had the two poor children in a tizzy,

81

marching them up and down, then making them bow and curtsey while he pretended to be Her Majesty Queen Elizabeth in residence at Buckingham Palace.

Cousin Hepzibah was being her own feisty self, harassing some unfortunate colonel she had borrowed from the Citadel who was trying in vain to explain the mechanics of firing the long out-dated cemetery cannon. He looked most upset when she grumbled, "I still think I should have called in General Westmoreland."

Then an Episcopalian rector sashayed over to us, looking positively colorless and puritanical compared to Big Shot's daddy in his flamboyant Catholic Bishop's regalia. "Aha," he exclaimed, slapping Mr Pee so hard on the back that he nearly knocked his partial bridge out. "So, I have caught my two turtle doves, and this time it will be a real church wedding! Miss Hepzibah, as cousin of the bridegroom, has asked me to help officiate at the newly-fashionable fully integrated ceremony. Oh, what wonders civil rights have done for all of us!"

Then he looked inquiringly at Mr Pee. "I...trust you have heard the shocking news about your late daddy's wife Number Two."

Mr Pee was incensed. "I do not care to hear that scarlet harlot's name spoken in front of my fiancee!"

The Episcopalian rector fidgeted in his tropical leather sandals that he had purchased while visiting a fellow clergyman in Palm Beach. "Apparently you *haven't* heard. In light of what happened, I am sure you would not wish to speak ill of the dead."

"Dead!" Mr Pee and I exclaimed together.

"It was on the early news," said the rector. "Your daddy's Wife Number Two and her lion tamer consort have gone to their reward. Snorkel fishing in the Bahamas. Disappeared in one last mad adulterous embrace into an underwater cavern known as the Lover's Farewell. So far their bodies have not reappeared. Only..." and the poor man blushed cherubically... "only your late stepmother's crimson-red bikini."

"Well", exclaimed Mr Pee, wiping what appeared to be a tear of sheer relief from his eye, "Our family honor is restored at last. At least in death my daddy has become posthumously respectable."

"Exactly," the rector nodded his head. "God works in a most mysterious way, His wonders to perform. Now you can be married in the church proper instead of in my study."

He might have said more if at that moment the local Gentleman's Chapter of the Flow-Blue China Society had not marched in, and he had to give the Salute. There were at least fifty of them, all twirling their matching umbrellas and wearing identical baseball caps and white shorts.

"Whoever asked them?" demanded Mr Pee, who was a conservative Republican, preferring traditional Canton porcelain to flow-blue china.

Then I caught sight of Miss Glory-Be, who had given up impersonating the Queen of England in order to replace the unfortunate colonel at Cousin Hepzibah's ancient cemetery cannon that had guarded the dead for so long.

Mr Pee was justly concerned. "With all due respect to the fact that Miss Glory-Be is a member of your household, I think we should make sure he really knows what he is doing..." He made his way over to where the under-butler was fiddling with the fuse mechanism. "Miss Glory-Be, begging your pardon...but is that thing really harmless?"

"Of course, Mr Pee, sir!" insisted Miss Glory-Be with great authority. "Your Cousin, Miss Alexis, has graciously donated three blank noisemaking shells, the kind they use to shoot unfaithful lovers in the movies."

"Well, I hope you are right," Mr Pee said, not totally convinced. "I haven't forgotten the African parrot that Mr

James sent you to collect from your Uncle Mr Amos Jeremiah Mikel over on Amherst Street, and how you swore both on the New Testament and the Confederate Flag that it had once belonged to two respectable Born-Again missionaries. Not only did that deceitful bird turn out to be a girl instead of a boy, she had a vocabulary fit for a brothel."

"Tolerance, Tolerance, Mr Pee, sir," Miss Glory-Be urged. "You know how attached Mr James is to Miss Sweet-Talking Harriett. Why, that bird has been a real blessing to him, ever since he became a widower twice in a single week, a record even in this Charleston."

Talk of angels and you hear the flap of their wings! At that very moment, Mr James, presumably having finished cleaning my family silver, arrived wearing the maroon Bermuda shorts with the little orange carrot motif I had given him as a remembrance of Big Shot. Miss Sweet-Talking Harriett was perched on his shoulder...and clinging to his arm as if she were a permanent attachment was a well-endowed lady wearing a purple see-through blouse set off with a pair of bright yellow pants, into which she had poured an enormously fat bottom.

"This plump-like-butter little lady," announced Mr James, adjusting his shades, "has consented to be my next fortunate wife. The Bible says man cannot live on bread alone, and this old body's gettin' awful hungry."

"I quite agree," said Mr Pee, ever practical. "What is the sense of paying two electric light bills when only one is necessary?"

"My name is Shirley-Mae," the hefty lady somewhat brazenly introduced herself. "Just as soon as I can find out if my husband, Mr Ezekiel Pott, is dead or divorced, Mr James can legally marry me."

She then turned to pat Miss Sweet-Talking Harriett, who all this time was sitting placidly on my old butler's skinny little shoulder. "There will always be a perch for this sweet cupid bird in my generous heart, for it was she, bless her little black beak, who brought us together."

"That's right," Mr James took up the story: "I was walkin' Miss Sweet-Talking Harriett on the Battery, as she likes to feed the seagulls, and there was Miss Shirley-Mae doin' the same thing. *'Hi, hot stuff!'* screams my precious parrot, so that Miss Shirley Mae quite naturally thought it was me hollerin' at her. One thing led to another, and then Miss Sweet-Talking Harriett, the fast little hussy, suggested we three take a room at the Last Chance Motel across the Ashley and watch some cartoons on TV..."

At that moment, a voice announced over a loudspeaker that the Princess Frances' plane would be landing momentarily. Mr James escorted his lady love over to join the others. "He certainly didn't waste any time," I observed. "He's scarcely out of double mourning."

"At least he's doing the honorable thing by marrying the lady," Mr Pee remarked. "I use the term 'lady' advisedly, of course."

"Instead of keeping her on the hook for ten years, you mean," I couldn't help but comment, but the intent was lost on Mr Pee. "At any rate, now there'll be two weddings to prepare for. I wonder if anyone else will join the bandwagon?"

"Possibly Her Royal Highness," Mr Pee dared to suggest. "I understand she is a widow-woman too. Apparently her husband, the Prince, was out walking their pet toy poodle, Miss Brigette-Simone, in Monte Carlo when they were run over by a tourist bus. Not only did the poor Princess lose a husband, but her little dog as well."

"Poor dear," I sympathized. "But if she ever recovers from the shock, it would be nice to have a royal wedding in Charleston."

This prompted Mr Pee to ask me: "Do you recall, Sugar honey, how we sat up in bed to watch the last one on TV?"

"*Fornication*!" screeched Miss Sweet-Talking Harriett from the safety of Mr James' shoulder.

At that moment Cousin Hepzibah, a vision in petunia pink, rushed over to where we were standing. "Cousin Pee," she began, gasping for breath. "I nearly forgot. You are to request that Her Royal Highness be guest of honor at the next St Cecilia's Ball. Thank God she comes to us as a respectable widow, and not some tarnished divorcee!"

Then she dashed off to take her place next to the Mayor in the receiving line, just as it was announced that the plane had landed. A red carpet was rolled out, and the gathered crowd prepared to welcome the royal guest.

As the cabin door swung open, hundreds of eyes opened wide and hundreds of jaws dropped. Even the Flow-Blue gentlemen suddenly stopped twirling their umbrellas and stood frozen. A loud gasp erupted from the Mayor's mouth, and was echoed by the crowd.

For the tall, Amazonic lady who stood surveying us disdainfully in her diamonds, mink stole and jeweled coronet was not exactly the vision any of us had expected. Her Royal Highness, the Princess Frances, was black.

In all the shock and confusion that followed, I do recollect Cousin Hepzibah croaking "Hells bells!" and dashing for the bathroom, for in times of stress she never could hold her water. And then Mr Pee was fanning Miss Topsey Piddleton, who had collapsed, with his large monogrammed handkerchief.

"VENGEANCE IS MINE, SAITH THE LORD!" the Princess shouted as she descended the steps and rushed by us with her bodyguards and royal attendants.

The voice was agonizingly familiar. So were her words. And so was the stern face.

All that was missing was the thunder and lightning which had accompanied Miss Frances Washington — my

86

former cook and jilted fiancee of Big Shot — in her stormy departure from my house many years ago.

As if in response, there was a flash of light and a thunderous roar, as the rusty cannon which Miss Glory-Be had been priming exploded, propelling my hapless under-butler — minus his powder blue shorts — into the midst of Princess Frances' entourage of dignitaries.

This letter, dearest Cousin Matilda-Madge, is being written from my cooling couch, where I am recuperating from the day's events. I have no idea what the return of Miss Frances — I mean the arrival of Her Royal Highness — will mean to Charleston Society, but I have a feeling things are never going to be quite the same.

Your affectionate, if thoroughly exhausted,
Cousin Gwendolyn.

# 10

Mr Pee was having his breakfast, seated at the head of the claw-and-ball footed Chippendale dining table in his white uncontaminated pajamas with the magenta piping around the collar. I sat opposite him, reading Lord Ashley Cooper's column in the Charleston News and Courier, wearing my best India silk summer nightgown patterned with red butterflies flitting around the middle. We were consuming generous portions of Miss Glory-Be's grits, hot biscuits, and home-cured ham.

Suddenly Mr Pee looked up at me, stomped his slippered foot and announced, "I am hot to trot, Miss Gwendolyn! When are we going to get married?"

"You may be hot to trot, Mr Pee," I cautioned him, "but it is not quite time for the final gallop. Your Cousin Hepzibah has put up the banns and plans a patriotic ceremony on the Fourth of July."

His face fell. "Well, we are neither of us getting any *younger.*" — as if I weren't painfully aware of it — "I have been a bachelor from childhood, while you have been a widow long enough. The only tomcatting I ever did was in my imagination, listening to the amorous adventures of my cousins Alexis and Lewis."

There was no time to reply, for we suddenly heard what sounded like a trumpet voluntary played on a motor horn....and the next thing we knew, a platoon of strange cigar-smoking men were running up and down the piazza, brandishing guns and gawking rudely through the windows.

"Good God!" Mr Pee said, spilling his coffee. "We are about to be *kidnapped*...or else the President is here to visit us!" He would have said more if Miss Glory-Be had not rushed in brandishing a wooden grit-stirring spoon to report that Princess Frances was on the doorstep. The intruders were her bodyguards.

Mr Pee got up and hoisted up his pajama pants. "I think if you don't mind, I'll go back to bed. Miss Frances never liked me when she was your cook." He hastily refilled his coffee cup, grabbed two more hot biscuits and three slices of ham, and ran upstairs, leaving me to face single-handedly the woman my late husband had jilted.

Thanks be to God and General Robert E. Lee, when the Princess strode in I saw that she had commandeered Cousin Alexis as lady-in-waiting. I opened my mouth but no words came.

*"How did he die?"* demanded Her Royal Highness. "Nobody will tell me a thing!" She glared at Cousin Alexis. "He didn't die of measles or chicken pox — I know he's had those because he gave them to me."

Cousin Alexis gave me a warning look. I cleared my throat. "He...he died of a gunshot wound. He — "

"Suicide!" shrieked the Princess. "He was already pining for me!" She stuck out her chest. "It took a woman like me to fulfill all his lustful desires..." She then collapsed weeping in the Martha Washington armchair with such brute force that it creaked.

I hastened to change the subject. "Miss Frances...I mean, Your Royal Highness...if I may be so bold as to ask you... How on earth did you manage to marry a prince? I'm sure it's none of my business, but I would be interested to know."

"Me, too," agreed Cousin Alexis. "It's the dream of all proper Charlestonian women to marry into royalty."

Princess Frances blew her nose and pulled her Russian red wig down over her prominent ears. "When I left your employ, I went to Detroit where I had some relatives. There I was fortunate enough to sell my idea for packaged frozen chittlins to a supermarket franchise. It was my own recipe, come down from my Mama and your Godmama, Miss Annabel Pincklea. In next to no time, with plenty of good juicy advertising of course, I was raking in millions."

She stood up abruptly and shouted, "MIRROR, MIRROR ON THE WALL — WHOSE FROZEN CHITTLINS ARE BEST OF ALL?"

"FRANCES' CHITTLINS!" the bodyguards chimed in through the piazza window like a barbershop quartet.

She sat back down in her chair. "With money to burn and no Big Shot to burn it on, I decided to travel — London, Paris, Rome... And it was while I was in Monte Carlo that I was introduced to my future husband, Prince Henri, who was then 79 years old and confined to a wheelchair. But after our wedding night, he never returned to his wheelchair again."

She grinned smugly. "Even Big Shot, a man of worldly experience, often said that my physical attributes were, to say the least, extraordinary."

"How inspiring," wept Cousin Alexis, dabbing at her purple-outlined eyes with a lace-edged handkerchief.

I nodded in agreement. "I must ask Miss Glory-Be to buy some of your frozen chittlins when he next goes to the store. After all," — I added hopefully — "Big Shot would wish us to be friends."

At the mention of Big Shot's sainted name, the Princess broke into sobbing again. "It was years before I even knew our Big Shot was dead." (At least she said "our"). "And I spent most of that time thinking of him. I need to know where he is buried. I want to arrange for his grave to be covered with blood red passionate Valentine roses every year on the anniversary of the day he forsook me at the Reverend Mrs Carmen Suck's tent meeting."

"How very romantic," interrupted Cousin Alexis. "I hope that one of my past husbands has the common decency to do that for me."

I saw no harm in revealing Big Shot's burial place, and raised no objection to her plan to provide flowers — anything to smooth over our differences. She blew her nose again with such vigor that I feared she would rupture a blood vessel, then got up to inspect a full length portrait of little Manigault that had replaced one of Osceola the Seminole Indian over the mantelpiece.

"This, I take it, is Big Shot's child..."

I started to correct her by saying "*our*" child, but simply answered yes.

"Well," she nodded, "she does have her daddy's big feet."

Cousin Alexis, having applied fresh orange lipstick and powdered her Grecian nose, walked over to the sideboard and poured two glasses of sherry, one for Princess Frances and the other for herself. Through the windows, some of the bodyguards were making suggestive gestures towards her. Where on earth, I wondered, had she found the time at this hour of the morning to have played her flirtatious games with them? No wonder poor Aunt Greta had retired to a convent.

Then Her Royal Highness rose abruptly and headed for the front door. "Come, Miss Alexis — there is work to be done. 'Operation Rescue' awaits!"

"'Operation Rescue'?" I echoed.

"Mr Pee's Cousin Hepzibah, as president of the Save-The-Poor-Horses League, has solicited my help — and a chunk of my money — to do something about an abysmal situation which exists in this town. One which requires *drastic action*!" And with that, she left the mansion with Cousin Alexis and all the bodyguards hastening to follow.

I breathed a sigh of relief and went upstairs to find Mr Pee finishing his breakfast. "I thought you were never coming," he complained. "Is that pretender to the throne gone yet?"

I assured him that Princess Frances had left, and he wiped his mouth with a damask napkin. Then he looked down at his bare feet. "Oh, dear — my toenails need trimming."

He looked up imploringly at me. "Do you suppose you could...?"

I raised an eyebrow. "Who cut your toenails while I was in exile?"

Mr Pee didn't reply, and sat sulking as I went to fetch my nail scissors. When I returned, he was sitting on the four-poster bed counting his toes. What hairy legs he has, I observed — Big Shot's legs were smooth as Manigault's bottom.

I sat down on General Robert E. Lee's mahogany bedsteps and started snipping away, while Mr Pee giggled and squirmed so much I feared I might cut him. When I had finished, he said, "How about a game of charades...to calm both our nerves. We'll do a scene from the Old Testament."

I hesitated, as Mr Pee had a strange glint in his eye. And besides, the last time we played it Miss Glory-Be was David and Mr Pee Goliath, with my best silver etui for the pebble. Between David, Goliath, and the etui, my Chippendale mirror managed to get shattered. I thought Mr James would never stop hollering when he discovered the mess.

"Oh, come on!" urged Mr Pee, and proceeded to take off his pajamas and strike a pose on General Lee's historic bedsteps, covering himself discreetly with a zinnia from a vase on my Louis XIV table. "Guess who?"

At that moment, Miss Glory-Be appeared in the bedroom door with Mr Pee's midday mint julep. "Why, the Garden of Eden!" he squealed. "Let me run back to the kitchen for an apple..."

Blushing profusely, Mr Pee snatched Great Uncle Frederick Pincklea's sword that he wore at the Battle of Shiloh and chased Miss Glory-Be down the grand staircase and out into the rose garden. I sank into my pink chaise lounge and drank the mint julep myself. This morning's chaotic events were beginning to take their toll on my nerves.

Mr Pee returned in a rage to my boudoir shortly, having scratched his bare bottom rather frightfully on a rose bush. I have never been much of a nurse, and found it no easy task to successfully apply a large band-aid to that cushiony part of his lower extremities. He was so mortified at having sustained such an intimate injury that I had to climb in bed beside him before he was pacified.

It didn't take long for me to fall fast asleep. Perhaps it was the mint julep or the traumatic encounter with Princess Frances — or both — but it was nearly noon when I awoke.

I slipped quietly from the bed, careful not to awaken the snoring Mr Pee, and was about to go down the stairs when the phone rang. The house seemed unusually quiet, and nobody was answering the phone, so I went back and picked up the bedroom extension.

It was a gruff voice from the Charleston Police Department. "Are you aware, madam, that at last count, you were harboring a dozen horses of various colors and sizes, plus a mule and a jackass? All your neighbors are complaining about their whinnying, while the Garden Club has already requested the manure. Would you be so kind as to give them some hay, then get someone to remove them?"

I dropped the receiver, hurried out onto the upper piazza, and stared over the railing just in time to see the jackass devour our miniature prize star magnolia. The other horses were milling about, trampling down flowers and nibbling at the bushes. Mr James and Miss Glory-Be were nowhere to be seen, which left me to deal with the situation.

At that moment, I caught sight of Mr James coming down the street, wearing his funeral top hat and proudly leading a big dappled gray horse wearing a straw hat. Behind him was the Princess Frances in tweed jacket, riding breeches, and her mid-day coronet, leading a patchy white mare who had seen better days. Cousin Alexis, never to be outdone, wore a green velvet riding habit with feathered hat, all of which would have done justice to Scarlet O'Hara. She was riding a white horse — her own Miss Penelope — sidesaddle.

"I will require your assistance, Miss Gwendolyn," Her Royal Highness called up to me. "I've purchased — or rather *rescued* — every overworked tour horse in this fair city. 'Operation Rescue' has been successfully completed, and 'Operation Judith' can commence!"

For a moment I thought I must still be asleep. "'Operation Judith'? I...don't understand."

"You will — because when I've corralled the lot into your walled garden, I'm having them all trucked off to your Cousin Judith's horse farm in upstate New York."

94

I had visions of Cousin Judith having a nervous break-down. "Does she know they are coming? And is she aware that one of them is a jackass? You know how fussy Cousin Judith is since one of her brood won the Kentucky Derby."

"Of *course* she knows about little Millie!" snapped Princess Frances in an impatient voice reminiscent of the days she ruled over my kitchen. "Besides, that little jackass is my favorite and the reason for my overwhelming generosity in the first place. I was taking a stroll with Mr James on the Battery just going over old times — you know, Big Shot and his affinity for my shredded fig and mashed potato salad — when we were shocked to observe poor little Millie desperately pulling a carriage with a purple fringe on top that contained six enormous ladies, three black and three white, all with oversized posteriors."

She rubbed the mangey old animal's muzzle. "At first, considering their red polyester pants, I thought they were ladies of the evening from Miss Potty's establishment. But no, they were on a teachers' convention at Myrtle Beach and had driven over to Charleston for the day. They were quite upset when I threatened to call the humane society and have them all arrested with their driver, a stringy-haired filly sadly in need of a good scalping, for cruelty to a dumb animal."

"That's right," chimed in Mr James, taking off his top hat to dab at his brow with a red polka dot handkerchief. "What's more, Miss Frances...I mean Her Royal Highness here...was about to shove the lot of them, carriage and all, into the harbor. It was all I could do, at my advanced age, and after wrestling all night with Miss Shirley-Mae, to restrain her."

"That was when the driver called me a *liberated maniac*," Princess Frances snorted.

95

"Well, we did throw *her* in," Mr James said, rubbing his boney old hands together for sheer satisfaction. "Last we saw, she was swimming towards Fort Sumter."

"What happened to the ladies from the teachers convention?" I quickly asked, fearing the worst.

"Oh," the Princess chuckled, "they all scrambled into St Philip's Church screaming 'Sanctuary!' We would have followed if the rector hadn't slammed the door in our faces."

She paused for breath. "I went home to the late Miss Minnihaha's mansion to get some money, which I intended to deposit in the Charleston First National Bank, and bought up every endangered horse in the Holy City. Money talks — when I told the owners what I was prepared to pay, the Simon Legrees couldn't refuse me. Even Miss Topsey Piddleton, who has never forgiven me for saying that her organ recitals were a sure cause of migraine headaches, declared that the Mayor should erect a statue of me leading a horse right in the front of City Hall. Said she was sick and tired of gawking tourists being driven past her ante-bellum house, wanting to use her lavatory."

At that moment, Mr Pee, his thinning hair in disarray, came out onto the piazza, yawning and stretching. At least he had had the presence of mind to don his powder blue shorts, even if they were several sizes too small, leaving little to the imagination.

"Good God!" cried Princess Frances. "Have you two eloped?"

At that, Mr Pee retreated indoors as fast as a Yankee deserter at the Battle of Bull Run.

"We did *not* elope," I replied quite icily, mustering as much dignity as I could with those wretched horses all whinnying their disapproval in the background. "Mr Pee is obviously just passing through."

Without another word, I turned and went back inside, where I was sorely tempted to remain until "Operation Judith" was over.

# 11

Mr James returned not a bit refreshed from a two-day vacation spent with his new fiancee, Miss Shirley-Mae, she-crabbing at Shem Creek. During that time, they managed to tidy up the graves of his two wives, the Misses Olabelle and Lillybelle. He was in a terrible mood, having been bitten on his right big toe by a dissident she-crab who had demonstrated in militaristic terms that she was not quite ready for his soup. He hobbled in, wearing one black patent leather butler's shoe and one of Mr Pee's red plaid carpet slippers from Scotland.

The old hypocrite pretended to be most upset at finding Mr Pee still in an unwed state in my bed, and told him quite bluntly it was time to go home — Maum Sarah with Miss Landine and her overgrown kitten were due back from their own fishing trip at any moment.

Mr Pee complained that he hadn't had his lunch yet, or his breakfast either for that matter, and the tomb-like emptiness in his stomach simply insisted on being appeased. Mr

James was not impressed, but did relent long enough to pack him a Champagne lunch. The Champagne belonged to Cousin Alexis, who never travels any place without a bottle, and had conveniently left one in the aspidestra pot by mistake.

Mr Pee gallantly insisted on sharing his picnic lunch with me, but Mr James said that if we did we would both have to drink out of paper cups, as he was still officially on vacation until dinner time that evening and was in no mood to wash our best crystal champagne glasses. This was a little awkward, as Big Shot had received the paper cups as a wedding gift from one of the hard-working ladies at Miss Potty's Health Club. Each was engraved with the warning: YOU CAN MESS WITH ME, BUT DON'T MESS WITH MY WIFE.

We had our picnic under the live oak tree, sitting on the white ante-bellum cast-iron benches, which were sheer torture on our unpadded bottoms. The champagne was warm, and the fried chicken — courtesy of Miss Glory-Be who had won a bucket full in a Sunday School raffle two weeks before — was stale and tough. Even Miss Margie and Miss J-J, who had never been known to refuse anything in the food line, turned their noses up when offered a morsel. The dogs eventually retired to the lower drawing room to sulk under a mahogany Sheraton side table.

"Am I still invited to your candlelight supper?" Mr Pee asked as he wrestled the joints of a chicken wing apart.

"Of course, Mr Pee. Cousin Hepzibah is coming, so we are sure to learn everything that the Princess Frances has been up to lately. Your cousin has apparently managed to wangle herself into Her Royal Highness' confidence."

"I cannot stand any more shocks," he moaned. "I am still getting over that awful business with the horses. I hope at least that Cousin Alexis has returned to her plantation in Ridgeland — I am in no mood for her salacious stories, which are better suited to the stables."

"I'm afraid Cousin Alexis will be there as well. And Cousin Lewis. Cousin Hepzibah insisted."

He sighed and wiped his mouth. "I think I had better go home, or Maum Sarah will go into one of her tizzies. Ever since Mama bequeathed her the exercise bicycle, she has had more energy than me."

"Well, get some rest." I patted his arm. "Cousin Hepzibah expects you to pick her up at seven."

He gave me a chaste kiss and vanished over the wall before being spotted by Maum Sarah's telescope, which she kept perpetually aimed in the direction of my house.

As it was sort of a special occasion, I asked Miss Glory-Be to bring out the Venetian glass epergne as a centerpiece for the dining table. Normally we only used it for Thanksgiving, Christmas, and the anniversary of the firing on Fort Sumter. It had been buried with the kitchen silver during the Yankee occupation of the Holy City and subsequently forgotten, only to be uncovered later by The Earthquake. Godmother Annabel's grandmother had the compote meticulously repaired, even the little baskets that hung from the bottom of its three tiers, which on special occasions were filled with sweetmeats and nuts. A nosegay of flowers graced the silver bud vase on top.

We set off the epergne with the blue and white Canton dinner service that some long-dead ancestor had ordered from China in trading-ship days. Each cup of the enormous brass chandelier was supplied with a new candle, and there were additional candles in Georgian sticks on the carved mantel and on the sideboard. Miss Glory-Be was delighted. "It's like a *fairyland*!"

With Cousin Hepzibah coming, we were all expected to dress formally, since she always insisted on doing things properly. In due course she arrived, her flowing blue gown offset by an enormously long train embroidered with her initials. She immediately complained that my staircase (which was as historic as any other in Charleston) had too many bends it, making it difficult to manipulate her train and causing her to nearly trip twice. "I could have broken my *neck*," she pointed out, causing uncharitable thoughts to flash through my mind.

Cousin Hepzibah was escorted somewhat reluctantly by Mr Pee, who looked simply delicious in his white tuxedo jacket and black pants, although he did complain several times that his shoes were pinching him. Cousin Alexis, not to be outdone by giant trains or Venetian epergnes, arrived in an above-the-knee Roaring Twenties apple-green silk lamé dress, hung with rows of little wooden beads in all colors of the rainbow. She was carrying a hula hoop, currently all the rage, and every time she gave a demonstration she noticeably rattled.

Cousin Alexis had picked up Cousin Lewis at his *All Passion Spent* Plantation house, and he, bless his little Confederate heart, looked resplendent as usual in his gray military uniform with all that braiding. His outfit did, however, look a bit rumpled, so I presumed that Cousin Alexis had again seduced him on the way into Charleston (those little groups of lob-lolly pine trees and magnolias always looked so intimately inviting). In fact, no sooner were we all seated and Mr James had offered grace — praying for everybody in turn including his two dead wives — than Cousin Lewis turned to his Cousin Hepzibah, a practicing Episcopalian in good standing, and asked whether she thought the church would ever allow first cousins to marry.

Cousin Hepzibah was aghast. "Cousin Lewis, have you no sense of propriety? It's bad enough that you insisted in corrupting your poor innocent cousin when she was still in the bloom of youth...but now you wish to *legalize* it! No wonder our Poor Aunt Greta resorted to voluntary penance at the Shrine of St Thomas-a-Becket in Canterbury Cathedral."

"I was only inquiring..."

"And I'm sure Cousin Alexis has better sense than to marry you even if you *weren't* first cousins. I know *I* wouldn't."

"And I wouldn't marry *you*, you old buzzard," retorted Cousin Lewis, "even if you were as rich and beautiful as...as the Princess Anastasia!"

Fortunately, Mr James hobbled in just in the nick of time wearing the brand new pair of heart-covered Valentine sneakers that his fiancee', Miss Shirley-Mae, had given him to help his damaged foot. "PEACE, dear brothers and sisters, peace!" he ordered. Then, as things quieted, he began solemnly serving the she-crab soup, assisted by Miss Glory-Be in a yellow polka-dot pinafore.

The soup was followed by roast possum and rice, with three roast potatoes for me because I was British and had never developed a taste for rice. The meal was consumed in relative peace and quiet, with Cousin Hepzibah and Cousin Lewis exchanging occasional venomous looks. For dessert, we had sherry trifle and lemon pie, and diet chocolate cookies for Cousin Alexis.

After coffee, Cousin Hepzibah led the way on Mr Pee's arm onto my lower drawing room as if she owned it, where she told us she was ready to announce Princess Frances' master plan for Charleston.

"The chittling-freezing hussy," Mr Pee whispered to me. "Who does that woman think she is?"

When everyone was seated, she licked her lips with relish at being the bearer of such devilish news. "The first news concerns you, Miss Gwendolyn. As your best friend, I have the pleasure of informing you that you have been granted a reprieve."

"A reprieve?" I echoed. "From what?"

"That should be obvious," she replied, a bit testily. "It was Her Royal Highness' intention, upon returning to Charleston, to satisfy her lust for revenge."

"Upon whom?" demanded Mr Pee, reaching for one of Miss Glory-Be's home-stuffed olives. "And for what?"

"Why, Miss Gwendolyn, of course...after what she did, filling Big Shot Calhoun's head with pretensions of grandeur so that he saw fit to jilt her publicly at a religious tent meeting."

"I cannot say I blame him," interjected Cousin Lewis, whose chin was being tickled with a celery stick by Cousin Alexis. "After all, Miss Gwendolyn had a sizable inheritance, a German shepherd, a mansion full of antiques, and Mr James. By the mercenary standards of Charleston society, she was a very good catch." Then, eyeing Mr Pee, he added, "And still is, of course."

Cousin Alexis stuck a celery stick in each of Cousin Lewis' baby pink nostrils to shut him up, while Cousin Hepzibah snorted: "For a gentleman who repeatedly commits improprieties with his own first cousin, your comments are too indelicate for a lower drawing room. At any rate, Princess Frances has magnanimously agreed to grant Miss Gwendolyn a pardon, in the interest of maintaining a proper decorum in our social circle."

"How sporting of her," scoffed Mr Pee. "As my dear Mama used to say, it was a sad day for the aristocracy when royalty started marrying commoners."

"I quite agree," replied Cousin Hepzibah. "Next on the agenda are her plans for Aunt Minnihaha's house, in which she now resides. She plans to rename it 'The Princess Frances-Big Shot Calhoun Center for African Studies'."

"But Big Shot had never even *been* to Africa," I pointed out. "The only travelling he ever did was to Miss Potty's Health Club, where he was gainfully employed."

"That woman is creating a dangerous precedent," insisted Mr Pee. "It has always been one of Charleston's most cherished traditions to name houses after their original builders."

"Oh, I do hope she doesn't paint the civil war privies," groaned Cousin Lewis. "That would be sheer sacrilege."

"It's a distinct possibility," Cousin Hepzibah allowed. "She mentioned plans to mount a coronet on each of their doors."

"Such bad taste," sniffed Cousin Alexis. "Gloria Swanson did no such crass thing in *Sunset Boulevard*."

"Well, at least she freed all of those poor dear horses from slavery," Cousin Hepzibah reminded us. "I only hope that none of them got sick traveling to Yankee land."

Mr Pee said peevishly, "She could have left a couple to pull our bridal carriage on the Fourth of July. Now all we have to fall back on is my dear horse Estella, and she's never pulled anything in her life."

"You can always borrow two ponies from the Polo Club," Cousin Alexis suggested. "I'll be happy to inquire — a couple of the members owe me a favor or two..."

Cousin Hepzibah continued. "Then the Princess intends to repay an old debt to our own Maum Sarah before her date with the Angel Gabriel. It was Maum Sarah who, over the vocal protestations of all ten deaconesses at the Gateway-To-Heaven-Free-For-All-Repented-Sinners Church, had the then cook Miss Frances Washington raised to their exalted ranks, in return for twenty-five dollars and a jar of her extraordinary kumquat preserves."

This met with general approval.

"To continue," Cousin Hepzibah said, adjusting her pince-nez glasses. "It is Princess Frances' opinion that Miss Potty is a blot on the standards of our fair city, and should be encouraged to vacate the premises. I expressed my opinion that for many and sundry reasons, this is unlikely to transpire, but Her Royal Highness seems determined to take some measures toward that end."

Cousin Lewis scoffed. "The real reason she wants Miss Potty out of the picture is that — you'll pardon me, Miss Gwendolyn — she not only performed as Big Shot's mistress, but she had the audacity to bear his child." He poured himself another large glass of gin, and did the same for Cousin Alexis.

"Quite so," Cousin Hepzibah agreed. "And indeed I find it difficult to believe that, during their engagement, she and Big Shot did not make at least some effort toward the same end."

This speculation fell like a ton of bricks on my head, leaving me momentarily speechless. Finally, I did manage to say, "At least Big Shot's son is a credit to his daddy."

Cousin Hepzibah ignored my stepmotherly remark and proceeded with matters at hand. "And finally, as the *piece de resistance*, Princess Frances would also like to do something for Cousin Alexis for functioning as a temporary lady-in-waiting upon her return to Charleston. Her Royal Highness plans to rent the Dock Street Theater for Cousin Alexis' long-threatened debut on the Charleston stage."

Cousin Alexis' jaw popped open at the news. Then her bow-shaped mouth widened into a toothy grin and her eyes flashed. She bounded from her chair and ran back into the dining room with all of us scrambling after her. With some effort, she mounted the table where Miss Glory-Be shouted "Right On!" and handed her a glass of champagne.

"I shall create a sensation as Miss Norma Desmond in *Sunset Boulevard on the Ashley*," Cousin Alexis announced like a shimmering antelope. "And *you*," swinging a foot toward Mr Pee and unfortunately making contact with his nose, "shall be the ungrateful lover whom I shoot in the swimming pool."

For a moment, Mr Pee was too engrossed in his injured nose to respond. Then he shouted, "I'll have *none* of this!" and dashed, bleeding profusely, for the nearest powder room.

"Spoil-sport," grumbled Cousin Alexis, slugging down the Champagne. "We might even have done a remake of *Gone With The Wind*, and he could have played Rhett Butler."

Cousin Lewis giggled, spilling his drink. "I cannot imagine any man in his right senses having the nerve to desert you, even if he didn't really give a damn. You would have shot him!"

"So we re-write it so that I *do* shoot the son-of-a-bitch!" Cousin Alexis whooped, and spun around on the table top, arms flung wide. As she did so, her feet became tangled in the damask tablecloth. Losing her balance, she clutched wildly at the chandelier, divesting it of handfuls of glass ornaments. Then over the edge she went, landing in a heap on the floor, an overturned bowl of pitted olives in her lap.

Cousin Hepzibah muttered "Hells bells," and stalked from the dining room, declaring that she had never witnessed such uncouth carnage. I saw her to the door, while Cousin Alexis kept hollering, "Take me to the Casbah!" as Cousin Lewis struggled to get her back on her feet.

Finally, with Miss Glory-Be's help, we got the two of them out the door. Mr Pee left as well, still holding a bloody tissue to his wounded nose. I returned to the living room and collapsed into a chair.

I had no more breathed a relieved sigh than the phone rang. I answered it hesitantly, wondering, "What now?"

It was Western Union, and the message read:

KINDLY SEND TWELVE MORE CHARLESTON HORSE
DIAPER BAGS. MY RACE HORSES TERRIBLY
JEALOUS OF THOSE WORN BY NEW ARRIVALS.

COUSIN JUDITH.

# 12

I was in bed eating my breakfast and reading the classified section of the News and Courier. Except for the comforting sound of a brisk wind whipping at the palmetto fronds outside, all was quiet around me. Manigault was in nursery school, Miss Glory-Be had brought me my breakfast in bed and then retired to the maid's sitting room to peruse the latest issue of *Muscle-Man* Magazine.

Mr James had been advised in no uncertain terms by his doctor to take two days rest to recharge his old batteries that were badly depleted after courting Miss Shirley-Mae. While she was away burying her first husband, who had expired from drinking Wild Irish Rose in a flop house, Mr James had taken Miss Sweet-Talking Harriett to Big Shot's Daddy's religious retreat in Ridgeland for Exhausted Sinners, of which The Princess Frances and Cousin Alexis were patrons.

Then an ad in the "Help Wanted" section caught my eye:

---

**WANTED    IMMEDIATELY**
SIX STALWART FEMALES WITH VISIBLE
MUSCULAR ATTRIBUTES TO ACT AS
BODYGUARD. NO SKINNY ANNIES NEED
APPLY. FREE FAMOUS SHRIMP PATTIE
AND AFTER-HOUR FRINGE BENEFITS.
APPLY IN PERSON
    MISS POTTY'S HEALTH CLUB,
        RADCLIFFE STREET.

---

One of Miss Potty's aristocratic clientele must have warned her that Princess Frances was on the warpath and that she was a marked woman. I was reflecting on this when I heard a commotion out on the landing. In rushed Cousin Hepzibah, who looked plumb terrible — she had even forgotten her white gloves, and it was only nine o'clock in the morning. And not only was she wearing a long, old-fashioned bathrobe that would have looked quite at home on Mr James, her head was still a mass of pink plastic curlers from Woolworths. With her was Miss Topsey Piddleton, looking not much better.

Something terrible has happened, I thought. And, short of the end of the world, it had.

Cousin Hepzibah was in tears, and threw herself bodily across one side of the bed with such force that all four posts rattled. Miss Topsey collapsed like a dying swan on the other side. I sat up in bed, trapped, my legs pinned by the two bodies, a half-eaten grapefruit in between. If I had been Cousin Alexis, I would have asked what Bette Davis would have done in such a predicament.

Miss Glory-Be, hearing all the commotion, fluttered into the bedroom. He stopped, assessing the situation. "Let me guess," he teased. "Mr Pee's come down with a hernia."

Miss Topsey gave him a very nasty look. "Miss Glory-Be, I am shocked at your lack of respect for Miss Hepzibah's terrible grief. Didn't you hear this morning's newscast? Miss Hepzibah is Charleston's latest orphan!"

His eyes widened. "You mean she's been committed to the Jenkins Orphanage?"

Cousin Hepzibah stopped weeping just long enough to glare at him like the Bride of Frankenstein.

I was confused. I had been told by Mr Pee that Cousin Hepzibah's Mama gave one first and final look at her new-born child, then shuddered and expired. And of course it's family history that her Daddy died three weeks later from over-exertion while enjoying his second honeymoon at Flat Rock, North Carolina. So I said, trying to extricate at least one of my legs, "But both your mama and papa are enjoy-ing eternal rest in St Philip's Churchyard..."

"You are quite right, Soon-to-be Cousin Gwendolyn," Cousin Hepzibah managed to tell me, "but I still qualify as a new orphan. It was *Maum Sarah* who raised me, along with your own Cousin Pee and that frivolous filly, Cousin Alexis. She sustained all three of us at one time, a record I am sure for our long-suffering wet nurse. Why, she liked to boast that all three of what she termed her triplets owed their clear milky complexions to all the lactic nourishment she had so freely donated."

Cousin Hepzibah drew a breath to gain strength for her supreme moment. "Last night, in all that wind, Maum Sarah left us to suckle the angels. I am more of an orphan than the others, for Cousin Pee still has you" — she admitted this almost grudgingly — "and of course his horse Estella, while Cousin Alexis, for some unnatural reason, can always claim Cousin Lewis in times of dire emergency."

By this time, Miss Glory-Be, in a gesture of respect for the dead, had joined in the weeping, so that between them my bedroom had been turned into a funeral parlor. As if this were not enough, Mr James arrived like the Wizard of Oz, still wearing the purple penitente outfit complete with conical cap that Cousin Alexis had so graciously made him during his sojourn in the Exhausted Sinner retreat.

"Hush up, the lot of you!" he shouted, "You gonna scare the Angel Gabriel into droppin' his golden trumpet while he's whiskin' Maum Sarah up into heaven." He rolled his eyes skyward. "I dun heard the news durin' Miss Alexis' Bible study class. She ordered two minutes of respectful silence, then lowered the Confederate Flag to half mast. She was too upset to go on with the lesson, so we never did find out what happened to the Prodigal Son."

He patted Cousin Hepzibah's arm gently. "Miss Hepzibah, you have my heart-felt sympathy down to the soles of my feet. Maum Sarah is marchin' with the saints."

"Oh, I do hope they let her keep her exercise bicycle," Miss Topsey sniffed. "She'll be lost without it."

Mr James had no sooner left the room than Cousin Hepzibah dropped to her knees next to the bed, mercifully releasing one of my legs, and yanked up the bedspread. "Okay, where is it?" I heard her say. "Princess Frances told me this is where Mr Pee used to hide the gin."

Miss Glory-Be then obliged her by miraculously producing a bottle of Dixie Belle pink gin — from where I never did discover — together with three glasses. He then poured Cousin Hepzibah, Miss Topsey and himself each a drink. "Not too much," cautioned Cousin Hepzibah. "Can't have liquor on my breath when I go shopping for Maum Sarah's casket."

"Well, I'm shocked at Maum Sarah's sudden demise," I ventured to say. "The day I took over her birthday cake, she looked in better health than I."

"As the Princess will tell you, being present at Maum Sarah's death bed, it was all too terrible. One of her gallstones cracked. Or whatever it is that gallstones do."

"I never was aware that she suffered from gallstones," I remarked, rubbing at a charlie horse in my leg. "Perhaps all that bicycling she's been doing lately hastened the end."

Miss Topsey shifted her weight, freeing up my other leg, in order to pinch a hot biscuit from the breakfast tray. "What's going to happen to Miss Landine, her old she-cat?" she asked.

"I suppose we'll have put her up for adoption," I ventured.

"That won't be necessary," Cousin Hepzibah informed me. "With her dying breath, Maum Sarah left you and Cousin Pee her most treasured possession — Miss Landine."

I suppressed a shudder...and I knew Mr James and Miss Glory-Be would be none too happy at the prospect. But in Charleston, it is considered exceptionally bad manners to refuse or return gifts.

"If it is any consolation," Cousin Hepzibah went on, pouring another glass of gin, "I will give shelter to Miss Landine until after the blessed Fourth of July. I have promised to care for Conniving Connie, Miss Topsey's tomcat, while she is attending a sky-diving convention in Natchez."

Miss Topsey polished off a thyme-sprinkled sausage and reached for a peach. "I do hope Miss Landine will compromise and try to get along with Conniving Connie. I don't want to spend the whole time up there worrying about my baby boy."

I excused myself to shower and dress, leaving Cousin Hepzibah to drown her sorrows in pink gin and Miss Topsey to polish off the rest of my breakfast. I chose a white summer mourning dress, out of respect to the other orphan, Mr Pee, who would probably show up any minute in need of sympathy.

When I returned to my bedroom, Miss Topsey had fallen asleep on my bed, and Miss Glory-Be had escorted Cousin Hepzibah to the maid's sitting room, as she stubbornly refused to relinquish the gin bottle. I went downstairs to await Mr Pee.

It was only moments later that I heard the familiar sound of his faithful horse, Estella, galloping through the wrought iron gate outside. Mr Pee dismounted and, leaving the horse untethered in the rose garden, rushed inside, choking back great sobs.

"Oh Miss Gwendolyn — have you heard the terrible news?"

"Yes, I have, Mr Pee. Cousin Hepzibah just told me."

He wrung his hands. "I was preparing to go heron-watching in Washington Park when Cousin Alexis telephoned me. Oh, I am so distressed!"

"There, there," I tried to console him. "Would you like me to fix you some tea?"

"I'm too upset to touch a thing," he insisted. "First my dear mama, now Maum Sarah. Whatever am I going to do without them?"

I couldn't help but be a bit miffed at this. "Mr Pee, I remind you that *I* am still here."

"Yes, of course." he sniffed. "I didn't mean..."

"It's not like you were totally *alone.*"

"No, of course not," he admitted, rather ashamedly. "Besides, there's Alexis, Hepzibah and Lewis. Not to mention my faithful horse, Estella..."

At that very moment, a blood-curdling whinny broke the silence. "Estella!" cried Mr Pee.

We both rushed out into the rose garden, but Estella was not there. She had wandered into a shadier spot where she had completely devoured Mr James pride and joy, the century shrub, even the seed pods which he was saving to peddle to the tourists.

The horse lay flat on her back, kicking up her legs like a four-legged go-go dancer. I knelt and propped up her head while Mr Pee frantically rubbed a front hoof. "We must call an ambulance!" he insisted.

But a moment later Estella gave a final grunt and expired.

Mr Pee collapsed with grief. I felt terribly sorry for him...but I couldn't help wondering if he would have shown the same emotion if I had been the one to eat the poisoned shrub.

It was Mr Pee's wish to have Estella stuffed, like Roy Rogers' horse Trigger. I thought this rather macabre...but at least he didn't insist on the same initiative for Maum Sarah.

The problem was that, in this climate, we had to get things cracking (as they say in my country). Obviously, trying to track down Roy Rogers' taxidermist was a hopeless task, so I called up the only other person I knew in Hollywood, Miss Joan Crawford, who was a family friend of long standing and a role model for Cousin Alexis. Joan was very understanding and sympathetic, and in no time at all had made all the necessary arrangements.

And so, covered with three Confederate flags, Mr Pee's faithful Estella left Charleston for the last time to be preserved for posterity.

# 13

The Hosea Pincklea Mansion
Dear Cousin Matilda-Madge

I am a battered shipwreck, so much so that I have been ordered to bed for three days where Miss Glory-Be, the underbutler, has been feeding me nothing but nourishing Low Country She-Crab Soup.

We have all just returned from Maum Sarah's going home obsequies, which proved to be the most nerve-wracking I have ever attended since one of Cousin Alexis' multiple husbands was cremated by mistake in Brooklyn's Greenwood Cemetery. It was the most fully integrated event in Charleston since they finally took down those disgusting WHITE and COLORED signs from the public washrooms at the Greyhound Bus Station.

Then, too, Mr Pee still had not fully recovered from the double shock of losing his beloved nanny and his faithful

115

horse in one fell swoop. I could only pray that he made it through the ceremony without collapsing.

The Princess Frances graciously arranged and paid for everything, although Cousin Hepzibah, Mr Pee, and Cousin Alexis all chipped in to purchase a hand-painted baby-blue copper casket with sterling silver handles and matching Venetian lace inside for their faithful old nurse. Her Royal Highness thought of everything, including a white doctor accompanied by two horsey no-nonsense nurses (one white and the other black), wearing their credentials pinned to their ample bosoms, just in case Cousin Hepzibah fainted, as she is inclined to do. As it was, she collapsed three times during the proceedings.

Mr James walked solemnly down the aisle, accompanied by his voluptuous fiancee Miss Shirley-Mae, wearing an orange sword of the Exalted Sons of Osceola (Mr James, not Miss Shirley-Mae), liberally encrusted with fake rubies, diamonds, and sickly green emeralds (the sword, not Mr James). Miss Shirley-Mae (did I tell you she's expecting, and they have to get married?) proudly carried the Exalted Sons embroidered banner which depicts, somewhat inappropriately for a funeral I thought, Adam and Eve in their birthday suits. (Were you aware that Adam and Eve were black?)

Wearing the crepe veil that Miss Topsey Piddleton had worn to Queen Mary's funeral at Windsor, Cousin Hepzibah (being the eldest of the three bereaved childhood charges) was designated Chief Mourner, leading Miss Landine (Maum Sarah's orphaned she-cat) on her half-mourning purple leash with a large black bow respectfully adorning her neck. Seeming to understand the solemnity of the occasion (thinking no doubt of the clotted sour cream which no longer would Maum Sarah provide so liberally every breakfast-time), the cat let out the most blood-curdling howls during Miss Topsey Piddleton's moving organ prelude. Miss Topsey had cancelled her sky-diving trip to Natchez in order to perform at the service.

There I sat where the pair of militant nurses had bodily placed me in the second pew from the front, feeding fresh shrimp from a Canton export porcelain saucer to Miss Landine who, following one of Cousin Hepzibah's collapses, had to be handed to me for safekeeping. Her regal manner seemed to suggest that she realized she was now an heiress, as Maum Sarah had left her everything... even the valuable Thomas Elre chest of drawers that half of Charleston so coveted that there had already been fifteen offers from some of the oldest and best Charleston families to legally adopt its new owner.

Directly below the appointed places of the Princess Frances, Big Shot's Daddy and the Jewish Rabbi who had asked as a good-will gesture if he might take part, lay Maum Sarah in her fancy casket, looking far more cheerful than she had ever done in life. Indeed, there was a suggestion of an enigmatic smile on her face, the reason for which was soon to become apparent.

She was attired in watermelon-pink satin from head to toe, clasping in her gloved hands a picture of Cousin Hepzibah, Mr Pee and Cousin Alexis taken on their confirmation day at St Philip's Episcopal Church. On her wizened old head had been lovingly placed an enormous beehive wig offset with cascading brown kiss curls that the Princess confided had been worn by no less than Vivien Leigh as Scarlet O'Hara in *Gone With the Wind*. With her petunia blush lipstick and lavender eyelashes, I never would have recognized the cadaver in the casket as the grim-faced old woman who so recently rejected her ill-fated birthday cake. Down on Broad Street, where everybody knows everything, it was whispered that the Princess Frances had even imported her own royal embalmer from Paris. Mr James, who never missed a funeral if he could help it, declared that

117

Maum Sarah's send-off was quite the finest he ever remembered.

The six unisex harpists from Grand Rapids with their identical short peroxide blonde hairdos began to pluck graciously at their strings, which was the signal for Miss Glory-Be, not one to be outdone by six fake angels, to appear attired in the white lace bridal gown in which I had married Big Shot, complete with that same pair of wings that Mr James always wore to serve supper on Christmas Eve, and a skull cap made of sequins. Miss Glory-Be carried a golden cage, which he opened to release a dove — which, in spite of all the makeup, looked suspiciously like Mr James' parrot, Miss Sweet-Talking Harriett.

Big Shot's Daddy then clapped his ring-bejewelled hands, which was the cue for the harpists to all stop their twanging and allow Miss Topsey Piddleton to really get down to business. Starting with a vigorous rendition of "The Battle Hymn of the Republic", she then launched into her own special interpretation of "Dixie". This was followed by Purcell's "Trumpet Voluntary", the sheer volume of which nearly cracked our eardrums — and if Miss Sweet-Talking Harriett, alias the dove, had not descended onto her bare neck and sunk her claws in, Miss Topsey probably would have gone on until the walls caved in.

Mopping his graying brow with a black-edged handkerchief, Big Shot's Daddy called for order, and when he didn't get it he used Princess Frances' gold knobbed parasol to bang lustily for silence. At last he was ready to begin his funeral oration.

"My chosen brothers and sisters," he began, "today we gather here united in our common grief for the lioness snatched from our midst."

"Amen!" cried Mr Pee, just like his late beloved Maum Sarah had taught him to do in the plantation Sunday School when he stood a little whippersnapper at her bony old knee.

"Amen!" Her Royal Highness the Princess Frances echoed, then yelled "Hallelujah!" and everyone in the church followed suit, with the noticeable exception of Miss Shirley-Mae, Mr James enceinte fiance, but then only because she was a Jehovah's Witness and had a sore throat.

By that time, Cousin Hepzibah and Mr Pee were sobbing so loudly that Big Shot's Daddy, as officiating minister, had to tell them to kindly shut up. This upset Mr Pee even more, for Maum Sarah herself had always said that anyone who didn't shed copious tears at a funeral showed no respect for the departed.

I tried to console him, offering my black lace handkerchief, as Cousin Alexis had used up all of hers. Then, with no prior warning, the sickly aroma of arum lilies and sweet peas became too much for me. I began to sway, and as my knees were caving in, one of the enormous nurses charged forward like Joan of Arc, knocking poor Mr Pee right out into the aisle.

As he struggled to his feet, the white clad Amazon attacked me, pressing on my neck so hard that she nearly broke it. As my head was thrust down, my chin came into sharp contact with Miss Landine, who shrieked and immediately clawed me so badly that the nurse had to stop her physical assault and apply an outsize band-aid that she had kept ready in her pocket.

At that moment, Miss Topsey mercifully struck up "God Save the Queen", causing my karate nurse — a loyal Jamaican by birth — to leap to attention and salute, leaving me to slide bodily to the floor.

Miss Landine, outraged at the disturbance, must have decided that she preferred her old dead mistress to the new live one, and with a gigantic leap, which belied her advanced years, landed plumb on top of Maum Sarah's sainted head.

Instantly, to the horror of all assembled, the blessed corpse sat bolt upright in her casket, like the reincarnation of one of the Pharaohs, and in that voice we all knew so well, screamed, "You God-Damned Cat! Get your mangy little pink ass off Miss Scarlett's wig!"

The music stopped, the congregation gasped, and Big Shot's Daddy choked on his new two thousand dollar dentures. Cousin Hepzibah and Miss Glory-Be both fainted at the same time, while Miss Topsey Piddleton sat frozen on her organ seat and wet herself.

Maum Sarah was the only one who was calm. "I always wanted to see who would come to my funeral," she announced with satisfaction. "And thanks to Princess Frances, who helped me set it up, I have achieved my dying wish and can now get on with the rest of my life."

By this time, most of the palpitating angels and distraught mourners had stampeded for the exits. Cousin Alexis had taken cover under the font with the undertaker. I was still woozy, but managed to pull myself back onto the pew seat.

"As a Southern gentleman of the old school," Her Royal Highness commanded the trembling Mr Pee, "perhaps you would kindly help Maum Sarah out of her casket before she breaks her neck."

On that exhausted note, I close.

Your faithful cousin
Gwendolyn

# 14

Mr Pee lay groaning on my Charleston Chippendale four-poster rice bed, wearing his white boxer shorts with the red valentine hearts embroidered in each corner. His frail body was covered with scratches, his hands were blistered and his feet were swollen. He sucked in his breath as I applied cold compresses to his wounds.

"Oh, Miss Gwendolyn...I don't think I'll ever be able to move again! Every muscle aches, and all the bones in my body seem to have been rearranged. Do you still have that wheelchair that belonged to Grampa Pincklea?"

"You don't need a wheelchair quite yet, Mr Pee," I assured him. "You'll recover, just as you did each time you fell off your horse Estella when you played polo."

"I was much younger then," he whimpered.

"Enough of that! You talk as if you had one foot in the grave."

"Please don't mention the word 'grave'," he moaned. "Two funerals in as many weeks — the next one will surely be mine!"

121

I had to admit that Mr Pee had had his share of traumas lately. First, Maum Sarah's staged funeral, which left us all quite shaken for days. The 'corpse' recovered much more quickly, and along with her old she-cat Miss Landine had set off for New York to visit her niece, the Reverend Mrs Carmen Suck and Miss Landine's surviving son, Mr Praise-The-Lord, now a respectable church cat.

Then there was the demise of Mr Pee's faithful horse, Estella, currently in the hands of a Hollywood taxidermist. Mr Pee had shown no interest whatever in seeking a replacement, and indeed had effectively retired from the demanding sport altogether — which was probably just as well, given that his health was not what it once was. And the most recent experience had not helped matters...

This morning, Mr Pee had attended the funeral of old Mr Amos Abraham Simons. The faithful retainer had expired from colic at the ripe old age of ninety-seven. Mr James blamed it all on eating green apples. Mr Pee's late sinful father had made him promise to see that Mr Amos Abraham was given a respectful sportsman's funeral, since he had taught Mr Pee's daddy the rudiments of hunting possum when he was a little boy. A generation later he tried to teach Mr Pee the same thing, but every time a gun went off the poor child got palpitations of the heart and wet his pants. For this reason, he became known on the plantation as Mr Amos Abraham's other failure — the previous one being his marriage at 87 to one of those fast hussies from Harlem, New York, who was visiting her home folks. It had been love at first sight, but when the bride discovered that her husband had invested his life savings in the fraternal organization arranging his funeral, she lost interest and took off again for New York where she got a divorce on the grounds of failure to consummate the marriage. For the rest of his days, Mr Amos Abraham never stopped hollering about the wedding ring (which Cousin Alexis found second-hand for him at a thrift shop in Savannah), since Miss Fast-Cheating Dolly, as he called her, had never returned it.

Mr Amos Abraham had lived a long, hectic life, having outlasted all of his sons, whose mothers he had steadfastly refused to marry because his mama had warned him about fast women (although he did go to Miss Potty's Health Club once and had to be carried out on a stretcher). Even his two grandsons had proved minor disasters — dissatisfied with life on the plantation, they had taken off for someplace in the liberal state of New York, where they grew marijuana in a flower pot and now resided in an upstate prison in Attica.

So now there was only Mr Pee left to bury the old man. While on his deathbed, Mr Amos Abraham insisted he heard harps playing Dixie, which touched Cousin Alexis' generous heart so much that she rashly promised him that he should be buried next to his Grandpappy and Grandmammy in the old plantation cemetery. No one mentioned that the cemetery hadn't been used in years, and had been taken over by weeds, brush brambles, and those horrible prickly little pine trees. Not to mention snakes.

"I didn't mind being a pall bearer," groaned Mr Pee as I rubbed soothing Ben Gay ointment into his aching shoulder blades, "I just wasn't up to carrying the casket all that way — the hearse could only go so far. Princess Frances never should have sent little Millie the mule to your Cousin Judith's in New York. She would have been a Godsend today."

He groaned again. "It took nearly an *hour* to get to the burial ground. Old Mr Burkee-Snout, Uncle Am's faithful hound, followed us, looking very woe-begotten.

"And when the woods got too thick, that top-hatted undertaker, who was prepaid for his services, had the audacity to hand me an axe and suggest that I start chopping. I had to clear a path through the woods before we could even get close to his Grandpappy and Grandmammy. Why, if Maum Sarah had seen me, she would have expired for good this time.

"When we finally got there, that scoundrel straightened the tails of his immaculate frock coat, handed me a shovel and said, 'You're doing mighty well, son. Just make believe you're working on a chain gang and start digging.' It took me all of *four hours* to plant Mr Amos Abraham!"

"That was a very noble thing that you did, Mr Pee," I assured him. "Your daddy would surely have been proud of you."

He nodded. "It was sheer torture...but the worst part was being driven back to the Holy City by Mr James. The man drives like a *maniac*. He dominates the center line as if he owns it!"

"Just be glad someone was there to get you home in the first place," I reminded him. "Mr James isn't perfect, but then none of us is."

I stressed these last words a little too emphatically, but as usual Mr Pee was oblivious. He pointed down toward his foot. "Kindly look at my right ankle... I think it might be broken. Or sprained. Or maybe I was bitten by a snake."

At that instant, a grappling hook sailed through the open window and dug firmly into the sill, bringing Mr Pee straight up out of bed. And a moment later a short apparition dressed in leder-hosen and rappelling boots hoisted itself into the room.

"I might have known," exclaimed Mr Pee, hastening to cover himself with a sheet. "Miss Topsey Piddleton..."

Miss Topsey proceeded to divest herself of all the hooks and rope. "You should take up mountain climbing, Mr Pee," she admonished. "It would give you much needed physical stamina, especially since Miss Henrietta is no longer around to give you your vitamins — " she glanced at me " — which after the Fourth of July will be *your* duty, Miss Gwendolyn. And speaking of physical matters, Mr Pee, you look *awful*. Were you involved in an accident?"

124

Mr Pee only groaned again and settled back down on the bed. "He has been out to the plantation to bury a much-esteemed family retainer," I explained.

"I am very sorry to hear it," sympathized Miss Topsey. "Good servants are so hard to get these days."

"This one lived to be ninety-seven," said Mr Pee, looking at his blistered hands. "I can only hope I'll last half that long."

Miss Topsey snatched a piece of fruit from a bowl and plonked herself down on the Queen Anne commode. "Miss Gwendolyn, I have a favor to ask..."

"A favor?" I knew these Charleston favors of old.

"Exactly. As you are aware, the Princess Frances has already engaged the Dock Street Theater for your Cousin-to-be Alexis' long-awaited stage debut — a benefit performance to aid that most worthy of all environmental causes, the Ban-Aluminum-Siding-In-Charleston Foundation, of which, naturally, Miss Hepzibah is the duly elected president."

"Having duly elected herself," Mr Pee muttered under his breath.

"That may well be. However, she has had the wisdom and foresight to place me in charge of the music for the production of *Sunset Boulevard On The Ashley*..."

"Music?" exclaimed Mr Pee. "Since when is *Sunset Boulevard* a musical? Cousin Alexis might be a fine dramatic actress, but I have it on good authority that she sings like a disillusioned pregnant toad. Cousin Lewis told me, and he of all people should know."

"It isn't exactly a musical..."

"She tried to sing him to sleep at her summer retreat in the Big Swamp, where she upset the occupants so much there was no fishing for a month." He chuckled. "And by the time things returned to normal, the elements opened up and it poured with rain. Cousin Lewis said all she did was complain that everything came down in torrents except men and money."

"As I said, it is *not* a musical," Miss Topsey went on. "However, Miss Alexis has extensively rewritten the original script, including moving the locale to Charleston and modifying the plot to make better use of her talents as a *femme fatale*. And since the actress in the movie, Miss Norma Desmond, always accompanies the private showings of her films with organ music, played by her servant Max, it seemed natural do do the same for the play. Incidental music, as it were."

It briefly crossed my mind that nothing in Miss Topsey's organ repertoire could even remotely be called "incidental", but I didn't pursue this. "So what is the favor you wish to ask?"

She helped herself to a biscuit and lathered it with butter. "I've been debating what kind of outfit to wear. Given the profound significance of the occasion, I need something more formal than what I normally wear to church services, funerals and workouts."

"You are welcome to look through my wardrobe," I offered, "but I'm not sure if — "

"Not *you*," she interrupted. "Mr *James*. He has some tuxedos with tails. That would be perfect."

The thought of the dumpy Miss Topsey Piddleton in suave formal attire was hard to imagine. But on reflection, for someone who had worn Venetian lace and three ostrich feathers when presented to the Archbishop of Canterbury, no outfit could be too outlandish.

"Well, Mr James isn't exactly your size either..."

She waved a hand. "A stitch here, a tuck there... I'm counting on you, Miss Gwendolyn."

I promised her I would talk to Mr James — a prospect I dreaded, given his decided lack of tolerance for Miss Topsey. Besides, Mr James had been out of sorts ever since he and Miss Shirley-Mae had gotten married. Big Shot's Daddy had performed the service in the privacy of his church study, because under the circumstances, nobody thought he should have a big wedding. Miss Sweet-Talking-Harriett was designated as bridesmaid. The bride and groom came back to the house for wedding cake and champagne following the ceremony, then had a terrible falling out when she overheard Mr James, after several glasses too many of Champagne, telling me that she looked like a pregnant water buffalo, even with her veil.

Then he informed her that their honeymoon in New York would have to wait because he had had all the honeymoon he could take for a while, and besides it was time to go to Edisto to dig up his crop of sweet potatoes. So Miss Shirley Mae took the nine p.m. train to New York City on her own, and every evening thereafter she called Mr James (collect) for spending money. After a week of this, even he conceded that the whole thing had been a bad mistake, but there was very little he could do under the circumstances. As Princess Frances reminded him unnecessarily, "A silly old goat like you didn't need a kid no-how!"

As Miss Topsey was gathering her gear and preparing to exit through the window, Miss Glory-Be appeared with a tray of stewed pigs feet and lima beans for Mr Pee — fixed just like Maum Sarah used to cook them for his supper when he was being weaned from her milk. "Mr James ordered me to bring this up, since he is still smarting from the unkind things you said about his driving. He said to inform you that you could *walk* home next time." He deposited the tray on Mr Pee's lap and tucked in a loose corner of the bedspread.

Mr Pee huffed and slowly began eating his meal, and Miss Topsey, seeing the food, delayed her departure and helped herself to a hush puppy from the tray. Miss Glory-Be opened the afternoon paper and drew our attention to a full-page paid advertisement in the Society Section:

THE UNIQUE, LUSCIOUS AND EMINENTLY TALENTED

# MISS ALEXIS PINCKLEA*

In the Three Act Melodrama

# SUNSET BOULEVARD ON THE ASHLEY

Completely Revised and Vastly Improved
by the LEADING LADY

## LUST.....MURDER.....ROMANCE.....LUST.....REVENGE .....DRAMA.....LUST .....SUSPENSE.....LUST

Also starring

**Mr Pee Pincklea as her Current Lover**

And Admirably Supported from Intimate Personal Experience by

**Mr Lewis Pincklea as an Ex-Lover and Current Butler**

Directed by

**Laurence LaChance of Buffalo and Broadway**

DIRECTOR OF MUSIC

**Miss Topsey Piddleton**

PRODUCED by

**HER ROYAL HIGHNESS**

**THE PRINCESS FRANCES OF PARIS, FRANCE**

CO-PRODUCER

**Mistress Hepzibah Pincklea Ravenal Jones,**

Exalted President of the

**BAN-ALUMINUM-SIDING-IN-CHARLESTON FOUNDATION**

*To Which All Proceeds Will Be Graciously Donated.*

---

*(Out of a loyal sense of Charleston propriety she thought it best to omit mention of her several married surnames)

Mr Pee nearly choked on a pig's toenail when I showed him the announcement. "I told that woman I wanted no part of this foolishness! Miss Gwendolyn, kindly get my cousin on that telephone contraption, and remind her of my resolve."

I did as he requested, since Mr Pee has always had an aversion to telephones and adamantly refuses to use them. I knew full well that Cousin Alexis would not take no for an answer, and wasn't sure just how I was going to deal with this.

Fortunately, she was not at home, so I left a message that Mr Pee wished to discuss a matter of some urgency. Mr Pee was in a bad mood now and lost his appetite, leaving it to Miss Topsey to finish the food on his tray.

I have to give Cousin Alexis credit for knowing just how to handle men, because she turned up at my door the following morning with an enormous cardboard box. There were holes punched into the sides and top, and a pink bow was scotched-taped to the lid.

Mr James helped carry the box into the dining room where Mr Pee, who was feeling somewhat better, was having his morning tea. Inside the box was a female Great Dane puppy with a ring around one eye and large floppy ears, one of which drooped over the unringed eye.

"This," announced Cousin Alexis," is Miss Pamela-Fay. She is a present for you, Cousin Pee."

Mr Pee scowled. "I dislike dogs. They get wet and smell like moldy dishrags. Why couldn't you have gotten me a nice Persian cat, like my mama's dear departed Miss Charmaine?"

Cousin Alexis ignored his protests. "Say hello to your new master, Miss Pamela-Fay."

The dog, also ignoring Mr Pee, rushed over and buried her face in Miss J-J and Miss Margie's breakfast bowl of

Happy Dog crunchies. Instantly, Miss J-J swatted the new-comer on the nose, sending her scurrying back to cringe behind Cousin Alexis.

"Serves her right," Mr Pee declared with satisfaction. "Now...I know why you're doing all this, Cousin Alexis. And I can tell you right now that it won't work."

"I have no idea what you mean, Cousin Pee," Alexis replied innocently. "I received an urgent message that you needed to speak to me. So — which family member has expired this time?"

"No one," insisted Mr Pee. "I have just read your self-serving announcement in the Charleston Evening Post. As well you know, Cousin Alexis, I am a polo player, a respected plantation owner, and Miss Gwendolyn's future husband. I am most definitely *not* your lover!"

"You should be so lucky," sniffed Cousin Alexis. "Most men would jump at the chance."

Mr Pee was not to be swayed. "I repeat, Cousin Alexis, I do not wish to be your lover in *Sunset Boulevard on the Ashley*, or any place else. I have to think of my bad heart. Besides, we are first cousins, so it would be incest. Poor Daddy would turn in his grave."

"Hmphh. Doesn't bother Cousin Lewis," Alexis remarked. "And considering that your Daddy, my late uncle Boniface Pincklea, kept a, er..." She struggled for just the right word for a Southern lady to decorously use "...*whatever*, in a little love nest on the banks of that same Ashley River, I fail to see where his decaying sensibilities would have been hurt at all."

Poor Mr Pee looked as if he had been clobbered at Gettysburg. "Miss Gwendolyn..." he whimpered, casting his helpless eyes over at me.

While all this was going on, Cousin Alexis had begun stroking Mr Pee's thinning hair, just as she had seen Gloria Swanson do to William Holden in the original *Sunset Bou-*

*levard.* "Come on...let's be friends again, Cousin Pee. Remember how I stuck up for you when we were all little? And how I blackened nasty Cousin Hepzibah's eye for saying you were just a watered-down version of your old sissy daddy?"

Mr Pee was weakening. He nodded his head in agreement.

"You will make a *splendid* on-stage lover. Why, you don't even have to take your clothes off. Nobody will see your legs."

Mr Pee looked hurt. "There's nothing wrong with my legs! I have very *nice* legs. Maum Sarah simply made me wear long pants so they wouldn't get sunburned." He looked at me for confirmation, but I evaded such a touchy issue.

"Besides," continued Cousin Alexis, putting on the finishing touches, "I know you to be a model of propriety. Now our Cousin Lewis on the other hand will probably get carried away by the torrid dialogue and remove his Confederate colonel's trousers right in the middle of the stage!"

"I am beginning to see your point," Mr Pee admitted.

Cousin Alexis sat back and folded her arms. "Good. Now, have we got all this settled?"

Mr Pee nodded. "I suppose. except..."

"Except?"

Mr Pee looked again at the newspaper ad. "Do you suppose my name could be in slightly larger letters?"

For the next six weeks, Mr Pee was so busy rehearsing with Cousin Alexis that I hardly saw him at all. He bequeathed me the new Great Dane puppy, Miss Pamela-Fay, to housebreak. Miss J-J, the basset hound, was furious at first, but later generously decided to become Miss Pamela Fay's surrogate mother, and together with Miss Margie, the

German Shepherd, commenced to train her to become a well-bred Charleston canine.

The whole cast of the play was being housed by Princess Frances in her mansion, so that rehearsals could continue any time during the day...and, in the case of Cousins Alexis and Lewis, the night as well. Miss Glory-Be had requested a paid leave of absence to be wardrobe master. Mr James said it was sheer heaven without him, although with Miss Shirley-Mae driving him silly with her morning sickness, he now had his hands full.

Because of his aversion to telephones, Mr Pee dutifully sent me a love letter every day, written on the pink note paper peppered all over with tiny lavender hearts that Miss Glory-Be had given him on Valentine's Day. The latest one read:

Dear Miss Gwendolyn

I am very lonely without you and I shall be glad when all this acting stuff is over and I can begin sharing your soft feather mattress again. In spite of all her money, the bed Princess Frances has assigned me is very hard. Miss Glory-Be, who has appointed himself to act as my body-servant, sleeps in a cot at the foot. Her Royal Highness is so heartless, she refuses me breakfast in bed and even rations the coffee.

Princess Frances has imported a famous director, Mr Laurence LaChance, to supervise the production. He flew in yesterday from France where he owns a chateau in Brittany. Her Royal Highness met him at the Film Festival in Cannes which she attended with the Prince, her late husband, and their equally late beloved French poodle.

Mr LaChance has a very high-pitched voice and wears a wretched yellow wig that has known better days. By that I mean there are only a few bristles left growing bravely at the hair-line, so he looks like a large aging canary bird that is moulting. He dresses in a pair of sailor's white bell bottomed pants, a blue and white striped t-shirt, and hand-crafted leather sandals. I have no objection to his sandals, although I do wish he would wash his feet. Cousin Alexis says he is an *artiste* and, being European, should not be judged by our impeccable Charleston standards. I have it on good authority, however, that he is actually from Oshkosh, Wisconsin, but feel it would be ungentlemanly of me to call attention to this.

At the first rehearsal, he had the sheer impudence to call Cousin Alexis a "true professional", and me a "rank amateur"! Fortunately, Cousin Lewis, red hair a-flying, rushed up to defend my reputation. "Mr LaChance, Sir," he informed him, "I would have you know that my Cousin Pee is a member of the esteemed Polo Players Society, and that his great-granddaddy fell nobly at the battle of Bull Run!"

Mr LaChance sniffed and tossed his head so that his toupee rose an inch or so before resetting. Rudely mimicking Cousin Lewis' proper Southern accent, he replied, "And *my* great grandaddy was Napoleon's valet and kept him warm at the Battle of Waterloo!"

At this, Cousin Lewis, God bless him, always prompt to defend our family's honor, then turned to me and said in a loud voice: "Cousin Pee, I am growing tired of portraying a cuckolded butler, as I am sure you must be of acting as our Cousin Alexis' swan song. Perhaps we should just turn in our resignations and go home. Miss Gwendolyn's roast possum seems awfully tempting!"

"But...but you can't do that!" Mr LaChance protested. "What will Her Royal Highness say?" We both ignored him as Cousin Lewis took my arm and led me to the nearest fire exit where, if I hadn't experienced a sudden urge to visit the bathroom, we might have made good our escape.

When I came out, Cousin Lewis and I were confronted by a furious Princess Frances, her ample bosom shaking with anger. "What's this I hear about you two lily-white turncoats resigning! I knew I should have taken Miss Alexis' advice and replaced Mr Lewis with her lighthouse-keeper friend in the role of the butler."

Poor Cousin Lewis looked as if he had been mortally wounded. "How *could* she?" he asked. "I will never understand that woman..."

Princess Frances shook her head sadly. "I was brought up in this Charleston to believe you were both true Southerners and gentlemen whose word was their bond. We cannot possibly get substitutes at this late date. And as for the lighthouse-keeper, following his last tryst with Miss Alexis he has applied for leave to recharge his faltering batteries. Besides..." she chucked him under the chin "...I have *personally* cooked up a batch of delicious lima beans and fried chitlins with turkey giblet sauce for your suppers tonight, just like the old days!"

To make a long story short, Cousin Lewis looked at me and I looked at him, as both of our stomachs began to growl. "Cousin Pee," he said rather sheepishly, "perhaps we were too hasty. Mr LaChance has doubtless been subjected to primitive European customs for so long that he has quite lost touch with our civilized sensibilities, which must account for his nasty disposition."

So, my dearest Miss Gwendolyn, unless the lima beans and fried chitlins upset my stomach and I have to send Miss Glory-Be home for some medicine, you will hear no more from me until tomorrow. I hope you will sleep peacefully with Miss Pamela-Fay, my Great Dane puppy, who must remain my surrogate until I return.

I remain

Your faithful fiance
Mr Pee.

I read the love note to Mr James, whose only comment was that if I didn't need his valuable services for a couple of hours he would mosey over to the Princess Frances' house and sample those lima beans and fried chitlins for himself.

# 15

There was a great rush on tickets for the performance, as resident Charlestonians always support their own. And as is typical in the Holy City, everybody was trying to outdo his neighbor in extravagant attire. Those who couldn't afford new tuxedos and evening gowns and tiaras were frantically selling off family heirlooms to buy them.

Mr Pee sent me three Chippendale chests of drawers and two highboys that desperate relatives had persuaded him to buy so that they wouldn't go out of the family. At the rate my hope chest was growing, I could soon have enough furnishings to open my own antique shop.

The Mother Superior of Poor Aunt Greta's convent had given Cousin Alexis' mother gracious permission to attend her daughter's starring performance in *Sunset Boulevard on the Ashley*. She would be chaperoned by another nun, Sister Augusta Benedictus, who had lived a sheltered life and was of a no-nonsense disposition. She was told specifically by the Mother Superior, who was once a go-go dancer in Baltimore and therefore knew all about sins of the flesh, "to see that poor Sister Doubting-Thomas Greta is not led into carnal temptation by her renegade daughter."

Mr Pee thought I should ask Cousin Matilda-Madge to fly over from England, but as it turned out she was off chaperoning a group of nubile Girl Scouts on their first trip to China.

Cousin Alexis sent a special invitation to the only one of her former husbands who was still in the land of the living, and then only because he was three months behind on his alimony payments. She had divorced him on the grounds of incompatibility, since he was unable to come to terms with having found her in bed with a bishop of the cloth (and he wasn't even an Episcopalian). When her poor mother in the convent learned of it, she came down with the shingles and couldn't sit down at Evensong for a month.

Maum Sarah felt it her duty to attend — after all, she was the one who had suckled the leading lady, Miss Alexis, along with her two cousins, Mr Pee and nasty Miss Hepzibah. But she would come only if she could be assured of a front row seat, that her old she-cat Miss Landine and Miss Landine's daughter Miss Fiddle-Dee-Dee could also attend, and that liquid refreshments would be served afterwards...and she didn't mean cherry soda. Even if the weather was hot, she intended to wear the white ermine fur coat that Miss Henrietta had left her, together with an appropriate tiara.

As it happened, I had to donate the tiara, since Miss Henrietta's kept slipping over her eyes and there wasn't time to fix it. By the time I had finished, I had also loaned her a pair of black lace see-through drawers, a Parisian negligee decorated with golden butterflies, and a red satin evening gown with only one sleeve, allowing the other arm to remain stylishly bare. Big Shot's Daddy, who was her spiritual adviser, was sent to the dime store for a pair of silver leashes for the pet cats, who already had green rhine-stone collars that Mr Pee had thoughtfully given them for Christmas.

In a burst of generosity, Princess Frances gave her not one but three front row seats for herself and feline entourage. She drew the line, however, at Maum Sarah's request to have her face lifted, reminding her of what finally happened to Miss Henrietta, God rest her sweet soul. Princess Frances had already paid for one funeral extravaganza, and really couldn't justify another to her accountants. Besides, Maum Sarah had already turned the copper casket into a daybed for Miss Landine and her daughter, and Miss Fiddle-Dee-Dee had immediately thrown up over the real Venetian lace lining.

Princess Frances also extracted a promise that Maum Sarah wouldn't use Mr Pee's grandmama's silver plated ear trumpet at the performance, since her ears were in fine condition for a woman of her age. Besides, when she pressed the wrong knob, as she frequently did, it emitted the most unladylike of noises.

She also solicited Miss Glory-Be to put a finger wave in her best church-going wig. Big Shot's Daddy observed that with the ankle length white ermine coat and the big ebonized walking stick with the silver lion's head for a handle, she looked just the Queen of Sheba. Or maybe Louis XIV.

As might be expected at a Great Occasion in Charleston, the pre-event ceremonies nearly overshadowed the event itself. There were numerous spotlights, without which no extravaganza would be complete. Television crewmen were there in force from as far afield as New York, Richmond, and Savannah, Georgia, where Cousin Alexis was still best remembered for the astonishing Dance of the Seven Veils she had performed at her high school graduation.

Princess Frances truly outdid herself...and everyone else in recent memory. Regally attired in the vintage gown that the Prince's first wife, Her Royal Highness Dena Irena, had worn to King George VI's coronation in Westminster Abbey, she arrived at the theater atop a big snow-white elephant named Miss Helen-Ethel, which Mr James, standing on a stepladder, had whitewashed. She sat majestically in one of those elaborate carriage boxes like they use in India where elephants are plentiful. Miss Glory-Be, attired in shimmering white satin with feathered scarlet turban, was perched astride Miss Helen-Ethel's obliging neck and guiding her down Church Street to the Dock Street Theater.

Immediately behind came a second, smaller elephant named Miss Jo-Ann, bearing Cousin Hepzibah. She was a sight to behold in apple-green lace with a crown of fake rubies on her head (I know they were not the real thing because Mr Pee's stepmama wore them to the Mardi Gras in New Orleans), and for some unknown reason she was carrying a scepter. Miss Jo-Ann was plain gray, Mr James having run out of whitewash, and was guided by none other than the director, Mr Laurence LaChance, splendidly arrayed in black velvet tights with sequined zipper, golden Roman sandals, a pink silk blouse, a silver neck chain, and his moth-eaten toupee.

Big Shot's Daddy, being a simple man of the cloth and therefore not given to such ostentatious exhibitionism, arrived wearing his clerical style collar and a dark cassock, which contrasted starkly with the glittering gowns worn by the two beaming starlets who clung to his arms.

Somewhat anti-climactically, I arrived in a sober gray limousine that was hired for the occasion (the one which had been used at Miss Henrietta's funeral), dutifully chauffeured by Mr James in a new bowler hat. I was dressed to match the car, in widow-woman grey, with white gloves and a string of real pearls. I had chosen not to bring my daughter Manigault, because with Cousin Alexis, one never knew quite what to expect.

139

We were accompanied, however, by Poor Aunt Greta, a little apprehensive as she recalled what happened at her only child's high school graduation, and her bodyguard, the abrasive-tongued Sister Augusta Benedictus, who was clutching a book entitled *How to Successfully Recognize Pornography*. They both wore long black habits and those stiff white headpieces that look like airplanes. I felt sorry for anyone sitting behind us.

As I walked between the two nuns, some hussy with dyed orange hair pointed at me and cackled: "Big Shot's old lady dun taken the veil!"

When Princess Frances had dismounted from Miss Helen-Ethel, the beast extended her trunk and picked up a ticket someone had dropped and thrust it through the ticket window. But as her size made it impossible to use the front entrance, she was led, reluctantly, by Miss Glory-Be around to the rear loading dock. As things were getting a bit crowded in the rear of the auditorium at that point, her co-worker, Miss Jo-Ann, was relegated to being tied to a tree outside, which angered her sufficiently that by the evening's end she had uprooted the tree, along with a whole row of palmettos and live oaks.

Inside, it was standing room only. Every seat had been sold, so Princess Frances had been forced to borrow all the folding chairs that three local funeral homes could muster to put in the aisles. To make matters worse, late-comers found it more and more difficult to get to their seats because, in true Charleston fashion, most attendees remained standing until the last minute in order to see and be seen by everyone else.

As the lights finally began to dim, Miss Topsey Piddle-ton, wearing Mr James' full dress suit complete with tails that dragged on the floor since she was so short, marched in and bowed professionally to the audience. Then she swung one leg, followed by the other, over the organ bench, squirmed into position, and immediately struck up "The Star Spangled Banner". The audience rose to its feet and sang patriotically.

At the conclusion, as everyone was sitting down, she launched into "Dixie". Once again, the audience rose, and sang even more patriotically.

We had hardly sat back down when Miss Topsey began playing "La Marseillaise", in honor of Princess Frances' deceased husband. Back up went the audience, noticeably slower this time. And since almost nobody knew the words, Miss Topsey compensated by increasing the volume of the organ.

As everyone was collapsing back into their seats for the third time, Miss Topsey must have remembered that I was British, because "God Save the Queen" rang out. This time, only about half the audience, knees popping, struggled back to their feet. And at the conclusion, most of them remained standing until they were sure the organist was not about to spring another anthem on them.

From my vantage point in the front row, I could see the director, Laurence LaChance, standing in the wings, busily giving last-minute instructions to the crew. Looming behind him, her eyes curiously fixed on the flamboyant gentleman, was Miss Helen-Ethel, the whitewashed elephant upon whose back Princess Frances had made her grand arrival at the theater.

As the director signaled for the curtain to be raised, Miss Helen-Ethel's long trunk reached out and plucked the weedy toupee from atop his head, apparently mistaking it for a leafy treat.

It never reached the beast's mouth, however, because once the moldy odor of the hairpiece registered on her nostrils, she sneezed, sending it sailing out into the audience. It landed with a plop in the lap of the hussy with the dyed orange hair, who promptly shrieked, swatted it onto the

141

floor, and proceeded to stomp on it until there were only scattered shreds left. The lady poked cautiously at the remains with her Woolworths Japanese fan until she was convinced that the danger was over.

Meanwhile, the curtain was slowly rising to reveal a white-columned ante-bellum plantation house standing under the magnolias, live oaks, crepe myrtles and ginger lilies. A large trough had been constructed across the front of the stage and filled with water to represent the placid blue waters of the Ashley River.

Cousin Alexis, in an apricot see-through chiffon nightgown that left little to the imagination, lay on a French Empire bed shaped like a gigantic swan that Princess Frances insisted had once belonged to the Empress Josephine. She wore sunglasses and puffed on a cigaret supported by a thin rod attached to her ring.

She was portraying Miss Norma, a rich and glamorous actress, who had a problem:

"Are there no real gentlemen left in this world?" she lamented. "I am so tired of lighthouse keepers, truck drivers, and bisexual hairdressers."

No sooner had this sage confession left her vermillion-painted lips than in marched her faithful butler Max, played by none other than Cousin Lewis, wearing a bald wig. In place of his Confederate Colonel's uniform, he was attired in another of Mr James' butler's outfits, which was as many sizes too small for him as Miss Topsey's was too large for her. Mr James had charged him twenty dollars to rent the suit and seventy-five cents to buy a lottery ticket.

He cleared his throat. "Cousin Alexis...I mean, Cousin *Madam*...no, I mean *Madam* — there is a news reporter from Savannah on the doorstep. Shall I throw him bodily into the river, or will you take coffee with him under the archway of scarlet oleanders?"

As one might expect of Cousin Alexis, she opted to stay put on her comfortable swan bed, but requested that the reporter be shown in. Then who should appear — looking a bit cocky, I thought — but my own Mr Pee, carrying a notebook and pencil, a press card in the band of his hat, and Big Shot's instamatic camera hanging from his own darling little neck. Mr Pee's real-life polo team, who were there in the audience to the last man, all stood and cheered at their blood brother's entrance, obviously irritating Cousin Alexis who liked to hog all the applause for herself.

True to form, her immoral intentions quickly became obvious. She dismissed her butler Max for the day and set about seducing Mr Pee. Pure-minded Aunt Greta and Sister Augusta Benedictus quickly caught on to what was happening and leaned in my direction, covering my innocent widow's face with their stiff white wings and causing me to miss most of the seduction scene. In spite of much squinting and wriggling, all I managed to observe was a glimpse of Cousin Alexis' apricot bottom and Mr Pee's black patent leather walking-out shoes, which he was never given the chance to take off.

After the seduction, Cousin Alexis, as Miss Norma, persuaded Mr Pee to live in her mansion and write a script worthy of her immense talents. "I shall be a *sensation*, darling, and you shall be famous!"

When Mr Pee left to fetch his clothes and typewriter, the door chimes rang. Since Max the Butler had been dismissed, Miss Norma swept aristocratically across the room and opened the door.

"I'm Lance Sterling, editor of the *Savannah Gazette*," said the husky gentleman standing there. Miss Norma's eyes lit up. He was tall, broad-shouldered, with wavy hair, and was smoking a pipe. "I'm looking for one of our reporters who — "

"Come *in*, come *in*!" Miss Norma insisted, grabbing his arm and pulling him into the room and over toward the couch.

The seduction was fast and furious, and the editor was out the door only minutes before Mr Pee reappeared with his belongings. At this point, Miss Norma was just getting wound up, and the poor man was once again subjected to the full force of her amorous will.

When he had dragged himself up the stairs to his room, the door chimes rang again.

The visitor this time introduced himself as a famous stage director, which was appropriate since he was played by none other than Mr Laurence LaChance, who felt that no one else could possibly do justice to the role. He had replaced his stolen toupee by a floppy beret, which itself became dislodged several times during the vigorous seduction which followed.

No sooner had the director staggered out the door, clutching his beret onto his head with one hand and carrying his shoes and socks in the other, than Mr Pee came back downstairs, dressed in a short white terry-cloth bathrobe. This sight of his fragile body and dimpled knees set Miss Norma off again, and within seconds they were thrashing around on the couch.

At this point, Poor Aunt Greta produced a little flask of brandy — for medicinal purposes, of course, should anyone faint. She gave me a swig after each episode in which my husband-to-be lost the virginity which he was supposed to be saving for me. (These scenes apparently upset her as well, as she resorted liberally to the flask, and it wasn't long before Sister Augusta Benedictus was following suit.)

When Mr Pee had returned back upstairs, the door chimes sounded once again. This time it was a fireman, dressed in heavy yellow coveralls, rubber boots and headgear. "Madam, are you aware that your house is on — "

As Miss Norma grabbed him by his lapels and yanked him into the room, the curtain fell on Act I.

In the course of the next two acts, Miss Norma seduced Mr Pee six times, along with a parade of visitors which included the mailman, a delivery boy, the electric meter reader, and two Jehovah's Witnesses, who always travel in pairs to reinforce one another's efforts. (One of the visitors was a Tupperware lady, who had the door rudely slammed in her face). Each seduction was accompanied by increasingly frenetic music from Miss Topsey's organ.

Finally, near the end of the play, Miss Norma was grappling with Cousin Lewis, playing Max the Butler, when Mr Pee happened to wander in. He was horrified. Seeing the error of his ways, he announced his intention to leave and return to the sweet little girl who has been waiting faithfully for him for ten years.

Well, no man had ever dared to leave Miss Norma, on stage or off. She reached under her scarlet lace-edged pillows for her revolver and aimed it at the departing Mr Pee.

That was all that Maum Sarah from her front row seat needed to see. "Don't you dare shoot him!" she shouted. "That's my baby's baby!" But Miss Norma had already pulled the trigger.

With an agonized cry, Mr Pee clutched his chest and staggered to and fro across the stage to the edge of the trough through which the Ashley River had flowed. Miss Norma fired again, and Mr Pee toppled over the edge.

Instead of the expected splash, however, a hollow *CLANG* echoed from inside the trough, accompanied by a yelp of pain. During the last intermission, no one had noticed a thirsty Miss Helen-Ethel, the whitewashed elephant, systematically reducing the Ashley waters to a bare trickle.

"Oh, what have I *done*?" wailed Miss Norma. "The only real gentleman I have ever known...and the only man I ever really loved!"

145

At this revelation, Cousin Lewis, as the butler Max — who had always secretly loved Miss Norma — uttered a cry of despair. Then he grabbed her favorite silk scarf, looped it quickly around his neck and strangled himself.

As he collapsed to the ground, and the curtain began to fall, Maum Sarah hobbled sprily up onto the stage where she pulled a startled Cousin Alexis across her knees and smacked her bottom smartly several times. Then she dashed over to assist Mr Pee, who was trying to extricate himself from the trough.

Moments later, the curtain raised again to allow the principals to take their bows. As they all lined up before the footlights — Cousin Alexis rubbing her stinging posterior, Mr Pee nursing an injured leg, and Cousin Lewis trying to fasten his trousers — Miss Helen-Ethel, insisting on participating, lumbered onto stage behind them, as a dozen stage-hands struggled unsuccessfully to restrain her.

At that moment, Miss Topsey Piddleton played a final tumultuous chord on the organ, nearly shattering all our eardrums...including those of Miss Helen-Ethel, who reared up on her hind legs, eyes wide, and trumpeted a blast of alarm. Then she thundered off toward the rear of the stage, dragging the stagehands behind her.

She ripped through the canvas backdrops, crashed through the construction area and out the loading dock entrance, and rumbled down Church Street, joined now by an equally frightened Miss Jo-Ann.

Cousin Alexis was furious that she had been upstaged by all the activity, but the tumultuous applause quickly restored her spirits. Charleston audiences had never enjoyed such a spectacle since the local Opera Guild's production of *Aida in the Holy City*.

# 16

The two rampant elephants were eventually brought under control, but not before they had overturned three cars, sent several fire hydrants geysering into the street, demolished a number of historic landmarks, and uprooted numerous live oaks, sending flocks of nesting herons shrieking into the air.

Princess Frances rather extravagantly ordered an ambulance for Mr Pee, who was carried out of the theater in a stretcher with the two nuns, Poor Aunt Greta and Sister Augusta Benedictus, in solicitous attendance. Someone had applied a temporary splint to his leg, which he insisted was broken. He looked completely devastated, and was moaning and groaning as the ambulance doors closed behind the three of them. He was to be taken to my house where the good Sisters would minister to him, since Maum Sarah was too exhausted by the whole evening's events to take care of anybody.

I gave Poor Aunt Greta the key to the mansion, because Princess Frances declared that it was my duty, knowing that my fiance was safe in such good capable hands, to represent him at the reception at her mansion to celebrate tonight's unprecedented triumph. The party would have to do without the help of Mr James, who had apparently taken up with a lady visiting from Columbia — he and Miss Shirley-Mae were still at odds after their separate honeymoons. And Miss Glory-Be was at the vets where Miss Jo-Ann's stomach was being pumped out from having devoured several bougainvillea vines before being constrained.

Mr Kent Brown-Tivoli, a theatrical museum director from New York, had been recruited to transform Princess Frances' restored mansion into a mock-Hollywood extravaganza for the reception. The mantlepieces were all covered with theatrical masks, while large cardboard cutouts representing exciting screen star stars such as Miss Bette Davis, Miss Gloria Swanson, Miss Joan Crawford, Miss Marilyn Monroe and Dame Margaret Rutherford mingled lifelike among the guests.

At the far end of the lower piazza was an equally large cutout of Rhett Butler embracing Scarlet O'Hara, another of John Garfield clasping Lana Turner, and others of Robert Taylor with Ava Gardner, Gregory Peck with Susan Hayward, Gary Cooper with Ingrid Bergman, and King Kong with Fay Wray. The only jarring note was at the entrance to the ladies powder room, where a large blow-up displayed Big Shot wearing his overly-short shorts, with Princess Frances — then plain Miss Frances Washington, my cook — sitting on his plump knees and showing off her short-lived engagement ring. I thought it was tacky to leave this reminder of the past on display on such an occasion, but as usual I said nothing.

Cousin Alexis, the leading lady, still wearing her dark movie star glasses, paired me off with Cousin Lewis who gallantly fetched me a lemonade. Unfortunately he became flustered at the persistent attentions of Miss Topsey Piddleton, who kept trying to drag him out onto the dance floor, that he gave me his triple vodka on the pink rocks with three cherries by mistake. Cousin Alexis later informed me that I passed out dancing the Charleston with her lighthouse keeper friend who had borrowed me for the dance.

I awoke at six the next morning in the Martha Washington armchair, with Cousin Lewis still in his full Confederate Colonel's uniform curled up puppy-like on the floor. Careful not to awaken him, or any of the other equally catatonic souls strewn about the room, I found a phone and called a taxi.

When I finally got home, it was to be confronted with a large notice on the front door which read:

### QUARANTINE

This was certainly puzzling. But as it was still my house, I disregarded the sign and marched right in... and nearly stumbled over the empty brandy bottle which Poor Aunt Gretta had produced during the play.

Upstairs, the door to my room was locked from the inside, and another sign, mounted on an artist's easel, displayed the warning:

### STOP
### DO NOT ENTER
### TEMPORARY CONVENT HOSPITAL

From inside, I could hear strange noises which sounded like Sister Augusta Benedictus giggling and Mr Pee moaning. I rushed to the adjacent room, which led out onto the upper piazza, and looked through the glass door into my room.

To my horror, I saw Mr Pee, secured to my four-poster bed by restraining straps, his injured leg elevated by a pulley. Poor Aunt Greta was forcing large silver tablespoonsful of lime Jello into his protesting mouth, while Sister Augusta Benedictus was sadistically tickling his bare foot with a turkey feather. "Now, stop struggling, Mr Pee," she insisted. "This will help to get the circulation back in your leg."

But Mr Pee continued to squirm and emit squeeking sounds like a distressed bat, when suddenly he saw me. "Miss Gwendolyn!" he hollered. "Stop them, stop them! They're disciples of the Marquis de Sade!"

The glass doors were locked and the Sisters paid me no mind whatever. I rushed downstairs to the telephone and dialed Cousin Alexis, hoping that she had returned from the reception.

When she finally answered, I shouted, "This is an emergency! Come and remove your mother and Sister Augusta Benedictus, her obnoxious bodyguard, from my bedroom before they give Mr Pee a stroke!"

She groaned. "I think it's high time for those two to return to the sanctity of their convent before they are both defrocked." Then she said to someone, "Kindly wriggle back into your polo breeches and then drive me post-haste to Miss Gwendolyn's."

She arrived in short order and dashed upstairs to rescue Mr Pee. The door was still locked, so we returned to the outer glass doors, which were also still locked. Cousin Alexis rapped sharply on the pane. "Mama, if you don't unlock this door right now I shall have to break it down! And your Mother Superior will have to pay for it!"

At that moment, Mr Pee gave a scream of sheer desperation: "Cousin Alexis, for the sake of my dear departed mother, Miss Henrietta, please rescue me! They're trying to make me use a *bedpan*!"

"Shouldn't we let them in?" I heard Poor Aunt Greta ask her sister nun. "Alexis is so impetuous. I never did take to her. She really *would* smash the window, like she did her poor dead Daddy's tombstone when he wouldn't let his ghost come out for her Halloween party. Besides, I would hate to have Reverend Mother bar us both from Miss Gwendolyn's next wedding. Oh, my, the eats will be so good!"

"Do we have to?" moaned Sister Augusta Benedictus. "It's been years since I've had such close contact with a man. Did you know that I was a professional tattoo artist before I took the veil?"

"Mama?" Cousin Alexis persisted. "Tell you what — if you open the door so that I can release Cousin Pee, I'll do something special for both of you. A real treat."

"Oh goody!" exclaimed Sister Augusta Benedictus, her narrow pointed face alight with ecstasy. "Pray tell us what."

"On our way back to the convent, we will take a short diversion to Myrtle Beach," Cousin Alexis promised.

Sister Augusta Benedictus clapped her hands. "Ooh...Myrtle Beach!"

"Can we go to the fun fair?" begged Poor Aunt Greta. "And have a ride on the Big Dipper?"

"And a dip in the Atlantic Ocean?" begged Sister Augusta Benedictus. "I always wear a bathing suit under my habit, just in case the need arises."

"As long as it is not a bikini," promised Cousin Alexis. "With my marital record, I cannot afford to upset the church."

Poor Aunt Gretta frowned. "The Reverend Mother is going to be displeased if we go to Myrtle Beach."

"We can pick up some toffee apples and chocolate donuts for her," Sister Augusta Benedictus suggested. "She has such a sweet tooth."

151

"Yes, let's!" the two nuns chortled together, holding hands and dancing around in circles. Then they unlocked the door.

By the time we cut him down, Mr Pee was ready for two weeks in a rest home. His heart was pounding like a trip hammer and he looked pale as a sheet. Cousin Alexis generously offered to call the ambulance back. I was beginning to think that, the way things were going, it might be better to simply buy one of our own.

# 17

After all the excitement of *Sunset Boulevard on the Ashley*, Miss Topsey Piddleton suggested that a nice, quiet, British-style tea party — at my house, of course — would be just the thing to allow us to unwind. Cousin Hepzibah accepted, although she complained that drinking hot tea always gave her indigestion. So Mr James agreed to provide her with a substitute — homemade herbed tomato juice, which she adored.

Cousin Alexis also had qualms, on the grounds that she wasn't a member of any women's liberation movement, and made it a point not to attend any function which didn't include men. With some coaxing, she relented, and preparations got under way.

Mr James made his delicious cucumber sandwiches — cutting his ring finger in the process, putting him in a bad mood for the rest of the day. Miss Glory-Be was in charge of the buttered scones, into each of which he stuck a miniature French flag, in honor of Princess Frances. I made my specialty, a very potent sherry trifle.

Miss Glory-Be dusted off the portrait of Big Shot on the mantle, and concocted a touching representation of his grave in Sissinghurst, copying from a photograph and using small pieces of watercress. Mr James, in spite of his wound and his worsening relationship with Miss Shirley-Mae, generously polished the Hester Bateman silver teapot to perfection. We had fetched it from the bank together that morning. Ever since a tourist had pinched Mr Pee's christening mug for a souvenir, we had prudently locked all the best silver up.

Miss Viola-Ball took Manigault out to Hampton Park for the afternoon, and the guests began arriving shortly before two o'clock. Princess Frances wore a French chiffon gown with frills. Cousin Alexis wore a red tight-fitting dress which was at least two sizes too small for her. And Cousin Hepzibah wore a pink linen two-piece suit with a short skirt and fitted jacket, which looked slightly bizarre on her large frame. Miss Topsey arrived last, puffing and panting, outfitted in a powder blue sweatsuit and beige Keds.

When everyone had arrived, Mr James offered grace, ignoring the impatient twitchings of Miss Topsey as she hungrily eyed the scones. I was afraid that, in her haste, she would devour them, miniature French flags and all.

"Ah," Cousin Hepzibah exclaimed. "I can see you are using the Rockingham cups and saucers. How well I remember the day we drank China tea with your dear mother in the sun lounge at Gerrards Cross."

"Mother always loved her Rockingham china," I agreed.

"And *cream puffs*," She recalled, smacking her ample lips. "The best in the whole of England."

"Alas, she took the recipe to heaven. I couldn't find it in any of her cookbooks."

154

"I do hope Saint Peter doesn't lose it!" exclaimed Miss Topsey, biting hungrily into her cucumber sandwich.

Cousin Hepzibah sipped her tomato juice. "Delicious. Reminds me of the time I portrayed The Bride of Frankenstein in the School play. We had to use tomato juice in place of blood."

This in turn reminded Mr James of his wounded finger, which he proceeded to suck gently. Miss Topsey made a face and said "Yuck".

All this time, Princess Frances had not said a word. She just sat there, looking glum, and hadn't touched her tea.

"Are you feeling ill, Your Royal Highness?" I inquired. "Or is it just the aftermath of *Sunset Boulevard on the Ashley*?"

Princess Frances shook her head so hard that her new golden wig momentarily absented itself from her head and landed on the floor in front of Miss Glory-Be, who had just entered the room with another tray of scones.

"*Oh* — finders, keepers!" he trilled, snatching it up and waltzing over to the Chippendale wall mirror to try on his prize. Her Royal Highness appeared not to notice, and sat looking waif-like with her own hair plastered down with hairpins. Then she started to cry.

"Oh Miss Gwendolyn," she moaned like a wounded cow, "I want to have a *baby*!"

Cousin Hepzibah choked on her sherry trifle. "Hells bells! This is *not* the proper topic for a British tea party," she protested. "You need to see your gynecologist."

Princess Frances did not appear to hear. "I never did have any babies of my own...and as for my fairy Prince, he was well past the age to accommodate me."

"Well, he *was* almost eighty," Cousin Alexis tried to console her.

Mr James snorted. "Well, I'm *more'n* eighty, and obviously I can still make babies."

155

Cousin Hepzibah turned white as the linen tablecloth. "This is all *most* indelicate...and to think I almost invited the rector of St Philip's." She rose and retreated to the nearest lavatory, taking her sherry trifle with her.

Cousin Alexis and Miss Topsey didn't seem to be bothered by Princess Frances' revelation, and the latter reached for another cucumber sandwich. Her Royal Highness dried her eyes on her sleeve. "I tried hard enough, God knows. Why, I even made the Prince wear boxer shorts like *Dear Abby* advised in her column. But it didn't make the slightest bit of difference. I still didn't have a baby."

I tried to sympathize, but she just glared at me with reddened eyes. "And *you*... Not only do you make off with my own beloved Big Shot, but you get yourself a baby with just one night's effort!"

"Well, there *are* other ways," Cousin Alexis mercifully broke in. "With all your money, you could always hire a surrogate mother, pay her ten thousand dollars...and when she delivers, the offspring is yours!"

Princess Frances blinked. "You mean for ten thousand dollars, *you* would be my surrogate mother?" She reached into her pocket book for her checkbook.

Cousin Alexis looked horrified. "*Me*?! Be a surrogate mother? I *detest* babies...nasty, messy little things."

Princess Frances looked imploringly over at me. "Miss Gwendolyn — "

"No!" I spluttered. "I have to consider Mr Pee and his heart condition. We have already decided that, even after we are married, such luxuries as making children might be hazardous to his already imperiled constitution."

She sighed, then turned her attention toward Miss Topsey Piddleton, who was cramming another scone into her mouth. Princess Frances winced and shook her head.

Then I suggested, "Couldn't you advertise for a donor in the morning paper?"

Princess Frances appeared not to hear me as she snatched Big Shot's portrait, silver frame and all, from the mantle and clutched it to her ample bosom. "My love!" she cried, "My greatest love! If I could only hold you in my arms once more!"

This was more than any legal widow could take, even from royalty. "Well, I can't allow you to dig him up," I snapped. "I don't think the Vicar of Sissinghurst would like it. And in any case you would need official permission from the British Home Office."

"I could speak to the Archbishop of Canterbury," offered Miss Topsey Piddleton, who was about to demolish the last of my sherry trifle. (I am still wondering about her and His Grace.)

Princes Frances gave her a nasty look. "If I *could* dig him up, I would. Just like whats-his-name...Heathcliff...did with Catherine in *Wuthering Heights*."

Miss Topsey made a face. "*Gross.*"

I had no doubt that, given the opportunity, Princess Frances would do exactly as she threatened, and I thanked my lucky stars that I had seen fit to bury Big Shot in England, where he would always be safe from her clutches.

Cousin Alexis then took a little silver flask of Dixie Belle gin from her pocket and poured a generous amount into her tea cup. "Let's not get into a tizzy about this," she said. "I'm sure that — "

"I deserve my share of Big Shot!" Princess Frances insisted. "I can *still* have his child of sorts. Miss Potty shall be the surrogate mother!"

"Miss *Potty*!" Cousin Alexis exclaimed. "But she hates you, ever since you publicly threatened to run her out of town on a rail."

"Well, it is high time I forgave her. Come, Miss Alexis, let us proceed over to Radcliffe Street."

Cousin Alexis hesitated. "I'm not sure I'm up to this. The last time I was an honorary guest at the Health Club, I didn't get home until six the next morning. It was a very busy place."

"Strictly business this time," Princess Frances assured her. "I have my checkbook...let's go."

"Miss Potty only accepts cash and traveler's checks," reminded Miss Glory-Be as he saw them to the door. "Ever since that Republican senator's check bounced, Miss Potty's policy is strictly cash on your bottom."

Miss Topsey Piddleton seemed a little under the weather; too much sherry trifle, I suspected. She was sitting with the Queen Marie Antoinette's golden harp, her eyes slightly glazed, playing "Cherry Ripe", which seemed a little out of place for a British tea party.

"I think I had better drive her home," suggested Cousin Hepzibah, who had returned to the drawing room. "From the looks of her, she'd be lucky to make the corner alone."

I would have volunteered Mr James do do the honors, but he was fast asleep on the Aubusson rug with Miss Pamela-Fay beside him. I was reluctant to disturb him, since he needed all his strength to cope with his demanding wife.

When Cousin Hepzibah had left with Miss Topsey, I asked Miss Glory-Be to bring a cup of tea up to Mr Pee, who had retired to my room to escape what he referred to as our "hen party". Actually, I could hardly blame him.

Mr Pee was sitting up in bed reading the afternoon papers, the Misses Margie and J-J on either side of him. I told him about Princess Frances' revelation.

"Don't trust that woman," he warned. "She'll do whatever she sets her mind to. *Including* digging up Big Shot."

When Miss Glory-Be arrived with our tea, he announced that Mr James was still out for the count, and that he would fix our dinner instead...including his very own special version of a French omelet. "That's the best news I've heard all day!" Mr Pee exclaimed. "One can take only so much of Mr James' possum, pigs feet and creamed Edisto rattle-snake."

Miss Glory-Be beamed at the compliment. "And I will make your favorite side dish — fried chicken livers and giz-zards, just like your Maum Sarah used to make as a treat when you were a good little boy and didn't wet your pants. Also fried rice, fried tomatoes, *and*... he rolled his eyes in sheer anticipation "...freshly baked corn bread."

As Miss Glory-Be trotted off to the kitchen, Mr Pee re-marked: "That boy is indeed a treasure!"

We ate by candlelight alone that evening. Mr James and Miss Pamela-Fay were recovering in the butler's pantry, the former from the day's exertion, the latter from a hangover from being fed too much sherry trifle.

The intimacy was soon broken when Cousin Alexis dragged herself in and collapsed on the couch. "I *knew* it would be sheer murder going to the Health Club," she groaned. "Do you mind if I borrow the guest room for the night?"

I assured her she was welcome to stay the night. "But what happened at Miss Potty's? Did she agree to be a sur-rogate mother for Princess Frances?"

"On the contrary," Cousin Alexis replied, removing her shoes. "Miss Potty was outraged that Her Royal Highness would even *suggest* such a thing. She said she had the repu-tation of her establishment, her employees and her clients to consider. No amount of money was going to change her mind...and that went for her girls as well."

"I can't imagine Princess Frances taking 'no' for an an-swer," Mr Pee remarked.

"She may not have to," Cousin Alexis said. "When Miss Potty stormed out of the room, all her girls rushed over and wanted to know how much she would pay. But for the moment, Princess Frances seemed determined that Miss Potty would do the honors herself."

She took a healthy swig from her gin flask. "At this point, I became involved in...eh, other things, and had to leave her to pursue the matter on her own. The last I saw of Princess Frances, she was showing a curious interest in Miss Potty's little boy, Rhett Cartland."

Mr Pee sniffed. "The unfortunate issue of Big Shot's indiscretion."

Cousin Alexis yawned, stretched and announced her intention to retire to her room and collapse. When she had dragged herself up the stairs, Mr Pee commented, "In all the years that I have had the pleasure of knowing my Cousin Alexis — and I have known her since I was a baby — I never recall her retiring so early. The poor girl looks worn out."

"That should come as no surprise," said Miss Glory-Be as he applied Big Shot's lighter to his flaming parfait. "A freighter just docked from Argentina."

At that moment, somebody started vigorously ringing our doorbell. It was Miss Christmas-Candle Hawkins, Miss Potty's number two evening hostess, who really looked quite drab without her makeup, bearing a urgent message written in pencil on the page of a child's exercise book.

As I had left my glasses in my bed, Mr Pee had to read it for me:

Dear Mistress Gwendolyn

THIS IS AN EMERGENCY!
That royal trollop has stole my baby! I beg you Miz Gwendolyn for Big Shot's sake if nothing else to come to my Health Club at once and I will even roll out the red carpet which I only do for VIP's. Let us let bigones be bigones, forgive my past transgressions, Religiously, Miss Potty.

"How jolly sporting of her," said Mr Pee. "I always did say that Miss Potty had a heart of pure gold."

"I can't believe that Princess Frances would kidnap a child," I said. "Whatever must have possessed her?"

"How old is the boy?" Mr Pee asked.

"Five or six, but he knows more than some teenagers," Miss Glory-Be informed us. "Her Royal Highness may have taken on more than she can manage. Once he put live frogs in all the beds at the Health Club. You could hear all the screaming way down on the Battery."

"Well, we are not going anywhere until we have partaken of Miss Glory-Be's flaming parfait," I insisted.

"That's right," agreed Mr Pee, and with some effort managed to blow out the recalcitrant flame.

After dinner, I put on Big Shot's dark sunglasses, grateful now that they had not been buried with him, since I had no wish to be recognized during my visit. Miss Glory-Be drove me to Miss Potty's establishment, first hanging an "Off Duty" sign in the car window.

"Big Shot," I said, gazing up towards heaven, "I hope you can see all the trouble you are causing me by your indiscretions. First the domineering Princess Frances, and now the infamous Miss Potty. Will your doxies never leave me in peace?" I think he must have heard me, because there was a low rumble of thunder in the darkening sky.

Miss Potty's Health Club was housed in what once had been a Victorian mansion, now painted pale pink. The fading remains of a sign, painted by Big Shot in a weak moment, could still be deciphered: "PRAISE THE LORD AND HAVE A SEXY CHRISTMAS."

Miss Glory-Be rang the doorbell, and we were ushered in by the tallest butler I had ever seen. His name was Gullah Jackson, and he served as Miss Potty's personal bodyguard when her lady ones were off duty. Miss Glory-Be said that he was also Miss Potty's current side dish.

Gullah Jackson showed us into the reception room. I had instructed Miss Glory-Be not to leave me, or to accept anything for us to eat, because Big Shot always maintained that Miss Potty was in league with Devious Julius, the conjurer man, and I wasn't about to have her put a spell upon me.

It was no surprise to me that room showed little evidence of any of the usual health club trappings — no weight-lifting or rowing machines, no reducing bicycles, no chinning bars, no climbing ropes. Instead, the walls were painted a garish shade of psychedelic pink, with loveseats, plush chairs, and sofas upholstered in velvet to match. On the arm of each chair and on the sofa backs, Miss Potty's girls had placed crocheted white lace mats in the shape of hearts, in case any of their clients suffered from dandruff.

The doors, trim, and window frames were tinted gold, and from the middle of the duck's-egg-blue ceiling hung the late Miss Minnehaha's crystal chandelier, which she had sold to Miss Potty during her last days when she was hard up. Over the mantel piece, in a mahogany frame that obviously had been painted gold with radiator paint, hung the worst color enlargement of Big Shot I had ever seen.

None of Miss Potty's working girls were in evidence although I distinctly heard giggles and laughter coming from distant parts of the house. At a large desk, which Mr Gullah Jackson had painted silver and purple, sat Miss Potty, her wisps of graying hair peeping out from beneath her chestnut brown wig. She looked like an embalmed Egyptian mummy dug up after four thousand years, even more frizzled up than I remembered her.

Miss Potty was sobbing, which did little to improve her looks, and wringing her black-edged handkerchief. "Oh, Miss Gwendolyn," she cried. "Do you know where that awful woman has taken my Rhett Cartland?" I confessed that I had no idea, and asked her if she had notified the police.

She hesitated, sniffling. "That would be a little...awkward. Many of my clients might feel...well, *antsy* about having a slew of cops and newspaper types nosing around."

At that moment, a gentleman dashed out into the room and across to the front entrance, clad only in his azure-blue underdrawers. He was pursued by a large plump female in a daffodil-yellow nightgown who was screaming to be tickled. He was out the door and down the street in the direction of East Bay before I could get a good look at him, but I felt sure I had seen his face before — in the Society page of the local paper, perhaps, or on a campaign poster.

The large, panting woman, frustrated in her pursuit, was introduced to me by Miss Potty as Mama Calhoun. She pumped my hand vigorously, and proudly announced that we were first cousins by marriage.

Miss Potty then called in some of the other girls to meet me. Most wore Scarlett O'Hara crinolines and bonnets, and their appearance was heralded by great puffs of choking cigarette smoke. They all curtsied, and two of them even asked for my autograph.

Miss Potty introduced each in turn. There was Miss Pansy-Crepe Myrtle, Miss Shelley-Cherie, Miss Lurleen-Beth, Miss Big-Ass Mabel (who could stand to use Maum Sara's reducing machine), and Miss Reba-Crystal. Miss Potty apologized that Miss Patty-Colleen had been forced to take the day off because of cramps.

"Pleased to meet you all," I said, trying to be friendly.

"Likewise, we're sure," the girls replied in chorus.

"I hope I didn't interrupt your dinner," Miss Potty said. "I can offer you some backbone pork stew, which we got cooking in a pot in the kitchen."

"That won't be — "

"We don't do a lot of cooking in the club, since most of our gentlemen callers like to send out for their suppers. Of course, the more genteel of them still have their cooks prepare them covered baskets...with a nice bottle of Champagne, of course."

"Miss Potty," I interrupted her, "I did not come here to discuss food. Am I really to believe that Her Royal Highness has actually *kidnapped* your little boy?"

"Indeed she has!" insisted all the girls together, their layers of petticoats rustling. "She has disrupted our whole evening! How can we keep our minds on our work?"

"She took him right from under our noses," wailed Miss Potty, breaking again into tears. "She and some white chick come here, telling me I had been chose to surrogate a kid for her! I told her *no way*, but she kept right on — said you and me both owed her, being recipients of Big Shot's glee and whelping his offspring when by rights it should of been her!"

She blew her nose. "Then the white chick disappeared with Alonzo Gomez, the baseball star, who just happens to be our best customer and still owes Miss Big-Ass Mabel eighty-five cents for his strawberry cooling-down ice cream cone with sprinkles."

"Did anyone actually *see* Princess Frances take Rhett Cartland away?" I had to ask.

Miss Reba-Crystal hesitantly raised her hand. "I come through the room after Miss Potty left, and that lady was just talking to the dear, sweet little child, telling him about Big Shot, his daddy, and how she knew him before he went to meet the Angel Gabriel. Little Rhett Cartland told her he wanted to grow up and be a preacher man like Big Shot's own daddy.

"Then the child asked if that big bodacious car parked out front was hers, and she allowed as how it was. That's when I left, and when I come back, they was both gone."

"And now you are the only one in this cruel world I can turn to," Miss Potty insisted. "I beg of you — save our Big Shot's baby!"

Miss Glory-Be was tugging at my sleeve to alert me to the sky outside, which had turned an ominous greenish-black — it looked like a fierce storm was brewing, as it often does on short notice in these parts.

"You could stay the night," Miss Potty offered.

"I would be glad to give you my bed," volunteered Miss Big-Ass Mabel. "I have a feeling that white chick ain't gonna return my Alonzo any time soon."

I declined politely, thanking her for the offer, and promised to do what I could about finding Rhett Cartland.

Mr Pee had retired to bed by the time we got back home, since he was deathly afraid of lightning.

"Is that you, Miss Gwendolyn?" his voice sounded from under the covers. "I am so relieved. I do wish you would go and see if my Cousin Alexis is all right. She keeps hollering for somebody named Alonzo."

Princess Frances showed up at my door bright and early the next morning as we were finishing our breakfast. Cousin Alexis was still in bed, suffering a strained back.

"Where is Miss Potty's little boy, Rhett Cartland?" I asked before she was even out of her coat.

"With his mama, I presume," Princess Frances replied as Miss Glory-Be poured her a cup of coffee.

"You didn't *kidnap* him, then?"

"Of *course* I didn't kidnap him," she replied indignantly. "He just wanted to go for a ride, so I obliged him. Just like his papa — loves big cars."

165

"Miss Potty was terribly upset..."

"Serves her right. When I brought him home and offered to buy him, she had six fits and threatened to have me assassinated."

"You offered to...*buy* him?"

"Of course. Same as being a surrogate mother, except that you save six years. And nine months."

She sighed sadly. "The final blow was when I was just leaving...before she could sic Gullah Jackson on me. Little Rhett Cartland said he wished I could stay a while and go on his rounds with him."

"His...rounds?"

Princess Frances grimmaced. "Little Rhett Cartland has more in common with his daddy than a fascination for cars. He pimps for his ma."

"*Pimps?*"

"You know — hands out visiting cards to gentlemen walking on the Battery, helps set up his mama's girls with their 'dates'... And she had the nerve to call *me* immoral!"

"Oh dear," I exclaimed. "Something really ought to be done!"

"Just what I thought," Princess Frances nodded. "So I went and did it."

"What do you mean?"

But Princess Frances just smiled cryptically, and asked, "Do you suppose Miss Glory-Be could fix me up one of his delicious omelets? I haven't had time for breakfast."

As she left for the kitchen, Mr Pee turned on the television to catch the morning news. "Good gracious!" he exclaimed. "That looks like Miss Potty...and she's all wet!"

The screen showed a thoroughly drenched Miss Potty, a blanket around her shoulders, being helped into a car. The reporter said: "Early this morning, a well-known resident of Charleston, Mistress Potty de Veux, was abducted by several masked figures, one wearing what appeared to be a coronet, from her place of business on Radcliffe Street. She was taken to a remote spot on the Ashley River, where she was submerged fully clothed in an ancient ducking chair. She was then tied to a nearby palmetto tree, still wearing her crinoline, where she was found by a shocked Methodist minister walking his dalmatian, Miss Galloping-Angel. According to a local preservationist who examined the victim's vacated ducking chair, it was a genuine antique and not a reproduction."

# 18

"I'm getting too old for all this activity," admitted Cousin Alexis when she finally managed to drag herself out of bed. She was wearing one of my teagowns since her other clothes were covered with sand from Folly Beach where her previous evenings "activity" had culminated. "Maybe I'll just join Mama in her convent."

"But you've never tolerated women as a steady diet," observed Mr Pee, who was feeding the two Chinese gold-fish, Mr Wok and Miss Soy. "You would find it insufferably confining."

She poured sand from one of her shoes. "Well, I could always borrow Miss Topsey's mountain climbing gear and scale the wall for an occasional nightly diversion. There's plenty going on after hours in Atlanta...although I do find male stripteasers rather tedious. I prefer — "

"Good heavens!" Mr Pee exclaimed suddenly. "So *that's* what became of the rest of this morning's paper."

He was staring into Miss Sweet-Talking Harriett's cage, which was filled with shreds of what had been the financial section of the paper. In the middle of the paper sat a large speckled egg. "I do declare she is about to become a mother!"

Indeed she had! Miss Sweet-Talking Harriett seemed mighty proud of her achievement as she softly crooned, "Who's in love with a drunken sailor?"

"But how is that possible?" Mr Pee asked. "Has she been keeping company with another of her species?"

"Birds do not need to mate in order to lay eggs," I informed him. "However, it has been years since she has done either, so I am truly bewildered."

"Perhaps Mr James slipped a little of Devious Julius' fertile turtle potion into her drinking water," Cousin Alexis suggested.

"There is no reason for him to have done so," I insisted. "Besides, he's too frugal to have wasted it on her."

At that moment, Mr James came into the room with the morning mail. "Miss Gwendolyn, I'm supposed to tell you — " He stopped suddenly and stared into Miss Sweet-Talking Harriett's cage. "Well, bless my soul — it *worked*!"

"Mr James, what do you know about this?" I demanded.

"Weren't my idea, Miss Gwendolyn," he insisted. "Miss Shirley-Mae, she got it in her head that one expectant mother around here weren't enough...that Miss Sweet-Talking Harriett needed a young-un to liven up her cage. So she bundled up the bird in a wicker basket, and we traipsed down to the bird-house at the zoo."

"You mean you — ?"

"Took a bit of doin', but we snuck her inside and loosed her where a lot of other birds like her was hangin' out. Then we moseyed around a bit while she occupied herself. Later we come back and fetched her back in the basket. She weren't too happy about leavin' and proceeded to raise a real ruckus."

"Don't blame her," Cousin Alexis commented.

"Next thing we know, a guard come up and accused us of tryin' to steal their birds. Miss Shirley-Mae explained that we just brought her in for a visit, but he weren't havin' no part of that...until he got a good look at Miss Sweet-Talking Harriett and she squawked some rude things at him. Then he said sure nuff that weren't one of theirs, and we'd better get her out before we contaminated the whole bunch."

"So now we just have to wait and see if the egg hatches," I said. "I hope it does. It would be such fun to watch Miss Sweet-Talking Harriett raise an offspring."

Mr Pee frowned. "As long as it doesn't inherit its mother's vocabulary. Every time she carries on about sailors, it makes me uneasy."

"Now, Mr James," I said, "you were about to tell me something when you came into the room..."

"Yessum. Before Princess Frances left, she said to tell you that she brought Mr Pee a present — she forgot to tell you about it, what with all that business about Miss Potty's kid."

"A present for Mr Pee? Where is it?"

At that moment, there was a shriek from the piazza. We hurried out to find Cousin Alexis pointing to an object in the garden.

"Great snakes alive!" exclaimed Mr Pee, "Someone's planted a corpse during the night!"

Propped up against the big live oak's trunk was an enormous white marble tombstone, decorated with a carved wreath of Charleston banana leaves. "Where on earth did that come from?" I exclaimed.

"That's the present," Mr James explained. "Princess Frances said she promised to have one made when old

Uncle Amos Abraham died and Mr Pee had to go traipsin'
out there to bury him."

We walked over to examine it. Cousin Alexis, whose
eyes were better in sunlight than mine, read aloud the in-
scription:

In Grateful Memory of Our Childhood Friend
Mr Amos Abraham Simons
Known to
Miss Alexis, Miss Hepzibah and Mr Pee
as their old Uncle Am.
"I have jumped into my chariot and gone up."

"Why, how very sweet," said Cousin Alexis, wiping
away a tear and smudging her mascara. "Just the other
night, I dreamed Charlton Heston took me on a sightseeing
tour of the Roman coliseum in *his* chariot!"

"It certainly is big," Mr Pee remarked, examining the
tombstone more closely. "And undoubtedly quite heavy."

"He said I kissed better than Raquel Welch," Cousin
Alexis sighed, still lost in her dream.

"This presents a serious problem, Mr Pee," I pointed
out. "In spite of your devotion to Uncle Am, surely you do
not intend to dig him up and replant him in my garden."

He shook his head. "Uncle Am needn't be moved to
your garden...or even to the hallowed ground of St Philip's,
where I am sure his mere presence would please those
meddling integrationists. We will transport his marker to
the plantation cemetery tomorrow."

This brought Cousin Alexis back down to earth. "If you
think I'm going to help carry that huge thing all the way out
to some overgrown cemetery in the middle of nowhere—"

"Not at all," Mr Pee assured her. "After my previous sojourn into that inhospitable territory, I am equally loathe to
return. And I am certainly in no condition to repeat my

physical exertion. Therefore, I propose we conscript the services of my faithful polo team brothers to assist with this venture."

Cousin Alexis' eyes lit up. "Count me in."

"To make the undertaking more palatable, I will request that each member have his cook prepare a tasty concoction, suitable for transporting, to be consumed on location once the primary task has been accomplished. Cousin Hepzibah can help with the arrangements."

Cousin Alexis grunted. "About time she did something useful..."

"We can do no less for our dear Uncle Am. 'Operation Tombstone' will commence at dawn tomorrow."

We set out next morning for Mr Pee's family plantation. Cousin Alexis, resplendent in my best afternoon teagown with a large floppy pink hat that had belonged to the youthful Miss Henrietta of blessed memory, drove me and Mr Pee in her bright red sports car with the top down. Mr James followed, driving my car, with Mr Amos Abraham's headstone lashed securely in the open trunk. Big Shot's Daddy, attired in his white fine linen surplice, sat in the passenger seat — he had graciously offered to dedicate the headstone, and besides we needed him to lift the massive object into the car. Cousin Hepzibah sat in the back seat, looking dour as usual.

Miss Topsey Piddleton declined to go because her hiking boots were in the shop being recleated...and besides, there was apparently not going to be any music, not even from a mouth organ. Princess Frances, donor of the headstone, declined also, having been arraigned for conduct unbecoming a Charlestonian for her role in the dunking of Miss Potty. Knowing Princess Frances, she would buy her way out of this litigation easily.

Miss Glory-Be wouldn't go, either, as he was deadly afraid of snakes. Even the prospect of the company of Mr Pee's polo team was not enough of an enticement to change his mind. As we departed, he lowered the Confederate flag to show that we were not in residence for the day.

After a very hot drive through the low country, we were delayed for half an hour when Cousin Alexis, her attention momentarily distracted by a strapping bare-chested gentleman launching a boat into the Edisto River, drove us into the water. It took the combined effort of Mr James, Big Shot's Daddy and the man with the boat — who, after all the trouble he had caused, turned out to be happily married to one of those saintly Porter girls — to get us out.

Most of the members of Mr Pee's polo team were waiting when we finally did arrive at Primrose Plantation. The sight which greeted us was depressing, for all that remained was the shell of its former glorious self — blackened chimneys and moldering columns, all overgrown with weeds, underbrush and palmetto trees. It had been burned to the ground by a group of rampaging Yankees during the War Between Us and Them and never rebuilt, which Mr Pee never forgot to mention to the United States Government when he was forced to pay his Federal income tax.

The plantation caretaker, Mr Rabshaker, had been ordered by his wife, Miss Fairy-Plum, to take her to the Old City Market in Charleston to sell the sweet-grass baskets she had made, a craft handed down from her African ancestors. He had left their ancient mule tied to a cast iron hitching post shaped like a horse's head, which somehow those inconsiderate Yankees had left intact. Miss Lucy was reputed to be nearly as old as her late master, Mr Amos Abraham, and every bone in her body was visible.

Miss Fairy-Plum had thoughtfully dressed Miss Lucy in her best straw bonnet with shocking pink ribbons and holes cut out to accommodate her big ears. The hat had been a present from Mr Pee for her last birthday, when he awarded her partial retirement and a silver medal on a neck ribbon for faithful service to his family.

She was in a most dreadful mood as she stood there with the little old wooden cart once used to carry the cotton bales. She deliberately stuck out her tongue at Cousin Hepzibah, who used to ride her roughly when she was a nasty little girl. Miss Lucy then perpetrated a dastardly act of nature right on top of Mr Pee's late grandma's prized ginger lilies which, along with the hitching post, had miraculously survived those churlish Yankees.

After a gallant communal effort on the part of Mr Pee's polo compatriots, Mr Amos Abraham's headstone was lifted from the back of my car where it had torn a long slit in the fabric, and duly loaded into Miss Lucy's cotton cart. The mule turned her head, took one long, lingering look at it, and sat down.

"I think she has gone on strike," observed Cousin Alexis, "and I can't say as I blame her."

"She looks about ready to be shot," Cousin Hepzibah said callously, adjusting her pince-nez spectacles to get a better look. "But horses, mules and donkeys are not in my domain. I am merely a dedicated preservationist."

Miss Lucy yawned and shook her silver medallion, as if to remind us of her retired status.

"Mr Amos Abraham used a special password to get her to up and go," Mr Pee informed us, "but I've quite forgotten what it was."

"Well, try to remember," grumbled Cousin Hepzibah. "My poor stomach is growling."

"Think of a likely word," urged Mr Pee, "and then perhaps Miss Lucy will start trotting."

"Sugar!" I shouted.

"Horsey!" yelled Cousin Hepzibah.

174

"Sex!" hollered Cousin Alexis. But Miss Lucy's rear end stayed firmly planted on the ground, her bony knees splayed outward.

"Up!"

"Giddap!"

"Play ball!"

"Mush!"

"Forward march!"

"Va-t-on!" (One of Mr Pee's polo brothers was French.)

"Ahoy!"

"Move it!"

"Up, up and away!"

"Liftoff!"

"Go!"

"Come!"

"Fetch!"

Miss Lucy nibbled at a ginger lily.

"Hoo-Ha!"

"Fire!"

"Hup!"

"Gee!"

"Haw!

"Tally-ho!"

"Yoicks!"

We would probably have been there until Doomsday if Big Shot's Daddy had not returned from tending to nature's call. "What's the problem here?" he asked.

"She won't cooperate," Mr Pee lamented. "If we can't get her up and moving, we're stuck here."

"Hell's bells!" snarled Cousin Hepzibah. "Just what we needed."

"What a *disaster*," groaned Cousin Alexis.

Big Shot's Daddy shook his head. "Amen!"

Miss Lucy's ears perked up, and an instant later she was on her feet and trotting off at a pace belying her age, heading toward the former slave cemetery. We quickly gathered our things and followed.

The path through the woods, cleared on his previous visit by Mr Pee, was narrow and often just barely navigable, but Miss Lucy plowed on doggedly, while the rest of us struggled to keep pace. Cousin Hepzibah, who was hardly dressed for a forage through the dense underbrush, kept muttering "Hell's bells!" and spent most of her time trying to untangle her Gucci scarf from the protruding branches of the multiflora rose bushes.

As we neared the site, our ears were met with a blood-curdling howl. We stopped dead in our tracks...except for Miss Lucy, who pressed on totally unflapped. A few seconds later, the howl sounded again, and Cousin Alexis, never at a loss for a convenient moment, swooned into the brawny arms of the nearest polo player.

"It's a werewolf!" hissed Mr James. "Damn thing comes out at midnight and messes up your throat."

"Mr James," I said reassuringly, "it is only eleven in the morning, so that is no werewolf. It sounds like Miss Pamela-Fay, our Great Dame, when she is upset about something. But we left her asleep on my bed."

We moved cautiously forward, not knowing what to expect. Just as we reached the clearing, the howl came again, much closer now. This time, Mr Pee began to laugh.

"It's only *Mr Burkee-Snout*, Mr Amos Abraham's old coon dog. Come on out of the ferns, Mr Burkee-Snout — it's your old friend Mr Pee! Why, you devoted creature, you must have stayed on to mourn your master after his funeral."

A mangey, gaunt hound dog with huge flat ears and drooping tail appeared from the underbrush and made his way hesitantly over to Mr Pee, who stooped to pat him. "That was a long time ago," I remarked. "The poor dog must be starving."

"Indeed," Mr Pee agreed. "His bones are sticking out like the spokes of an umbrella. Cousin Hepzibah, you're in charge of the food. Don't we have something to offer poor Mr Burkee-Snout?"

Cousin Hepzibah beckoned to the polo player carrying her own personal picnic basket and rummaged around inside. "I didn't really plan for such a contingency," she grumbled. "The dog will simply have to make do with whatever I can dredge up."

With that, she extracted a silver dish of caviar and a bottle of champagne. As the gentleman popped the cork, Cousin Hepzibah began to spoon-feed caviar to old Mr Burkee-Snout, who inhaled each bite greedily, nearly devouring the Sterling silver spoon in the process. The polo player poured a generous quantity of the Champagne into a Tiffany bowl, and when the dog had consumed enough caviar to generate a thirst, he lapped voraciously, pausing only briefly to emit a burp.

Finally, he stopped, backed away from the empty bowl and sat down, a quizzical look on his face. Then he grinned, his eyes rolled up into his head, and he keeled over sideways.

"Now you've done it!" Mr James shouted at Cousin Hepzibah. "The poor critter dun gone and joined his master!"

At that moment, a hiccup sounded from the dog's open mouth, and his front paws twitched.

Big Shot's Daddy leaned over for a closer look. "I think all he needs is some time to sleep it off. And while he's doing that, I believe we should get on with what we came here for."

Mr Pee's polo brothers dug a hole at the head of Mr Amos Abraham's grave and hoisted the massive tombstone into place. When it was firmly situated, Big Shot's Daddy preached a short sermon likening the Dear Departed to

Jeremiah the prophet, who was likewise always moaning about something, but then admitting that he (Mr Amos Abraham, not the prophet Jeremiah) was the best jackrabbit and possum catcher on Primrose Plantation. He probably would have said more if his eyes had not fastened on the succulent home-cured ham dotted with cloves which Mr James had removed from one of the picnic baskets. There followed some hasty "Amens", and it was time for lunch.

Mr James insisted that things be done properly, even in an overgrown cemetery. Two mahogany tea tables, one Queen Anne with padded feet and the other Chippendale with fretted sides in the Chinese style, were set up in the clearing between several faded tombstones. Over the tops of the tables, two polo players laid fine white linen tablecloths edged with Venetian lace, which the late lamented Miss Henrietta had bought on her honeymoon in Italy.

Two large Meissen candelabra, which Mr James had carefully transported from the Holy City wrapped in his best pair of long red winter underwear, were centered on the tables. Both candelabra were encrusted with a busy conflux of cherubs, each wearing purple drawers which had been painted on their anatomies years ago by Maum Sarah in deference to Mr Pee's childhood modesty. Each cherub in turn supported a porcelain tulip, into which Mr James had placed a tall scalloped candle.

The Champagne was chilled in solid silver Regency ice buckets and poured into long-stemmed crystal flutes. Tea was served from a Napoleonic tea-pot, donated for the occasion by Princess Frances. It was shaped in the likeness of the cast-off Empress Josephine, and the tea was dispensed through the tragic lady's snout into gaily-adorned cups with matching saucers, plates and accessories, gaudily crafted by the British Art-Deco designer Clarice Cliff.

Besides the spicy ham, which Mr James was presently carving into individual servings, the table was ladened with savory roast pheasant, crisp fried chicken, fresh corn bread, baked beans, lima beans, steamy portions of she-crab soup, and bread pudding and rice pudding for dessert. Big Shot's Daddy muttered a hasty blessing, and we commenced to enjoy the repast among the tombstones.

It was a sunny day, with not a cloud in the sky, so it was with some perplexity that we suddenly found ourselves enveloped in a deepening shadow. We looked up to see that a round object had imposed itself between us and the sun.

"It can't be an eclipse," Mr Pee noted. "My almanac would most certainly made mention of it."

"Whatever it is, it seems to be getting bigger," observed Cousin Hepzibah. "Or closer..."

"A flying saucer!" shrieked Cousin Alexis. "We're being invaded!"

"No," Big Shot's Daddy cautioned, squinting up at the phenomenon. "It's...a *balloon!*"

"A *balloon?*" everyone echoed.

"A hot-air balloon — you can see the basket suspended from beneath. And it's descending. I do believe it intends to land right here in the cemetery."

And indeed it did. We watched in amazement as the onion-shaped craft, its fabric sides emblazoned with a colorful Confederate flag, wafted to the ground between our tables and the nearby trees. A short, chunky figure leaped from the basket and looped the anchoring ropes to some nearby tombstones.

"I might have known," sighed Mr Pee. "Miss Topsey Piddleton..."

Setting the levitating flame jets to a position sufficient to keep the balloon inflated, Miss Topsey retrieved some items from the basket and joined us at our tables. "I brought a special treat," she announced. "A jar of jellied eel and peppercorns, which the Archbishop of Canterbury sent me for Christmas."

Then she unsnapped the locks on what looked like a wide, flat suitcase, which unfolded into a keyboard with telescoping legs. "It's a portable harpsichord. No meal is complete without a musical accompaniment!"

And so, for the next few hours, we enjoyed a leisurely banquet, consumed to the spritely strains of Scarlatti and Soler from Miss Topsey Piddleton's harpsichord.

As evening fell, and the pesky mosquitos began biting, we packed up our possessions — including old Mr Burkee-Snout, still a bit tipsy but contentedly sprawled across Mr Pee's lap in the car — and departed for home.

# 19

The Hosea Pincklea Mansion
Dear Cousin Matilda-Madge

As the wedding draws nigh, confusion reigns. Everyone wants to be in charge, and nobody consults me about anything. As usual, there are too many cooks, and the broth is rapidly getting spoiled.

Cousin-to-be Hepzibah is the worst, as you might expect — she has insisted that I have a bridal shower this time, since all those amenities got lost in the shuffle the first time around. In the interest of simplicity, I tried to dissuade her, but she wouldn't hear of it.

"Of *course* you must have a bridal shower. What would people think if you didn't?" She was standing in front of the mirror, adjusting her new platinum blonde wig which Princess Frances had given her. "And since I am Mr Pee's senior cousin, as well as your best friend, I am the proper one to organize it."

181

"And I suppose I will have to pay for it," sighed Her Royal Highness, who was giving Miss Sweet-Talking Harriett, the parrot, teaspoonfuls of cherry cough mixture liberally laced with Jamaican Rum. The bird had apparently developed a very sore throat after laying that large unexpected egg, because when she opened her mouth nothing came out...which suited Mr Pee just fine.

"Then I shall be in charge of the decorations," announced Cousin Alexis, never one to be left out. She was still in residence at my home, and was presently wearing my yellow terry cloth sunsuit with matching headband. Cousin Lewis lay on the couch with his head in her lap as she fed him brandied chocolate cherries with Mr Pee's much treasured apostle christening spoon. "The theme will be antebellum so that we can all wear our crinolines."

"I still have my great-grandmother's," bragged Miss Topsey Piddleton. "It is all black, because she was in mourning for her third husband. Poor dear, she lost all three in the War of Northern Aggression. Two died in battle and the third in a hospital tent from a ruptured hernia."

At that moment Mr James marched in with afternoon tea and asked us all to hold down the noise, as his Big Mistake, as he called his bride, Miss Shirley-Mae, had given him a migraine headache. Not only had she demanded he buy her a color television, but to do so he had been forced to once again borrow against his own funeral expenses.

Princess Frances then volunteered her new cook to help with the food. "I'm flying him in from Paris. I'm so sick of rice, fatty bacon and chitlins that I could spit. "And I'm also tired of having to do most of the work myself. I've had to fire five cooks in the last month — two whites, one black, one Cajun and one Chinese."

When the subject of music came up, Miss Topsey Piddleton promised to bring her collection of Elvis Presley records to play while the presents were opened. Seeing the stunned looks on all our faces, she hastened to explain that Elvis' songs, such as "Hound Dog" and "Heartbreak Hotel", extolled true Southern values and traditions.

Big Shot's Daddy agreed. "And the boy's a good Southern Baptist to boot."

Cousin Hepzibah was unconvinced. "I think something a little more in keeping with the dignity of the occasion would be in order," she told Miss Topsey. Then she added, for good measure, "Something your friend, the Archbishop of Canterbury, would approve of."

Miss Topsey snatched an apple from the fruit bowl and bit into it. "His excellency happens to *like* Elvis."

"Let's get back to the matters at hand," Cousin Hepzibah insisted. "The next item is the flowers. Who's in charge of that?"

Her Royal Highness volunteered to do the floral arrangements. "But I am fed up with the traditional white crepe myrtle. How about white roses?"

Cousin Hepzibah shook her head. "They're too sad-looking at this time of year. And besides, they've all been nibbled at by those hungry little June bugs."

"Then we'll settle for bouquets of white orchids and orange blossoms. I hope nobody's allergic to them."

"I'm allergic to anthuriums," Miss Topsey Piddleton said, but she was ignored.

"Now the guest list. Who is invited?"

"Why, all of us here, I would assume," Cousin Alexis said, popping one of the brandied cherries into her mouth. Cousin Lewis lay with his eyes closed and his mouth open. It wasn't clear whether he was asleep or simply awaiting another cherry.

"Plus Maum Sarah, of course," Cousin Hepzibah scribbled on a pad. I cringed, because Maum Sarah has practically become a fixture in my home in the last few weeks. It's Mr Pee's fault, actually, since he has been making less and less effort to keep his virtual residence here a secret any longer. He rarely returns next door to his departed mother's house, so Maum Sarah, in a last-ditch effort to guard her baby's baby's virtue down to the wire, has essentially moved in as well...complete with exercise bike, TV, and her old she-cat, Miss Landine, who promptly claimed the large potted palm in the hall as her private bathroom, much to Mr James' chagrin.

With the arrival of Maum Sarah, there has been no privacy at all — she sees to it that Mr Pee is better guarded than Fort Knox. He has been relegated to one of the remaining guests rooms, where he complains regularly about the quality of the mattress. I suggested that he simply wait until Maum Sarah has gone to bed, then come and join me in my room. But he declined, apparently fearing the inevitable nocturnal encounter with his old nanny en route to the bathroom.

He did, however, promise that if we survived our wedding he would send Maum Sarah and her she-cats on an extended trip down the Nile, since she is always telling us that she is descended from Queen Nefertiti, and that Moses in the bullrushes was her adopted cousin.

In addition to her and Cousin Alexis, I have to contend with Big Shot's Daddy, who has just painted his home and is waiting for the paint smell to dissipate, and with Cousin Lewis, who spends most of his time here now to be near Cousin Alexis. He, Big Shot's Daddy and Mr James play poker till all hours each night, so I have begun to realize what it must be like to run a boarding house.

But I digress — I was telling you about planning the bridal shower. We were finalizing the guest list when Mr Pee asked, "What about me? I've never been to a shower."

Cousin Hepzibah scoffed. "Men are not allowed at bridal showers!

"And why not?" he complained.

"It's...it's just not *done*. Would you invite women to your bachelor party?"

Cousin Alexis' eyes lit up.

"What bachelor party?" Mr Pee inquired. "I have not been informed of any plans for such a function."

"I believe your Polo Club members are preparing one," Cousin Hepzibah replied.

This prospect worried me. "I hope they are not planning anything too foolhardy. Mr Pee has a very low tolerance for alcohol. Two mint juleps and he is out for the count."

"Well, the solution to both problems is simple," Princess Frances said. "We'll allow men to attend the bridal shower, and in return women may attend the bachelor party...to assure that things do not get out of hand."

"No spitting or profanity," said Cousin Alexis.

"Or topless dancers," I added. "You know how easily Mr Pee is shocked. Why, he still undresses in the dark."

"Just as well," Princess Frances snorted. "All men look like monkeys with their clothes off."

Cousin Hepzibah objected. "The whole idea is *most* improper..."

"Proper, Schmoper," Cousin Alexis waved an impatient hand. "I *hate* going to women-only parties. I agree with Her Royal Highness — let Mr Pee and anyone else who wants to come to the shower...including Cousin Lewis." She tickled his nose, causing him to snicker in his sleep. "And *we'll* go to the bachelor party."

There were no more objections, although Cousin Hepzibah shook her head.

"Then it's settled," Cousin Alexis announced, carefully extricating herself from under Cousin Lewis' head. He was indeed sound asleep...whether from boredom or an excess of brandy from the potent cherries was anybody's guess.

This ought to give you some idea for how hectic things have become, dear Cousin. I really would have preferred to dispense with the whole bridal shower business, and I'm sure Mr Pee feels the same about the bachelor party. But as usual, I seem to have very little to say about anything these days.

At any rate, Mr Pee and I arrived at Cousin Hepzibah's house during a typical Charleston downpour. Mr James drove, grumbling all the way about the "bloody old sing-song" he was being dragged to. He insisted that he was going to remain in the car till the foolishness was over, provided Miss Glory-Be brought him out a big slice of the bridal shower cake with extra vanilla ice cream and purple sprinkles.

Miss Glory-Be had gone ahead to assist with the raffle, which Princess Frances had arranged as part of the entertainment. There was to be a drawing, in which everybody's names would be placed into a hat, and the lucky winner would get to accompany Her Royal Highness on a week's vacation in Hawaii, all expenses paid. She had already purchased the obligatory grass skirts at Woolworths, because the prices there were cheaper than in Hawaii.

Mr James parked our car in the large circular driveway which fronted Cousin Hepzibah's eighteenth century slate-roofed mansion. We managed to persuade him to join us, suggesting that he might win the drawing, which would get him away from the nagging Miss Shirley-Mae for a week.

We made our way past the boxwood shrubbery, trimmed in the shape of swans, and up the steps to the double-door entrance where a uniformed doorman stood ready with a period silver server to receive our visitors cards.

When our credentials had been properly inspected and we were deemed acceptable for admission, Maum Sarah appeared from behind the crepe myrtles to lead the way in, just as it would have been done on the family plantation.

Inside the spacious foyer hung a full-length portrait of our hostess, painted by a regional artist who "showed great promise", according to a local art critic. Cousin Hepzibah herself, outfitted in orange sequins and matching wig, appeared to greet us, followed by Princess Frances in a gown of golden lame, Cousin Alexis in a red mini-skirt with low-cut white satin blouse, and Miss Topsey Piddleton in an emerald green pants suit with a large red matador's hat.

"The other guests have already arrived," Cousin Hepzibah informed us. "We shall begin shortly."

We were then ushered past the grand staircase, which had a notice pasted to one of the bottom posts:

PRIVATE PROPERTY — KEEP OFF

"She should have hung that ghastly portrait there," Mr Pee giggled. "It would have discouraged any curiosity seekers."

We entered the Chinese Export Porcelain Drawing Room, with its genuine cypress paneling and obligatory chandelier. In the middle of the room was a massive mahogany table, the centerpiece of which was a sculpted ice swan floating gracefully in a miniature pond of 100 proof vodka. The Sheraton settee and every period chair, be it Queen Anne, Chippendale or Hepplewhite, had a piece of white satin ribbon tied around its immaculate seat. On each, Cousin Hepzibah had placed cards that read:

DO NOT SIT — FAMILY HEIRLOOM

Which, of course, explained why all of the guests were standing rather stiffly around the center table, refilling their glasses or shifting from one foot to another. Cousin Lewis had apparently been occupied at the vodka repository for some time, as he was having some difficulty transferring the potent beverage from ladle to glass.

When the ceremonies were ready to commence, we had to either remain standing or squat on the floor on one of the bridal cushions lined with real swan down (Cousin Hepzibah obviously had a thing for swans). Cousin Alexis said it was all too romantic, that it reminded her of Rudolph Valentino's forbidden tent in *The Sheik*, which she had just watched on the late show. Miss Topsey chose a cushion next to Cousin Lewis and batted her eyes at him. He winced and took another hefty quaff of vodka.

Miss Glory-Be busied himself collecting empty glasses, since Miss Hepzibah's current butler had just quit. Owing to her irascible temperament, she found it impossible to keep servants for more than a few days, and had to make do with an office maintenance crew to come in every week to clean up. Her long-time family butler, Mr Ernest, had got religion and hopped a train to New York City to live with Maum Sarah's niece, the Reverend Mrs Carmen Suck (they had been childhood sweethearts), where they spent their days and nights wallowing in religious ecstasy. Now Miss Hepzibah had to manage quite alone in her fine mansion.

Because she was short-handed, Cousin Hepzibah asked Miss Topsey Piddleton to help serve the refreshments, eliciting a sigh of relief from Cousin Lewis. Miss Topsey passed around the tray of cucumber sandwiches, supplying herself liberally as she did so. Before I could take my first delicious bite, Big Shot's Daddy strode into the room, elegantly attired in a white robe and bright green turban, like a Sultan from Morocco. Miss Topsey Piddleton nearly dropped the tray, then asked if he had become a Moslem.

"No Ma'am," he chuckled throatily, helping himself from her tray. "This is simply my fortune-telling outfit. As soon as I have lined my stomach, I will reveal your futures!"

"I didn't know you dabbled in the occult," Mr Pee said skeptically.

"Nothing occulty about it," Big Shot's Daddy insisted. "It's a Gift — given only to a select few. And like many Gifts, it should not be used frivolously." Then his eyes twinkled. "Course, I'm willing to make an exception from time to time..."

"Me first!" Miss Topsey waved her hand.

Big Shot's Daddy closed his eyes and concentrated. "I see...a *move* in your future. I see all your worldly goods in a new place... Someplace...in England."

Miss Topsey's eyes grew wide.

"Someplace...like a cathedral...and there's a man in a robe and wearing a mitre on his head."

Miss Topsey sat down hard on one of the cushions, the corners of her mouth twitching.

Big Shot's Daddy took a breath and opened his eyes. "Who's next?"

Cousin Alexis raised her hand. "Me!"

"I see... Yes, I see a big, handsome, strapping..."

"Yes?Yes?Yes?Yes?"

"...horse."

She blinked. "A *horse*? But I've already *got* a horse."

"This one is bigger. And sturdier. And pure white."

"Hmph. I would have preferred something darker, with just two legs. But I guess Miss Penelope won't complain."

"Miss Hepzibah," Big Shot's Daddy shifted his attention. "I see you in a strange, far-away place..."

"Not likely," she scoffed. "I hate to travel."

"...where no one speaks English..."

"Even worse."

"...and the food is...well, *different*..."

She winced. "I don't think I want to hear any more."

"And all there is to drink is vodka..."

189

Her face lit up. "Well, now...it can't be all that bad, then."

"Enough of her!" Maum Sarah rasped, jabbing at Big shot's Daddy with her rhinestone-studded fly swatter. "It's my turn!"

"Maum Sarah," Big Shot's Daddy began, in his best baritone preaching voice, "you must be the most remarkable woman in this Charleston. Why, I see you with a puny baby boy clasped to your ancient sagging jugs, just like Sarah in the Good Book." He winked at her. "Can it be that you are seeing some gentleman on the sly?"

Maum Sarah was so shocked that she nearly turned white. "A *baby*! Why, you...you wuthless old quack! I dun finished with all that business after raisin' my baby — Mr Pee's Daddy — and *his* baby...not to mention Miss Alexis and her nasty cousin Miss Hepzibah! Ain't been with a man durin' all that time, and ain't about to start now!" With that, she swung her fly swatter at Big Shot's Daddy, knocking off his turban.

"All right, all right — calm down, everyone," Cousin Hepzibah ordered. "We'll continue with the entertainment later. Right now it's time for The Drawing. So gather round..."

Miss Glory-Be passed around Mr James' top hat and all the guests dropped in slips of paper with their names on them. Then he shook the hat and held it out to Princess Frances.

"Isn't this exciting?" Miss Topsey Piddleton whispered to Maum Sarah, who was still fuming over Big Shot's Daddy's prediction. "Imagine — a whole week in Hawaii!"

"Ain't never been more'n fifty mile from Charleston in my life," Maum Sarah grunted, lighting up a crooked black cigar, "and don't expect I ever will. 'Sides, they probably got this thing rigged..."

"And the winner is..." Princess Frances unfolded a scrap of paper. The guests leaned forward on their cushions.

"...Big Shot's Daddy!"

Maum Sarah snorted. "What I tell you?"

Everyone congratulated Big Shot's Daddy, who grinned heartily as Princess Frances handed him one of the grass skirts. He wrapped it around his middle and wiggled suggestively, rolling his eyes and strumming an imaginary ukulele.

Cousin Hepzibah clapped her hands to restore order. "It's time for the happy couple to open their presents. Cousin Lewis, will you give me a hand?"

Cousin Lewis blinked groggily, then struggled to his feet, cracking his head on the table ledge and spilling his glass of vodka all over the oriental rug. Then his feet became entangled in his sword scabbard, and as he attempted to unbuckle it, a belt clip snagged his riding britches, splitting the rear seam.

"Oh dear," he muttered, self-consciously covering the exposed area behind him with his hand.

"This will never do," Cousin Hepzibah said with exasperation. "Go upstairs and find something to wear so we can get on with this thing!"

He nodded sheepishly, and as he turned and staggered toward the forbidden staircase, Miss Topsey Piddleton emitted a gasp.

"What's wrong *now*?" Cousin Hepzibah demanded.

"Mr Lewis is not wearing underdrawers!" she whispered, averting her eyes.

"He never does," sniffed Mr Pee, reaching for a glace cherry. "Like Henry VIII, he is always ready for action."

I gave my fiancee a rather icy look. He coughed, and suggested we proceed with the shower gifts.

Miss Topsey Piddleton gave us a stuffed ostrich — three tail feathers conspicuously absent — with a note that read:

191

In Memory Of Happy Times at the Court of St James

...whatever that meant; I didn't ask.

Then we opened a large box that had stamped on the top:

𝕽𝖊𝖑𝖎𝖌𝖎𝖔𝖚𝖘 𝕲𝖔𝖔𝖉𝖘 𝕺𝖓𝖑𝖞.

Inside was the most gorgeous white satin bedspread to be placed on the bridal bed. It was the handiwork of Poor Aunt Greta, Sister Augusta Benedictus the Terrible, The Mother Superior and several other nuns in the Atlanta convent. Embroidered into the fabric, and entwined in a true lovers knot, were the initials G & P — their customary order reversed as Poor Aunt Greta was somewhat dyslexic. The accompanying card read:

From Your Devoted if frustrated
Cousin Alexis
Hope you have better luck than I've had

Cousin Hepzibah cleared her throat and announced that Maum Sarah's gift was next. I grew a little nervous, since I was not exactly her favorite person. But Mr Pee was her baby's baby...

"I been up in the late Miss Henrietta's attic," Maum Sarah began, stabbing the butt of her cigar into a potted palm, "and I come across the cradle I rocked Mr Pee and Miss Hepzibah in when they was just tads...havin' farmed Miss Alexis out to Miss Potty's mama, Miss Wilma-Lou, 'cause I didn't have the equipment to nuss all three. So cute they was, one at each end of the cradle...until Miss Hepzibah started kickin' poor Mr Pee, and finally wounded me for life while she was sucklin'..."

Cousin Hepzibah muttered under her breath, "If the old bat had paid attention to what she was doing, instead of swatting at an Edisto swamp mosquito, I would never have bitten her."

"Anyhow," Maum Sarah concluded, "I'm givin' the cradle to Mr Pee, 'cause I don't guess either Miss Alexis or Miss Hepzibah ever gonna have any use for it."

I found all this talk about babies at a bridal shower quite disconcerting, and Miss Glory-Be's gift, which he had won at Big Shot's Daddy's church bingo, did not help matters. It was a large pink and blue plastic carryall containing two dozen diapers, with a card that read:

Be Prepared.

Big-Ass Mabel sent a book entitled *Sex for the Faint-Hearted*. Miss Potty sent us a matching pair of sunrise-red bikini underwear — mine came with matching top which was several sizes too large.

Next was an enormous package, long and narrow like a coffin, which from the royal cipher on top we knew to be from the Princess Frances. My heart started to pound, because I suddenly feared that she had followed up on her threat to dig up Big Shot. When the box was opened, I breathed a sigh of relief. Inside was a large grandfather clock, with her Royal Highness' own face substituted for the original.

"This way, you will never forget me," she informed us smugly.

Cousin Hepzibah's present was a bound copy of the Charleston Social Register. "Indispensable," She insisted. "And it comes with annual updates."

"And finally," she read from the card on the last present to be opened, "from Cousin Lewis..." She looked up. "Where *is* Cousin Lewis?"

He had not returned from upstairs where he had gone to seek a replacement for his torn trousers. Miss Glory-Be volunteered to go up and find him.

"Probably passed out," Cousin Hepzibah sneered, "judging from the vodka level remaining in the bowl. But never mind...it's time for treats and Champagne!"

Big Shot's Daddy, still wearing his turban, released a cageful of turtle doves from the stair landing. Mr Pee was sure they were pigeons because of the squeaking sound their wings made as they swooped through the drawing room and out through the open window, presumably to lay eggs or mate, whichever came first.

Monsieur Pierre-Henri, the new French chef, then wheeled in the outsize shower cake on a tea trolley. It was covered with white sugar icing to symbolize (I suppose) Mr Pee's purity...but the effect was decidedly offset by the miniature wax representations of a man and woman posed on top in their birthday suits, arms outstretched toward one another. I could almost hear Miss Henrietta turning over in Magnolia Cemetery.

"Well," said Mr Pee, "What can you expect from a Frenchman!"

I wasn't sure, but I couldn't help wondering, given the suggestive nature of the shower cake, just what Chef Pierre-Henri would concoct for the actual wedding cake a few weeks hence.

As the cake was being cut, a huge jeroboam of Champagne was brought out. It had been chilled in a large tub of ice, being too large to fit in the refrigerator.

The tin foil and wire capsule were removed, and one of Mr Pee's polo club members tried to extract the giant cork. When the chore proved too much for him, several other guests lent a hand. As they struggled with the bottle, I worried that the volatile contents might get too shaken up.

Just then Miss Glory-Be returned from upstairs, visibly excited. "Mr Lewis is *outside*, hanging onto the drainpipe!" He announced breathlessly.

"He's *what*?!"

"And he's wearing Big Shot's Daddy's grass skirt! I think he may have accidently locked himself out on the balcony, and tried to climb down the drainpipe. There's a big crowd gathering outside..."

At that moment, the cork came free from the bottle with a resounding *POP*! and shot across the room, decapitating the ice swan, and shattering one of the parlor windows. A huge geyser of Champagne foam gushed from the bottle and completely enveloped poor Cousin Hepzibah, who had been standing in front of the bottle and had narrowly escaped the same fate as the swan.

She shrieked, waving her arms against the deluge, as most of the guests responded instantly to the situation by extending their Champagne glasses toward the foaming barrage. Someone finally had the good sense to hold an empty bowl beneath the mouth of the bottle to catch the overflow.

While Cousin Hepzibah groped around for a towel, Mr James rushed in to announce that there was a policeman at the front door. Cousin Hepzibah cursed and strode into the foyer and flung open the door.

The tall policeman standing there blinked, staring at Cousin Hepzibah, drenched from head to foot, her dripping orange wig hanging in wet strands over her face, yeasty bubbles all over her clothes.

"Uhh..."

"We're having a *shower*," she announced impatiently.

The policeman nodded. "Yes ma'am...I can believe that. However..."

"Yes?" she demanded.

"...That doesn't explain the projectile that just took out your front window and almost clobbered the mailman. And then there's the gentleman wearing only a grass skirt, hanging onto the drainpipe halfway up the side of your house."

"There's a perfectly reasonable explanation for all of this," Cousin Hepzibah insisted. "Now, are you just going to stand there and stare, or are you going to do something useful and help get Cousin Lewis down from his perch before he breaks his fool neck!"

As you have probably gathered, dear Cousin Matilda-Madge, Cousin Hepzibah refused to be fazed in the slightest by all of this, and as usual had matters quickly in hand. The policeman was very accomodating, helping to disburse the crowds and get Cousin Lewis returned safely to earth. I guess it's just as well that he didn't see the naked man and woman in the shower cake, or we might all have been arrested on morals charges.

Looking forward to seeing you in a few weeks.

Your affectionate cousin
Gwendolyn

# 20

After the shower, Princess Frances and Big Shot's Daddy left for Hawaii – to my great relief, as that meant two fewer people under foot in my house. Cousins Alexis and Lewis were still around, but I didn't see much of them. And Cousin Hepzibah was busy trying to downplay the incidents at her house.

That left Maum Sarah, who was now beginning to get on Mr Pee's nerves as well as mine. Poor dear, his constitution has been somewhat fragile ever since his heart attack after my first wedding...and his role in *Sunset Boulevard on the Ashley* did little to help. Now, as our oft-postponed wedding was just over a week away, his nerves were beginning to fray.

Maum Sarah noticed this too, of course, and naturally blamed me for his tenuous condition. One morning, she announced that a visit to her cousin Devious Julius, the root man in Wadmelow Island, would provide some remedies to get him back on track.

Mr James volunteered to drive her in my car, but only if she agreed to leave her two she-cats at home — the last time Miss Landine had been in the car, she had thrown up twice and scratched a hole in the maroon leather cushions. I agreed to the arrangements, but with the condition that I be allowed to come along. This would give Mr Pee a full day alone to relax, which I felt would be better therapy than any conjurer's spells.

Maum Sarah was none too happy about this imposition, but reluctantly agreed when it was clear that she had no choice. Miss Glory-Be was recruited as well, as someone had to row the boat through the swamp, since both Mr James' arms were bruised from his latest altercation with Miss Shirley-Mae.

We parked the car near the water's edge and climbed into the creaky old boat, which was the only means of getting to Devious Julius' cabin. The water was full of alligators, moccasins and snapping turtles, and Miss Glory-Be had to negotiate carefully around numerous logs and other debris which stuck up out of the brackish water.

Devious Julius' cabin was surrounded by mossy oaks, chinaberry trees and poison ivy. The place was old and ramshackle, like its owner, and it wasn't at all clear just what was holding it all together. There was another boat tied up on shore, but no sign of Devious Julius.

Maum Sarah took us around to the back of the house where rusty old tanks with glass fronts, which in better days had been home to goldfish, now contained her cousin's live collection of snakes, frogs, lizards and salamanders. A large black bird of unknown species or sex sat perched on a big clump of mistletoe suspended from a live oak tree, as though guarding the premises. When we suddenly appeared, the bird hollered so much that Miss Glory-Be thought it would attack us, but when Maum Sarah made one of her evil faces, it blinked once and promptly shut up.

Inside the shack, the smoke from the open fire nearly choked us, mingled as it was with the horrendous aroma of fish, frogs legs and rhubarb which was cooking altogether in a large black iron stewpot. Around the walls were shelves stacked with old glass jelly jars filled with dead frogs, salamanders and mice preserved in a yellowish liquid, while from the ceiling hung bunches of dried herbs. A wooden crate of crawfish sat under the window, whose screens were in shreds. Miss Glory-Be looked pale, and had to borrow my smelling salts.

And then we saw, dozing in a rocker made of twisted branches roped together with vines, none other than Big-Ass Mabel. Devious Julius' flea-bitten old tomcat, Mr Attila, was curled up in her spacious lap, burbling asthmatically.

"What you doin' here, you fat hag?" Maum Sarah demanded. Big-Ass Mable's eyes popped open. "And where's my cousin?"

Big-Ass Mable yawned and scratched. "He's gone to fetch me some potions. If it's any of your business."

"Hmph," Maum Sarah grunted. "What's your problem?"

"My battery's run down," complained Big-Ass Mabel. "Ever since my Alonzo piccadiloed with that slick white chick name of Alexis, he's complained of my overall performance. I thought Devious Julius might be able to help me."

At that moment, a trap door in the floor creaked open and Devious Julius appeared, carrying a corn meal sack filled with a number of items. He bore an uncanny resemblance to Maum Sarah except he had a pointed beard like a billy goat, and retained most of his own hair, which she didn't. He was dressed in an old frockcoat that had once belonged to an undertaker, with scarlet art deco buttons which he had substituted for the originals. His black pin-striped pants, which had come from the same source, were hoisted up at the knees with string, since they were much too long, and his collarless shirt was secured at the neck

199

with a large gold stud he had relieved from a body he had found floating down the creek. His feet were bare, although a pair of size 12 sneakers that had known better days stood forlornly at the foot of his broken-down rocking chair. On his right big toe was a diamond ring, which to his delight he had found in the belly of a fish he was cleaning.

"Well, heighdy, Cuz," he greeted, depositing the sack on a table and unscrewing the cap of a half-empty jug of cheap red wine. He took a long swig, and wiped his mouth on his sleeve. "What brings you to these parts?"

"Hey — me first!" Big-Ass Mabel reminded him. Devious Julius nodded and rummaged around in the sack, extracting a necklace of chicken bones, assorted teeth (animal and human) and red cardinal feathers. He put it around his neck and rubbed his hands together.

"I remind you, woman," he said, "you ain't no ordinary case, with that big seat o' yourn...you kinda special."

"Flattery will get you nowhere," cooed Big-Ass Mabel. "Besides, I gotta do something before Miss Potty finds out. She's still plenty out of sorts since that princess critter tried to drown her, and she don't want to hear that one of her girls is burned out."

"It'll cost you," warned Devious Julius, "but you can afford it."

"How much?"

"Seven dollars and sixty-three cents," said the old root man, rolling the whites of his eyes.

Big-Ass Mable tried to get up from the rocker to retrieve her purse, but Mr Attila refused to budge, digging his claws in her leg. When she tried to extricate him, he hissed and swatted her on the nose, then bolted across the room.

"Damn cat!" she hollered, rubbing her nose. "Alonzo always says that next to my bottom, my nose is my best feature."

She fetched her purse and rummaged around in it. "That's a lot of money when you think that Miss Potty charges me a seventy percent commission on my earnings. Who you think I am, the Queen of Sheba?"

When all she could find was a five-dollar bill, she fiddled with her purple lace girdle to extract two worn one-dollar bills. She had to borrow the sixty-three cents from Mr James, who was sampling the rhubarb *et al* stew, promising to reimburse him on his next visit to the Health Club.

After counting it carefully, since he didn't trust women, Devious Julius grovelled in the sack again and removed a small package wrapped in baby-pink toilet tissue and tied with string. He shut his eyes and mumbled some sort of incantation. Then he blew on the package and handed it to her.

"Take two tablespoons of my love-explosion-potion now, two before goin' to work, and another one when you knock off."

As Big-Ass Mabel consumed the first dose, he danced around her three times and slapped her ample bottom real hard. "You now on the road to complete recovery, girl. Your tired old battery's a-ticking already."

"Much obliged. Now I gotta get back before my shift starts." She gathered her belongings and waddled out the door.

Devious Julius then turned his attention to Maum Sarah, who had joined Mr James at the stew pot. "What's up, Cuz...You got man problems?"

"Fool," snapped Maum Sarah. "My baby's baby dun takin' the plunge."

"Black or white?" demanded the root man. "Never can tell these days."

"White," said Mr Pee's old nurse. "He dun grown up and found him a wife. This one here," nodding in my direction, but not bothering to introduce me.

201

"Mr Pee takin' the death plunge at last!" Devious Julius grinned and tugged on his beard. Then he turned and considered me. "Well, I s'pose if Big Shot took a fancy to you, you can't be all bad."

"Problem is," Maum Sarah said, "my baby's baby, he lookin' awful pale these days. You still makin' your fertile turtle soup?"

Devious Julius nodded his wrinkled head. "But fertile turtles scarce this year...soup expensive."

"Rubbish!" snapped Maum Sarah, producing a little silver pipe and her cloisonne' tobacco pouch from her knicker pocket. Devious Julius lit it for her with an ember from the fire, and she sucked noisily on the stem. "Fertile turtles breedin' fine over on Edisto."

Her cousin shook his head and picked a piece of cornflake out of his beard. "We had problems — what with Lecherous Jack, the gator, escapin' before I could cook him, and then gobblin' up all the fertile turtles he could lay his beady eyes on, times have been hard." He looked sadly into the fire, as though reflecting on better times. "I did try snappin' turtles, but it didn't work...nearly lost a finger."

"You know better'n mess with a snappin' turtle, 'specially at matin' time," Maum Sarah said, puffing on her pipe. Then she put on her gold-rimmed glasses that had once been Miss Henrietta's, counted out five silver dollars — she never did trust paper money — and stopped.

The old root man smacked his lips, yellowed by chewing tobacco. "Two more and you got your fertile turtle soup."

Maum Sarah muttered something under her breath before parting with the extra coins. Devious Julius carefully placed them in a neat pile on the table, then disappeared under a raggedy green curtain leading into his sleeping quarters. Moments later he emerged, waving a jam jar full of a thick reddish-brown liquid which he handed to Maum Sarah.

"It better work," she warned. "This place of yours is already fallin' apart, and I'm likely to come back and hurry it up a tad!"

As we were getting ready to leave, Mr James took Devious Julius off to one side and whispered something to him. Devious Julius nodded and rummaged again in his sack. He handed Mr James a vial of something, and Mr James took some more money out of his wallet and handed it to the old wizard. Then he rejoined us, and we left the shack and returned to the boat. Miss Glory-Be shoved off and began to row us back the way we had come.

After a few minutes, Maum Sarah dozed off. I asked Mr James what he had bought from Devious Julius.

"Well, Missus, just a little something to put Miss Shirley-Mae in a better frame of mind...keep her off my back for a spell."

"It...It's not *harmful*, is it?" I asked suspiciously.

Mr James shook his head. "Just gonna cool her down a bit. Give my bruises a chance to heal."

"Do you really believe those potions of Devious Julius actually work? Personally, I think it's all a lot of mumbo-jumbo."

"Oh, no Ma'am — Devious Julius knows what he's doin'. This stuff is the real thing."

I was unconvinced. "Well, you wouldn't catch me trying any of it. And I'm glad to say that none of our other friends would be so foolish as to fall for all that malarky..."

At that moment, we heard the sound of an outboard motor, and a few seconds later we saw a motorboat with two women aboard heading for Devious Julius' cabin. It was some distance away, and the occupants didn't see us...but it wasn't hard to recognize Cousins Hepzibah and Alexis.

# 21

Thr Hosea Pincklea Mansion
Dear Cousin Judith

I'm writing this while waiting for Mr Pee to return from his bachelor party. I had great misgivings about the wisdom of this whole thing — I need him to be in good shape for the wedding tomorrow. And that goes for Cousin Lewis as well. However, Princess Frances and Cousin Alexis are also attending (don't ask me to explain this — it's too complicated) and they have assured me that things will be kept well under control.

The party is being given by Mr Pee's Polo Club brothers, some of whom have insisted on bringing their ponies. Thank goodness Aunt Minnihaha preserved the ante-bellum stables, so there will be some place to park them.

Mr Pee and I were delighted to receive your gift of a pair of cast iron hitching posts. Mr Pee wants them placed on either side of our four-poster bed, but I'm not sure if the historic floor is strong enough to bear all that weight. As it is, every floor in the house slants in a different direction. We'll probably situate them in front of the stable so Cousin Alexis has a place to tie Miss Penelope when she visits.

Speaking of four-footed beasts, Mr Pee's childhood friend, Miss Lucy the mule, to whom he awarded the family medal for devotion, service and endurance, is due for retirement on the family plantation. Would you consider accepting her as an appreciative permanent fixture and paying guest? She comes with her own endowment so that she may continue to have Southern grits instead of Northern oats every morning for her breakfast, and central heating in her stable during your brutal Yankee winters. Of course, she would have to bring along her down-at-the-heel cotton bale cart — after so many years of constant companionship it would be cruel to separate them.

How lovely it was to hear that three more of the former Holy City horses have adopted more worldly pleasures and are expecting little foals. Princess Frances was so elated at the news that she has promised to send her personal architect up to New York City to design you some extra stables (and, of course, she will pay for them), complete with bassinets, or whatever baby ponies sleep in.

We were surely shocked, however, to learn that little Millie has got herself in a family way with your donkey Nigel. I didn't think jackasses could experience the joys of motherhood — especially at her age, which was considerable when Princess Frances rescued her from a fate worse than death last year. Mr Pee, who fancies himself an expert on the subject of jackasses, suspects that Millie might be going through change of life. It might be a good idea to watch for evidence of morning sickness, or better still call in your vet to find out if she is getting hot flashes.

It is so disappointing that you cannot leave all your expectant mothers to come to the wedding. You must feel rather like the matron in charge of a maternity ward! Are you hoping for boys or girls, or some of each?

And thank you for offering to care for the Misses J-J, Margie and Pamela-Fay while we are away on our honeymoon, but I think it more prudent that Miss Glory-Be watch after them here at home. Given the frequency with which animals in your care are becoming pregnant, I would feel safer if they remained here. Besides, Mr Pee says we cannot contemplate puppies so early in our married life.

The wedding is purposely being kept low-keyed by Charleston standards. Goodness knows, the last one had its share of fireworks. Mr Pee insists that I follow established convention and promise to obey him, which Cousin Alexis thinks should be excised from the marriage ceremony altogether — maybe someday it will be.

Mr James and Miss Glory-Be have been very busy polishing the family silver, as it is the custom on such a joyous occasion to display everything one owns (or inherited). And since Mr Pee's family hasn't thrown out a teaspoon since 1768, we have amassed quite a bit.

We are spending our honeymoon at Cousin Matilda-Madge's castle at Sissinghurst, where Big Shot is buried in the local cemetery. You remember what an ardent feminist Matilda-Madge is, so she is making a special concession to accommodate Mr Pee, who of course is a male — though at times the way he carries on like a fussy old maid leads me to wonder. She did suggest that we put him up at the Bull Pub in the village while I occupy the bridal suite at the top of the tower (365 steps up!), but I wouldn't hear of it, saying I couldn't be alone because I was scared of bats.

We expect to fly back to Charleston by way of Alaska, as Mr Pee has always wanted to see a live moose. I have warned him that Alaska also has giant bears and earthquakes, but he remains steadfast in his intentions.

You inquired about Cousin Alexis' mother, Poor Aunt Greta. No, she is not the famous flying nun who is always turning up in the National Enquirer. She retreated to the Episcopalian convent in Atlanta when the classified section of the local paper offered Cousin Alexis a special Frequent User rate for engagement announcements. Cousin Hepzibah, who herself couldn't even hold onto a Baptist minister, even with all her money, said Poor Aunt Greta should have taken her oversexed daughter with her.

My own little Manigault is a real little lady. she has a lovely nurse named Miss Viola-Ball, who will be caring for her while Mr Pee and I are on our honeymoon. Of course, I doubt if she will ever be invited to the St Cecilia Ball, because of her...well, shall we say her father. But having Mr Pee, the "Crown Prince of Charleston", as he used to be known in society circles, as her stepfather will lend a modicum of respectability.

Princess Frances continues to make news in Charleston — although in the Holy City, what they don't know they make up. She has settled the suit brought against her by Miss Potty out of court by giving her the glossy purple Thunderbird she had bought for Big Shot. I wish she could find a respectable automobile salesman or something to marry and settle down with — she still pines unnaturally for Big Shot, and ever since she threatened to dig him up I've not been able to stop worrying that she really will. She even carries a screwdriver in her handbag, since she heard that British coffin lids are fastened on with screws.

The wedding rehearsal was this afternoon. Poor Mr Pee is so nervous — in spite of Devious Julius' fertile turtle soup — that he took me for a walk among the tombstones at St Philip's, pointing out where everybody who was anybody (and not already interred at Magnolia Cemetery) is buried. I suppose he felt that the very presence of so many Dear

Departeds would make us both feel at ease. Actually, it had just the opposite effect on me, but I said nothing.

The rehearsal was late getting started, as Cousin Alexis' red Thunderbird broke down outside of Charleston. She rode the rest of the way on a plow horse named Miss Amy which she borrowed from a farmer, promising to return him after the wedding tomorrow.

Manigault is the flower girl, and spent most of the rehearsal time playing with little Freddy Legare, the ring bearer. Freddy is the son of a rich undertaker whom Mr James has been paying on time for the past thirty-five years (and which he refers to as his "lay-away plan") and still shows no sign of dying.

Maum Sarah is as irascible as ever, and it will be such a pleasure to have some time away from all her cajoling. She chastised Mr Pee roundly for letting old Mr Burkee-Snout, the orphaned coondog he inherited from the family retainer Mr Amos Abraham, go around smelling like a cesspool. His patience wearing thin, Mr Pee suggested that she give him a bath, which surprisingly enough she agreed to do...in her jacuzzi.

Maum Sarah outfitted herself for the ordeal, and was a sight to behold in her long white bib and tucker apron that she hadn't used since Mr. Pee, Alexis and Hepzibah were babies. She had shrunk some since then and kept tripping over the bottom hem. On her head she had what she called her sanitary cap which had a crinkled blue frill around the edge, which bore the affectionate label "Maumy".

Miss Glory-Be led a very suspicious Mr Burkee-Snout next door to where the expensive jacuzzi was waiting. Maum Sarah had stuffed her accommodating apron pockets with Cousin Alexis' clematis, pomegranate and spring violet bubble-bath salts which Cousin Lewis had given her for Christmas, and filched my best monogrammed hairbrush to groom him.

Mr Burkee-Snout began trembling the minute he spotted the jacuzzi, as if he knew what was in store for him. It took Maum Sarah and Miss Glory-Be both to wrestle him into the water, where he sat rigidly, eyes clamped shut and teeth gritted.

When Maum Sarah turned on the pump, it made an awful noise and Mr Burkee-Snout rose straight up in terror. Since Maum Sarah had been holding onto his collar, she was jerked bodily into the jacuzzi, and for several moments there was a confusion of limbs, paws and splashing water.

Miss Glory-Be managed to pull Maum Sarah out of the churning water, while Mr Burkee-Snout made good his escape, all covered with bubbles, like one of Miss Potty's more innovative girls (Option #17), running home to hide for the rest of the day under Mr. Pee's bed.

I will write you all the news about the honeymoon when we return. Until then, I remain

Your ever affectionate
Cousin Gwendolyn

P. S.

Just as I had gotten into bed to read for a while, the doorbell rang. I looked at the clock — just after 11:00 PM. I knew Mr James and Miss Glory-Be were at the bachelor party, so there was no one but me to answer the door.

I threw on a robe and went downstairs and peered out the door window. To my surprise, it was Mr Pee.

"I lost my key," he explained as I unlocked and opened the door. "Is there any coffee?"

'I didn't expect you home so soon," I remarked. "Are you all right? Where are Mr James and Miss Glory-Be?"

He yawned. "I'm fine. I only had one small glass of sherry. Mr James and Miss Glory-Be, I'm sorry to report, both imbibed much more heavily and are still at the party, which was still going strong when I left."

"Then why did you leave? The party was in your honor."

"For one thing, I was bored," he replied, following me into Mr James' kitchen, where I reheated the coffee. "For another, I am sure that everyone quickly forgot the reason for the party. And besides, I thought it advisable to depart before the police arrived."

"The *police*?"

"Almost inevitable, I'm afraid, as the whole party had disintegrated into a veritable orgy. It's only a matter of time before someone files a complaint."

"But Princess Frances and Cousin Alexis promised to keep things under control..."

"Unfortunately, there was no one to keep *them* under control. When I left, Princess Frances and Big Shot's Daddy — who was wearing that capricious Hawaiian grass skirt — were performing what looked like a tropical fertility dance. And Cousin Alexis was riding that smelly farm horse bareback around the Queen Anne dining table, dressed only in a red see-through chiffon gown."

"Oh dear..."

He sighed. "It was all Cousin Lewis' fault — he should never have been appointed bartender. All the drinks were extremely potent, and became more so as the evening wore on. The last I saw of him, he was feeding spoonfuls of vodka to Princess Frances' teddy bear."

"Oh my..."

"And Mr James was swinging from the Czar of Russia blue crystal chandelier..."

"Oh no..."

"And Miss Glory-Be..."

I shut my eyes.

"...Miss Glory-Be mercifully went to sleep on the cooling couch early in the evening and slept through the whole thing."

He sat down at the kitchen table while I poured him a cup of reheated coffee. "And my Polo brothers all behaved quite abominably...certainly not in the spirit of Southern gentility. I trust that they will all awaken tomorrow properly contrite...and with splitting headaches to boot!"

'"Well, I'm proud of you for having better sense."

"My dear, I am *not* Cousin Lewis," he said.

"I am thankful for that..."

He pointed to his coffee cup. "I mean, I cannot drink coffee without milk and sugar."

"Oh." I looked around to see where Mr James kept these two essentials.

"And I have had nothing to eat," he complained. "Perhaps we could wake Maum Sarah to cook us grits and hot biscuits, like she used to do when I got upset about something."

I shook my head. "Maum Sarah has an early morning appointment at Miss Potty's to have her face made over for the wedding. Big-Ass Mabel is quite talented in that department, but she did say that with All Maum Sarah's wrinkles it would be a long job."

"Well, can't *you* make grits?" inquired Mr Pee.

"Since coming to Charleston from England, I've never been allowed to try," I admitted.

"Oh, dear," groaned Mr Pee. "I can't cook either."

At that moment, the doorbell rang again. "Maybe it's Miss Glory-Be," I said. "Or Mr James."

But when I opened the door, I was confronted with a stocky young policeman — fortunately, not the one who had interrupted Cousin Hepzibah's shower party. Behind him, in the shadows, was an ungainly horse, and snoring loudly on its back, in a flimsy red gown, was Cousin Alexis.

"Ma'am," the policeman tipped his cap, "we found this lady asleep on this horse in White Point Gardens. When we woke her up, she insisted she was your Matron of Honor."

At this point, Cousin Alexis slid off the side of the horse and fell into the marigolds lining the sidewalk. She blinked, then grinned up at me. "Cousin-to-be Gwendolyn," she hiccuped.

She struggled to her feet and handed me the horse's reins. "Kindly see to Miss Amy...I have to return her after the wedding tomorrow. Or is it today?" Then she disappeared into the house, leaving me to deal with yet another bewildered policeman.

Affectionately, as always
Cousin Gwendolyn

# 22

I was half an hour late for my own wedding because Princess Frances and too-soon-to-be-Cousin Hepzibah nearly got into a knock-down drag-out in the Victorian bedroom because each claimed the role of substitute Mother of the Bride. I thought this had been resolved long ago, but plans changed so fast from day to day that I had given up trying to keep track of them.

In the end, Maum Sarah, the bridegroom's old wet nurse, threatened to stand on top of Robert E. Lee's bedsteps and box both their ears if they didn't shut up. *She* would do the honors. After all, it was her baby's baby's big day, and it was only right that she have a part in the ceremony — even if it meant recognizing my role as well, however briefly. Knowing from past experience that Maum Sarah was a woman of her word, royalty and commoner quickly acceded.

Finally, Mr James, aided by Miss Glory-Be, got me and my train of off-white lace into the carriage which stood ready to be pulled by six polo ponies. The ponies were decidedly unhappy at being harnessed in such close quarters, and kept snorting and nipping at each other. One of them managed to bite a BBC TV cameraman as he was relieving himself on the white crepe myrtles just around the corner.

Cousin Alexis with little Manigault and Freddy had already left for the church in the undertaker's big gray limousine. Mr James, in his ceremonial top hat, and Miss Glory-Be, in white summer mourning, climbed up into the driver's seat of the carriage. Big Shot's Daddy, majestic in formal attire and top hat, squeezed in next to me — stepping on one of my toes in the process and nearly crippling me — and we were off to St Philip's.

They were having a few problems at the church too, as Mr Pee told me later. Miss Topsey Piddleton was blissfully playing her own special amalgam of "Love Me Tender", "Dixie" and "The Voice that Breathed O'er Eden". When Cousin Lewis weaved by, wearing his usual Civil War uniform complete with sash and sword, she suddenly stopped dead right in the middle, looked down at him and shouted, "I'll not play another note if that immoral sinner is in the wedding! I heard all about your shenanigans with your own Cousin Alexis at the bachelor party! Shame on you!"

Cousin Lewis went white as a sheet, and Mr Pee had to extend a hand to steady him. Then Mr Pee found a chance to repay Cousin Lewis for his support during the rehearsal of *Sunset Boulevard on the Ashley* — he leaned over to the organ and said coolly: "Miss Topsey, what do you think all these fine members of the Southern Aristocracy gathered here today would say if they knew about your two old-maid great-aunts, who were sent off to exile in Boston when it was discovered they were both slave-freeing abolitionists!"

A jarring discord blasted from the organ. Then Miss Topsey, faced with the facts of life, struck up "Dixie", just as the surrogate Mothers of the Bride — now arm-in-arm, sisters of the flesh — were marching up the aisle.

When I finally arrived at the church, I was relieved to see that the crowd was apparently a friendly one...except for one robed, bearded man in sandals carrying a sign that read, "The World Will End Tonight!" There would be none of the controversy or downright hostility which accompanied my wedding to Big Shot.

Society weddings always bring out the crowds in Charleston, and although the publicity for this one had been purposely kept to a minimum, it still required several policemen riding horses — which thus far had escaped Princess Frances' clutches — to assist us through the throngs.

There were a number of newspaper photographers and television crewmen, and I obliged by smiling sweetly while cameras clicked and rolled. Cousin Alexis, in a gorgeous vintage yellow gown that had formerly belonged to her idol Gloria Swanson, tried desperately to get into the pictures, but little Freddy Legare kept tugging at her skirt, until she finally gave up and rushed him behind a tombstone to relieve himself.

Then Miss Topsey struck up the Trumpet Voluntary, which was so loud I feared the church steeple would collapse. Clinging to Big Shot's Daddy, who kept nodding to everybody and thanking them in advance for donations to his church, we proceeded to where my bridegroom was waiting.

There were some awkward moments en route. I was nearly asphyxiated by the pungent aroma of five hundred Easter lilies that Maum Sarah had ordered (and which I had to pay for). I thought her choice of flowers more appropriate for a funeral than a wedding...but maybe she was trying to make a point.

Then Maum Sarah herself, dressed in full mourning in tribute to my late mother-in-law-to-be Miss Henrietta — who, she kept sobbing, was watching us all with a party of angels — started wailing like a banshee. Cousin Alexis had to once again relinquish her prominent position in the spotlight to come over and shut her up.

The only other hitch was that Cousin Lewis, who had nearly swallowed the ring during my previous marriage, had tied it on a string around his neck to avoid a similar embarrassment. However, having sampled a sizeable quantity of the reception punch prior to the ceremony, he managed to get the string hopelessly knotted, and Mr Pee had to use Cousin Lewis' own Civil War sword to carefully cut it off.

After that it was smooth sailing, and Mr Pee and I were soon pronounced husband and wife. As we made our way back along the aisle, I felt a strange mixture of relief, expectation and *deja-vu*.

The reception, quiet and small by local Charleston standards, was held at my home, with Mr James in his usual element officiating. Like the wedding, it was relatively trouble-free...with a few exceptions. Miss Topsey Piddleton once again caught the bridal bouquet, having elbowed the competition out of the way as I tossed it from the staircase. She then rushed over to Cousin Lewis, who was breathing on one of his ancestoral Civil War medals in order to polish it, and slapped him on the back to show that all was forgiven. Unfortunately this caused him to swallow the medal, and he had to be rushed to the hospital.

Then Mr Pee cut his finger with Cousin Lewis' sword, which we were using to cut the cake, and the way Maum Sarah carried on you would have thought he had cut his throat.

"My poor baby's baby!" she cried, while applying a bandage. "You never cut a piece of cake in your whole life, and now you had to go and use a *sword*." She gave me a very nasty look, as if I had been wielding the weapon.

216

When first-aid had been administered, she said, "Now I got to go and pack. Miss Glory-Be, fetch Miss Landine's travel cage."

"You're going somewhere, Maum Sarah?" I asked, dreading the answer I knew was coming.

"Course I am!" she replied testily. "You don't think I'd let that child go flying off by himself!"

I tried to remain calm. "Maum Sarah, *I* will be with him. In case you've forgotten, we are now married."

"And the first thing he does is near bout cut his hand off!" she sneered. "Nossir, this boy needs his old nanny!"

The thought of Maum Sarah sharing our honeymoon was just too much. I had to think fast. Then I remembered... "You realize, of course, that under British Law, Miss Landine would be quarantined for six months, in case she has rabies."

Her jaw dropped. "Rabies! My sweet Miss Landine?!"

"That's the law."

"Somebody should speak to the Queen!"

That, plus my mink coat, which I never wore anyway, did the trick. Maum Sarah went upstairs, grumbling, presumably to try on the coat. She didn't bother coming back down to wish us farewell. I was worried that Mr Pee might be upset, but he just smiled and said, "Free...free at last!" To which I quietly added, "Amen!"

Accompanied by Big Shot's Daddy, Mr James drove us in my car to the airport to catch our flight to New York City, where we were to pick up a flight for London. Miss Shirley-Mae, big as a horse, and Miss Glory-Be had decorated the car with pusilanimous pink and white ribbons, while Princess Frances had commissioned a gold-leafed sign that read, "Better Late Than Never".

En route to the airport we passed Cousin Alexis riding Miss Amy bareback home to her plantation in Ridgeland. She appeared to be wearing little but her slip and frilly lace drawers, having tied her gown around her neck so that it floated out in the breeze.

"Shades of Isadora Duncan," commented Mr Pee. "I do hope she doesn't choke."

At the airport, while waiting for the plane to depart, Mr James instructed us in the facts of life, to the delight of our fellow travelers. Then he gave Mr Pee what looked to be a mummified rabbit's foot, tightly secured by an old rubber band to a little bag containing a toadstool, some bones, and a small jar of Devious Julius' famous fertile turtle soup. "I dun spent four dollars and eighty-nine cents with Devious Julius, so Mr Pee, kindly drink the soup and put the rest of this stuff under your pillow. Then with a little effort on your part, we might get us a little master yet!"

Big Shot's Daddy prayed in a booming voice that we might be fruitful, to which our fellow passengers chorused a loud "Amen!" Then the old butler suggested we all join in the singing of "The Battle Hymn of the Republic". A sweet little old lady asked if we were all going to a military funeral.

Our first night was spent on the plane to London, which to say the least was rather public. Mr Pee promised on the ghost of General Stonewall Jackson that the second night would be better.

# 23

U pon arriving at Heathrow Airport, we were handed a
cablegram that read:

COUSIN LEWIS' CIVIL WAR MEDAL LOCATED NEAR
UPPER DUODENAL TRACT. PATIENT HAS
SUSPECTED ULCER. LOVE, GLORY-BE.

"Thank the Lord!" Mr Pee sighed in relief. "That medal
was irreplaceable."

On the train to Staplehurst, where Cousin Matilda-Madge
was scheduled to meet us and drive us to Sissinghurst, I fell
asleep and had a very strange dream. There was Big Shot,
large as life, surrounded by all these adoring lady angels, listening while he played on his mouth organ.

"Angel," he said to me, "now you be kind to Mr Pee. The
poor guy can't help the way that old witch Maum Sarah and
Miss Face-lift Henrietta raised him."

"Oh, Big Shot...does that mean you've forgiven him?"

219

"Nothin' to forgive, Angel. It was all in the cards. Somebody just dealt a bad hand." He winked. "Maybe the next one'll be better."

I smiled.

"Your Mama says to tell you that the cream puffs are awfully good up here..." At that point, there was a squeal of brakes, and I awoke as the train came to a halt.

We had reached Paddock Wood. Now I had to prepare Mr Pee for Cousin Matilda-Madge, whom he had never met in the flesh.

My cousin is really a good-hearted soul, if a little outspoken and overbearing at times — a rough diamond, but a diamond nevertheless. She never did take to girlish things like dolls and pretty frilly dresses. In fact, when she was fourteen years old she grew a moustache. It was hard on her father — Uncle Alfie was a widower, and did all he could to raise her in a normal fashion while trying to tolerate her eccentricities. All attempts to marry her off met with failure.

Then when she was twenty-one, having come of age and a woman — or whatever — in her own right, Cousin Matilda-Madge told her father flat-out that she had no interest in men, and that either he accept her as she was or she would enter the convent at Staplehurst and cause the nuns there many sleepless nights.

Poor Uncle Alfie — he nearly suffered a stroke. After all, she was Master of the Hounds, and he couldn't afford to lose her. So, faced with the choice between foxes and nuns, Uncle Alfie capitulated and never brought up the touchy subject of marriage again. When he died, she inherited the castle, which those nasty liberal London columnists dubbed "Honeymoon Palace".

Mr Pee looked somewhat perplexed as I told him all these things. "What a curious situation."

"Indeed," I agreed. "I just thought you ought to — "

"I mean, with all the products they advertise on television to combat surplus hair, I cannot understand why your cousin would want to wear a moustache..."

Cousin Matilda-Madge, dressed in a coarse tweed jacket and baggy wool trousers, was standing on the platform to greet us. With her were two other women of uncertain age.

"Good Lord," whispered Mr Pee, clutching my arm. "I see what you mean."

"My dears!" Cousin Matilda-Madge boomed. "How romantic you do look!"

She then enveloped us both in a bear hug as if we were Siamese Twins, kissing us profusely. I thought I heard one of Mr Pee's ribs snap.

Then she introduced us to her friends. "This," she said, indication a prim, plumpish woman as if she were describing a racing horse, "is Patricia Holyhead, doting wife of the vicar. And this," throwing her brawny arm around the slumping shoulders of a dwarfish girl with nearly impenetrably thick-lensed glasses, "is Miss Bluebell Cantwell, our church organist. Please mind your language in front of her — she is of the old school, and a virgin besides."

Miss Bluebell tittered. Mrs Holyhead had a worried look on her face. "I still think I should have gone straight back to the vicarage, Matilda-Madge. You know how cross my husband gets when he comes home from his rabbiting and I am not there waiting dutifully to pour his cup of tea."

"Don't mention that infidel to me!" roared my cousin, hoisting up her trousers with one hand and encompassing Mr Pee's reluctant shoulders with the other. "I am a fan of Beatrix Potter, and I love rabbits. That man should himself be shot. And skinned."

"I quite agree," snapped Miss Bluebell, giving Mr Pee a nasty look as if, being male, he were somehow a party to the vicar's barbarity.

221

Cousin Matilda-Madge piled us all into her station wagon, allotting me the front seat while Mr Pee was sandwiched somewhat uncomfortably between Mrs Holyhead and the cringing Miss Bluebell. We sped through Staplehurst village and out into the open countryside, past orchards and hopgardens, toward Sissinghurst.

"Have to get you home quickly, Pattycake," she yelled at the vicar's spouse. "Must be a good little wifey."

We turned into the vicarage driveway on two wheels, taking half a rhododendron bush with us. Mr Pee had turned white as a sheet, and later confided to me that after driving with her he felt safer with Mr James. Cousin Matilda-Madge, catching a look at him in the rear-view mirror, roared with laughter. "Didn't your blushing bride tell you how I once won the Grand Prix?"

"I won a race, too," interjected Miss Bluebell. "The egg and spoon race when I was a Brownie. I won a purple wooden yo-yo with a portrait of the Queen Mother on the side — it's still among my most treasured possessions."

"How nice," Mr Pee said, forcing a polite smile. Then turned to me. "Did you ever win anything, my dear?"

Cousin Matilda-Madge guffawed again. "The consolation prize — Gwendolyn won you!"

Mr Pee blushed. Miss Bluebell's lips muttered something to the effect that she would rather have her yo-yo.

We skidded to a stop in front of the towering grey walls of the gothic vicarage. The heavy front door swung open and out came a cherubic little pink-cheeked man with fading straight blonde hair, wearing a prim clerical collar. He carried a Book of Common Prayer in one hand, a shotgun in the other, and had a stern look on his face.

"Patricia," he reprimanded as if she were a member of his Sunday School class, appearing not to notice the rest of us, "once again you have failed to live up to our sacred vows, made on our wedding day in Rochester Cathedral.

We agreed that tea time should always be *our* time...and yet suddenly you are always off traipsing about."

Cousin Matilda-Madge snorted, and the vicar gave her an accusing look. Then he turned and marched indoors, with Mrs Holyhead running behind him like a dutiful Chinese wife.

"Nuts," sneered Cousin Matilda-Madge, stepping hard on the accelerator. "Poor little Pattycake is a slave to that pompous bore. Makes me thankful I've never had to put up with that kind of bilge!"

I briefly recalled Mr Pee's insistence that the line in the marriage ceremony about "love and *obey*" remain intact...but I could hardly envision my husband degenerating into another Vicar Holyhead.

We then unloaded Miss Bluebell at the door of her small red tile hung cottage in Sissinghurst village where Mr Pee, never forgetting his proper Charleston manners, said he hoped she would continue to enjoy her yo-yo for many years to come.

"Another sad case," mused Cousin Matilda-Madge, ripping off her tie and handing it to me as we drove away. "Her father was kicked in the head by his horse and never regained consciousness. Bluebell was born just three months after her father's cremation at Charing, and when her mother got her first look at the baby, she had a severe nervous breakdown and had to be admitted to Balmy Heath asylum, where she stayed for two years. Bluebell was brought in for frequent visits, but her mother just sat there and stared at her.

"Then she seemed to make a remarkable recovery, and was soon released...whereupon she marched straight to the cliff at Beachy Head and jumped off. Little Bluebell was raised by her maternal grandparents, but they are gone now — Pattycake and I are all she's got."

Mr Pee's head was nodding — he looked sleepy and a little gray. Then the towers of Cousin Matilda-Madge's castle loomed up like some prehistoric monster on the horizon.

Cousin Matilda-Madge screeched up to the front entrance, throwing a cloud of dust over the huge white marble horse which stood by the steps. "Welcome to my home," she announced heartily. "High tea is in exactly an hour. We will dispense with formality at dinner, as I refuse to get dressed up except for weddings and funerals...and of course coronations. Besides, Florence Appleby, my cook, cycles home to her fancy man in the village at seven every evening."

"How considerate," noted Mr Pee, and I smiled in agreement.

"Now, you turtle doves — all is ready in the honeymoon suite." She pointed up to some large diamond-paned windows at the top of a double-turreted tower. "Nothing but the white owls to disturb you. *To whit to whoo...*" she trilled in falsetto. "Three hundred and sixty-five steps up to the room. I'll have Florence carry up your luggage — she's strong as an ox."

Cousin Matilda-Madge bowed graciously and was gone, leaving us to our climb. I had a mind to call her back and ask for a room that could be reached more easily — I kept thinking about my dream, in which Big Shot had told me to be kind to Mr Pee, and I wondered whether it wise to allow him to exert himself.

"Mr Pee," I said, "maybe we should take a little walk in the garden before tea, so that we don't have to make the climb twice."

Mr Pee shook his head. "I never felt better! Must be the clean British air." With that he began to climb the stairs, while I followed right behind him.

After what seemed an eternity we reached the top, and there was our room, the door open wide, to greet us.

Mr Pee was trembling. He looked very pale. "I know I'm supposed to carry you over the threshold, but..." he took a deep breath "...I seem to have used up all my energy."

I helped him into an arm chair covered with crimson velvet. He looked around the warm interior of the room, the vases of white roses everywhere, and the four-poster bed with a white satin coverlet. "What a beautiful room. Mama would have loved it."

"Why don't you just rest until time for tea?" I suggested.

"It must be all the excitement of the wedding catching up with me," he said. "I believe I shall shut my eyes for a few minutes..."

He was still dozing when it came time for high tea, and I hadn't the heart to wake him. So I went down alone to find Cousin Matilda-Madge already in the dining room warming her considerable posterior in front of a log fire in the great fireplace, for the evenings here can become quite chilly, even in July.

She was very understanding. "Men just do not have the stamina of women," she insisted, pounding her chest like a mighty gorilla. "Let's eat."

Florence had done us well: a large cake with white sugar icing and the words Long Life spelled out on the top in red glace cherries that curiously enough reminded me of Cousin Lewis...a cut glass Georgian decanter filled with golden sherry...hot tea...fresh cucumber sandwiches with lots of home made butter, and...

"You remembered!" I exclaimed. "My favorite — pork pie!"

Cousin Matilda-Madge chuckled aloud. "I drove all the way to Tunbridge Wells to get it. I did not forget how as a child you were morbidly fascinated with cold, spicy pork pie."

"That's because dear old Aunty Doom was always telling us the story of her poor cousin Mabel Hall who went to Carpenter's Restaurant in Tunbridge Wells, fancied a pork pie, and ate it...only to expire exactly one hour later."

"At least she died happy," observed my cousin as she cut us each a generous helping.

I carried a piece back upstairs, along with a nice cup of coffee for Mr Pee, who had awakened, undressed and sat waiting for me in the crimson armchair, rather a sad-looking figure in his nuptial pajamas.

"The bridegroom cometh...or rather the bride." I gave him his snack while I prepared myself for bed. It was dusk and the nightingales were singing down by the lake. Somewhere, a fox barked.

Minutes later, I clambered up into the four-poster, where Mr Pee soon joined me. "Do you realize, my Gwendolyn," he sighed, "that we are alone at last?"

"Are you happy?" I asked him a short time later.

"Blissfully, my dear. But I do wish I had brought my ear plugs. Those bloody English owls kept interrupting what I was trying to do." He breathed a sigh and then lay quietly, gazing into the darkness. After a few minutes, he whispered, "Thank you, my Gwendolyn."

"For what?" I was already half asleep.

"For everything. But I must ask you for one thing more..."

"And that is?"

"You must promise that you'll not bury me in Magnolia."

And with those words, Mr Pee closed his eyes and joined Big Shot and the angels.

# 24

As is always the case with an unexpected death, especially one involving a foreign national, an inquest was convened at the Village Institute. The verdict was that the victim had succumbed to heart failure brought on most likely by over-exertion, complicated by the assault of a spicy pork pie on a delicate stomach.

Mr Pee used to remark that the British must have stomachs of cast iron to tolerate the frightfully heavy foods they consume. Why he chose to eat the pork pie that evening will always be a mystery.

Florence Appleby was distraught. "If only somebody had told me he had such a weak stomach, I would have served boiled mutton or..."

"It really wasn't your fault, Florence," I assured her. And to show my forgiveness, I gave her the small pearl mourning ring from my left little finger. Poor thing, she left the room in tears, mumbling something about my gesture being the nicest thing that had happened to her since her confirmation.

Having clearly spurned Magnolia Cemetery in his last words, it seemed the logical thing to bury Mr Pee at Sissinghurst where his predecessor was interred, with a space left for me between them. Funeral arrangements were begun, and friends and relatives were notified.

Someone managed to produce a confederate flag, which was flown at half-mast to greet the contingent of mourners that the Princess Frances flew in by private jet from the Holy City. She and Cousin Matilda-Madge hit it off at once, for which I was very grateful, and spent most of their time extolling the virtues of country living and exchanging recipes for Yorkshire pudding and chitlins.

Cousin Lewis was attired in full uniform, of course, while Cousin Hepzibah wore an ankle-length black dress, white collar and pearls. Cousin Alexis looked stunning in the same black riding habit, top hat and crepe scarf she had once worn in an Elks Club presentation of Charles Dickens' *Great Expectations*. Appropriately enough, the first thing that caught her eye was the enormous white marble horse that stood in the yew walk, reminding her of Big Shot's Daddy's prophesy at the bridal shower that she was destined to encounter one.

"What a magnificent statue!" she exclaimed. "What I wouldn't give for something like that at my plantation."

"Never cared for it, myself," grunted Cousin Matilda-Madge. "Our cousin Judith, who is obsessed with those beasts, unloaded it on me."

Others in the arriving party included Miss Topsey Piddleton, who wore her jogging gear, and immediately put in a person-to-person telephone call to somebody in Canterbury Cathedral; Big Shot's Daddy, wearing his cassock and collar so as not to seem out of place among his Anglican counterparts; Mr James, looking grim; Miss Glory-Be, looking heartbroken; and my own little Manigault and her faithful nurse, Miss Viola-Ball.

Mercifully, Maum Sarah was missing. Wearing her new mink coat, and accompanied by her old she-cat Miss Landine, she had taken off to go fertile turtle hunting with Devious Julius, to replenish his depleted supply. As their secret hunting grounds were known only to themselves, nobody could locate them in time to attend the funeral. For such small mercies, I was deeply grateful.

Florence Appleby prepared a delicious (porkless) lunch for the guests — all except Princess Frances, who had curiously disappeared. The cook seemed to be quite taken by Mr. James, being particularly impressed by the size of his swinging gold watch. She even suggested that her fancy man take him for a drink at the Bull that evening, but out of respect for the dear departed, my faithful old butler declined.

I noticed that Cousin Lewis also seemed unusually sober, hardly touching his wine during lunch. And Cousin Alexis had kept her amorous inclinations in check, having not to my knowledge seduced a single man since her arrival. Moreover, the two of them were presently holding hands.

Cousin Matilda-Madge, never one to mince words, remarked on this at the table, and Cousin Lewis seemed quite embarrassed. "I have always loved my Cousin Alexis," he confessed. "But in our family cousins don't marry in case they have weird children."

"Why, how ridiculous!" exclaimed Cousin Matilda-Madge, her mouth full of sherry trifle. "My uncle and aunt in Chelmsford were first cousins, and their only child is in the House of Commons."

Cousin Lewis' eyes lit up. "You mean...Alexis and I might be wed?"

"Of course, provided that she is a respectable widow."

"All of my previous spouses are now deceased," Alexis said, "including the one I divorced for infidelity. I always carry copies of their death certificates in my purse for identification purposes."

"Then," announced my cousin, beckoning Florence for a refill, "we will apply for a special license and marry you off a week from today at eight o'clock in the morning."

"So early?" Cousin Lewis cast a doubtful look at Alexis. "I'm not sure she can get up at that hour."

"We are still officially in mourning," declared Matilda-Madge with finality. "It's either now or wait one year 'til that's over."

The two cousins eagerly agreed, and Matilda-Madge said she would contact the Reverend Holyhead to make the arrangements right after lunch.

As we were finishing our strawberry and real Devonshire clotted cream dessert, it was observed that Princess Frances was still absent. At that moment, the door chimes sounded, and moments later Florence ushered a police constable and Princess Frances into the room. Her Royal Highness' clothes were disheveled and her face and hands were covered with dirt.

"Sorry to trouble you, Mum," the officer said, "but this lady claims she's a guest here."

"Well of *course* she is!" insisted Matilda-Madge. "Whatever is the problem?"

"Well, Mum...I come upon her in the village cemetery. She had a shovel, and was diggin' up one of the graves."

As we all sat in stunned silence, Princess Frances pulled away from the officer and brushed the dirt off her dress. "I *said* if I could, I would..." She glared at the confused man "...and I almost did!"

With all of the funeral-planning activities, the incident was soon forgotten. That evening, Matilda-Madge invited us to join her and a few friends in the library for their weekly poker game. Princess Frances, Cousin Hepzibah and Mr James accepted. Cousin Alexis and her now-fiancee Cousin Lewis preferred a romantic walk by the lake; Miss Topsey Piddleton, who had been asked to be guest organist at the funeral, had to go over the hymns with the Reverend Holyhead; Big Shot's Daddy retired to his room with the Book of Common Prayer to read up on the Church of England's Order for the Burial of the Dead. I was exhausted, and decided to turn in early that evening.

I had been moved from the honeymoon suite to a bedroom over the library, from which emanated the loud voices of the poker players. I had just put on my nightgown when I heard a sort of muffled *whump*, followed by a commotion from the floor below. I put on my robe and hurried down the winding staircase.

There on the floor of the library lay Princess Frances, a hand of cards still clenched in her large jewel-encrusted right fist. Mr. James was fanning her with the London Daily Telegraph, while trying to get a glimpse of her cards. I was so used to sudden expirations by this time that I feared the worst.

"No, just fainted, looks like," Cousin Matilda-Madge assured me. "Must have been one hell of a poker hand! I've sent Florence's fancy man on his bicycle to Cranbrook to fetch my family doctor. No good phoning him — it's his poker night too."

By the time the doctor arrived, Princess Frances had revived and was sitting up, sipping a cup of tea. We were all relieved, especially Mr James, who complained that his arm was near to breaking from fanning her.

"Been feeling whoozy all day," Her Royal Highness complained. "But I put it down to that boisterous plane trip." I was tempted to add that the exertion of digging up Big Shot's grave probably didn't help much...but I kept quiet.

At the doctor's insistence, she agreed to see him in his office first thing in the morning so he could run some tests. And on that note, I returned to my room as the poker game resumed...Princess Frances included.

There were the usual protocol problems the next day in planning for the funeral, with everyone claiming the right to escort the grieving widow. Princess Frances insisted her sovereign status entitled her to the honor; Cousin Alexis claimed me as her best friend; and Cousin Hepzibah declared herself as *my* best friend. Cousin Matilda-Madge won out, however, because she could lick anyone in the house.

Then Miss Bluebell Cantwell found out she was being replaced as official church organist for the occasion by Miss Topsey Piddleton, by special decree from Canterbury Cathedral. She stamped her feet and threatened to resign, right in the middle of the vicar's and Big Shot's Daddy's rabbiting. The situation was resolved, however, when Miss Topsey promised to take Miss Bluebell spelunking in one of the local caves, in return for relinquishing her organ for this one occasion. Miss Bluebell was delighted, having held a lifelong fascination for bats and other nocturnal creatures.

On the day of the funeral service, it was arranged that Miss Viola-Ball should take Manigault down to Hastings to visit Ocky the octopus. They would stay in my Tudor cottage where I would join them for a few days after Mr. Pee had been properly laid to rest.

Mr Pee was placed in the library so guests could pay their last respects. He looked very peaceful, as if he were simply taking a short nap, as he frequently did. Cousin Matilda-Madge gave me a cerise blossom from her rare prickly cactus to place in the coffin. Two heavy antique pennies from her personal collection had been placed over his eyes, because every time they were removed his eyes popped open. "Oh, how sweet," said Princess Frances. "He just hates to say goodbye!" In the end the pennies had to be buried with him.

Miss Glory-Be, who had sequestered himself in the castle wine cellar ever since his arrival finally emerged and busied himself arranging and rearranging the flowers in the parlor, to which he had added his own construction of a spray of flaming orange tiger lilies.

Mr Pee was carried into the church for the funeral service by six stalwart policewomen who were donating their services out of respect for their patroness, Cousin Matilda-Madge. She and Cousin Lewis led me in, so heavily veiled that one tabloid reporter wrote afterwards that I looked like the Duchess of Windsor. Behind us, Cousin Alexis was supported by Mr James and Miss Glory-Be, all weeping profusely. Cousin Hepzibah, who let everyone know that funerals gave her palpitations of the heart, maintained a more stoic profile.

Being royalty, Princess Frances was already seated in a choir stall in the chancel. Miss Glory-Be kept fainting and having to be revived by Cousin Alexis and her smelling salts, which she had brought with her in case such amenities were not available in a foreign country. She was noticeably miffed at being upstaged, having planned to do all the fainting herself.

The short dignified Church of England service was concluded appropriately by Princess Frances' rendering of "Swing Low Sweet Chariot" and "Dixie", followed by "God Save the Queen", in which everyone joined in. Then Miss Topsey Piddleton struck up "The Battle Hymn of the Republic", which signified to those present that Mr Pee was ready to begin his last journey.

233

We followed the coffin to the cemetery, where I noticed with relief that Big Shot's grave had been refilled. I resolved to keep a close eye on Princess Frances until she was headed safely out of the country.

Big Shot's Daddy managed to keep his graveside eulogy short, which for him was no small feat. Perhaps it was the proximity of his son's grave a few feet away, but he observed that in the end Big Shot and Mr Pee had each other while the poor widow is left with no one.

As we were returning to the house, Matilda-Madge's doctor joined us. He had just gotten the results of the tests he had run on Princess Frances.

"Well, am I going to live?" Princess Frances demanded.

"I see no reason why not," he replied. "You're in excellent health."

"Then why — ?"

The doctor lit his pipe. "To be expected, my dear. It seems you are in the first stages of pregnancy."

"*Pregnancy*?!" we all exclaimed at once.

"But..." Princess Frances began. Then she turned slowly and looked over at Big Shot's Daddy.

A scraggly grin came over his face. "I do believe it must have been that evening in Hawaii when we consumed countless rum zombies, and hula-ed until dawn..."

Princess Frances pondered the situation for several moments. Then she nodded. "Well, if I can't have Big Shot's son, I guess I can settle for having his *brother*."

We all congratulated the two of them, and told them how happy we were for them both. I felt an added measure of relief, knowing that Big Shot's grave would now remain safe.

# Epilogue

Mr Pee's two favorite cousins were wed in Sissinghurst and returned happily to Charleston. Now that the Anglican church had given Alexis belated respectability, it was only fair to suggest that Poor Aunt Greta might like to retire from her convent.

"Not on your life," she wrote back, "I've just been elected the Mother Superior."

After a few restful weeks at Hastings, I returned also to the Holy City with Miss Viola-Ball, little Manigault and Ocky the Octopus, whom we had rescued just in time from a Sicilian restaurant, since the aquarium was going out of business. Ocky travelled in a special tank.

Upon arrival, Mr James informed me that Maum Sarah had disappeared, lock, stock and jacuzzi, leaving behind a note pinned on my front door that said: "SO YOU WENT AND DONE IT AGAIN!"

I was resigned to the fact that Maum Sarah would always hold me responsible for the death of her baby's baby, just as Princess Frances blamed me for what happened to Big Shot. But Princess Frances had gotten over *his* death, so maybe there was hope...

It was only proper that I should take up residence in Miss Henrietta's house, Mr Pee's ancestral home, which had some of the best carved woodwork in the city. Princess Frances, now rapidly getting big as a horse, rented my house to accommodate the Prince's maiden sister, the Princess Genevieve-Marlene, who in due time arrived with her companion, Mademoiselle Maree-Pierre, who wore leather and had a tattoo.

In the months that followed, there were many arrivals and departures. Estella, Mr Pee's faithful white horse, came back from being stuffed. Everyone thought she looked terrible — Mr James was sure that a different head had been substituted onto the body. We placed her in Maum Sarah's old quarters where the exercise bicycle used to stand.

And speaking of horses, Cousin Matilda-Madge shipped Cousin Alexis the life-size white marble horse that she had admired so much, as a gift to the newlyweds.

Cousin Hepzibah surprised everyone by marrying a Russian cosmonaut whom she met at one of Princess Frances' soirees and returning with him to Leningrad, which Cousin Hepzibah described as "quaint". Her husband's profession required that he be away from home for extended periods of time, which gave her time to learn the language and bring some measure of Southern genteelness to Russian society. She seemed to be making some headway, although they persisted in using vodka in their mint juleps instead of bourbon.

On a less pleasant note, Miss Topsey Piddleton vanished during a snowslide while mountain climbing in Switzerland. All that was recovered was one cleated hiking boot, size eleven, which as part of her estate was bequeathed to his Grace, the Archbishop of Canterbury.

We also lost Miss Glory-Be, who up and joined the marines as a cook. He sent Miss Manigault a picture of himself wearing a tall chef's hat and toting a machine gun.

At the same time, there seemed to be a concerted effort to repopulate the Holy City. Miss Shirley-Mae gave birth to a beefy cantankerous girl, whom Mr James growled was "just like her mother", and who constantly harrassed poor Miss Sweet-Talking Harriett — now herself the mother of a brightly-colored chick — by pulling her tail feathers. Mr James expressed great relief when shortly thereafter Miss Shirley-Mae ran off with Cousin Alexis's lighthouse keeper's house steward, taking the dreadful infant with her. He quickly filed for divorce — which of course I had to pay for, since Miss Shirley-Mae had used up the rest of his burial insurance money on her new color television set.

Cousins Alexis and Lewis became parents of healthy twin boys, both with flaming red hair. They were named Stonewall Jackson and Jefferson Davis.

Then Her Royal Highness was safely delivered of a daughter, which she intended to name Princess Big Shotta. She came to Miss Henrietta's house to show me the infant, who was dressed from head to foot in cloth of gold.

"When are you and Big Shot's Daddy getting married?" I asked, rather imprudently.

"*Married*? And give up my title?" A look of horror crossed the regal face. "Never! But in gratitude, I am sponsoring his own television ministry. You'll be able to watch him and Miss Potty's little Rhett Cartland — his new protégé — every weekday morning right after breakfast. He's very happy with the arrangement."

My own contribution arrived exactly nine months from that fateful bridal night in Sissinghurst. Miss Manigault was presented with a brother, Ashley Heathcliff, who had his father's blue eyes and dimpled chin.

For all its size, Charleston is provincial in many ways, and news travels fast. On the very day of my return from the hospital, Maum Sarah turned up on the doorstep. She snatched Ashley Heathcliff right out of Mr James arms and hugged him to her bony frame. *"My baby's baby's baby!"* she cried. "Come to comfort me in my old age!"

She glared at us. "Good thing I decided to come back — you all would of let some other hussy bring up my little mournin' dove!" Maum Sarah then marched off with my poor puzzled child to her own private quarters, in which she had already reinstalled her belongings in my absence.

She did allow the stuffed Estella to remain.